PERCY'S GOLD OR THE TRUST FUND

A Novel

Marilyn M. London

AUTHOR'S NOTE

"Percy's Gold or The Trust Fund" is a symbolic story which illustrates the trust between family members and the importance of family ties. Percy and Sam's relationship is an allegorical saga of growing pains, as young adults struggle to discover meaning in life. The story of Emma and Jason is a parable suggesting the strong desire of children to connect with their parents. Finally, the "Trust Fund" is a metaphor for the valuable lessons passed from generation to generation. Some lessons are used well, some are wasted, feared or forgotten, and some are buried, waiting to be rediscovered. Love passed on is golden.

Marilyn M. London 10/16/15

DEDICATED TO

Estelle and Belle,
Sam and Percy
Like two roses on a vine, I've always got your back

ACKNOWLEDGEMENTS

My friends and I shared stories about cleaning out our parents' houses—the homes where we spent our childhoods. We agreed that "letting go" was difficult. I started this book as a reflective "look back". Both of my parents suffered from dementia in their final years. "So, what's new" was a favorite line of my dad's which we answered repeatedly each time we called home to see how things were going. My mom's anger and frustration about forgetting the very things that were important to her made it difficult for me to help her until she 'settled' into a calm "dis-connecting" mode as an Alzheimer's patient. Somewhere along the way, as I cleared out their home, I discovered that what I really wanted as keepsakes were the happy moments my parents created for me as a child, as well as my memories of their idiosyncrasies that I would never forget. And so, my serious writing journey took a turn in celebration of remembrance of their good humor, happy vacations together and their love of American History. Beyond that, I allowed my imagination to run free as I wrote. Thank you, posthumously, mom and dad. The most valuable "*Trust* Fund" that you could ever have passed along to me was having had you as my parents.

Thank you, David and Jared, for daily reminding me how essential the strong relationship between siblings can be, and for teaching me the joy that children bring to their parents. You are my daily inspiration to be happy. Thank you for helping us keep Cole and Mirabelle in our lives. As you can see, our dogs play very important roles in the story.

I am very grateful to my nephew, Michael Mitnick, for spending hours of his time reading the story, giving helpful and inspiring comments while showing me how to keep the characters in the action and cheering me on. His suggestions were invaluable, and I appreciate his support, encouragement and guidance. Thank you as well to his sister, Jenny Eckers, and his mother, Margy Mitnick, whose painstaking editing of my grammar and storyline--history helped me feel much more comfortable about the final copy.

At one point while I was writing, I asked my 94-year-old aunt about her most cherished memories of childhood. She said her uncle Percy visited her from Virginia—he only came once—and brought her a treasured book about a woodsman, published in 1884. Percy was such a wonderful name from the past that I had to include it in my book. She also noted that my grandmother had four sisters and one was named Rosie, and another, Sadie. Thank you, Belle, for inspiration. I found a picture of Percy in an overcoat, suit and tie, in my mother's picture album. He looks nothing like the Percy I picture in my story.

Percy's brother was my grandfather, Sam—my mom and aunt's father. I don't believe that Sam or Percy ever lived in Nantucket or Fort Laramie. Pictures I found in my parents' home of Sam and a man identified by my mother as my grandmother's Russian brother (He would have been Sam's brother-in-law, but apparently never made it to America) inspired my physical descriptions of the brothers in the story.

Thank you to the Dix Hills writer's club for your warm hospitality and inclusion. I've been inspired by all of you and deeply appreciate your patience, your ear and advice.

Thanks to Dr. Richard Bronson for suggesting "Percy's Gold" as the title. The Trust Fund really only tells half of the story, so Richard's suggestion was 'pure gold'.

Thank you Barry, Paul, and Ellen for correcting my history and reminding me to motivate the reader.

Thank to you to my friends who so patiently listened to "the part of the story I'm making up today."

Finally, I want to thank my husband, Manny. We plan to write the all American novel when we retire. I've had a head-start to practice. Please join me, dear.

PART 1

Late 1850's

SAM AND PERCY

A lone osprey spread its black wings as it swooped down for a sumptuous meal. The bird landed on a nearby piling to devour its prey as small skiffs rocked in unison over glassy waters by the inner docks. Large anchored schooners sat further out, patiently waiting for the tide to change, their holds filled with valuable whale oil. Church bells added to the cacophony of seagulls waking up on the shores, creating a concert of blessings over the calm Nantucket Harbor.

"Come on cry-baby, run! Run!" Percy yelled.

The startled osprey dropped its feast and fluttered away to join the mass of grey and white wings overhead, fleeing the sudden commotion.

A heavy set man wearing a stylish blue suit with a white napkin tied around his neck grabbed Sam by the collar and was yelling words you didn't say in public. He roughly snatched a partially eaten chicken leg from the boy's hand and was frantically waving it in the air. Sam wiggled loose and ran. When Ma saw his wrinkled collar covered with sauce and chocolate, there'd be hell to pay. His neck would remain black and blue where the man had held him, but he scrambled away and ran between the houses to hide in a doorway. He didn't start to sob until he saw the man walking back toward the hall where the party had been, swearing in a way that Quakers shouldn't. Sam watched him toss the chicken leg in the street, wasting perfectly good food, and shaking his head back and forth, gesticulating as if he was talking to God himself. Percy, also hiding, kept one eye on Sam and one eye on the man.

When he was sure no one would see, Percy ran and grabbed the chicken leg off the road. He and Sam would starve without something to eat. It had been days since they had had anything fulfilling. Percy pulled the sand covered skin off the chicken leg and tossed it away, putting the leg itself into his pocket. He headed down the alley to get Sam who was sitting on the ground crying and shaking, his knees pulled up to his chin. He looked small. Percy thought, "He'll have to grow up faster than I did to survive."

Percy helped Sam get up and brushed off his pants. He put his arm around him, and they walked down the alley. Percy stole a glance over his shoulder. They were alone. He squeezed Sam tenderly. Looking down at his frail, hungry brother, Percy remembered his mission to toughen him up. Dropping his arm from around Sam's shoulder, he said sharply, "Snap out of it."

Percy pulled the chicken leg from his pocket and waved it tauntingly in front of Sam. Sam smiled through his tears and they both started to laugh, as he reached up, jumping to get a piece. Percy smiled and handed it right over. He'd figure out his own meal. He had taken dessert first and seemed to thrive on the stress of the situation. Grinning, with hands in his greasy pockets, Percy watched Sam eat.

Sam was ten years younger than his brother, and still impressionable. His face was tense, even as he ate. Percy could tell that Sam felt uncomfortable, as if he would be punished by a power bigger than their Ma when she saw how dirty their Sunday best was, and especially when she realized why. He knew that Sam believed what they learned in Sunday school, whereas, he left Sunday school ten years ago and never looked back.

"Ma's gonna punish us good," remarked Sam seriously, licking his fingers on one hand as he still held the chicken leg with the other.

Percy grabbed Sam's hand to take a small bite out of what was left of the leg. He had a mouth full and just waved away the thought.

"Ma always tells us that Quakers are generous. They won't let others starve. Did that man back there look generous to you?" Percy asked Sam.

"I didn't ask him for the chicken. I took it. Maybe if I asked him, he would have been nicer," Sam replied.

"I think he would have just pushed you away," said Percy. "There hasn't been a day we haven't been hungry since Pa left on that whaling trip two years ago."

"But he'll come back. I just know he will," Sam said. "He's out there somewhere." Looking out toward the docks, he imagined his dad sailing into the harbor.

"He's not coming back, Sam, and no one is going to put food on our table, though Ma does her best."

Percy's gaze followed Sam's past the shipyards to the distant shoreline, at the end of the harbor. He remembered looking out at the same visage when he was Sam's age, holding his mother's hand. They were watching his Pa's ship coasting into the Harbor. Her other hand was on his shoulder, holding him close, anticipating her husband's return.

"Your Pa is a good man, Percy." Kneeling to straighten his hat, she smiled at him and wondered out loud, "I hope you'll recognize your father. You were so very young when he left."

Sam looked up at Percy, who had stopped walking and was lost in thought, mesmerized by the circling osprey. Percy caught his questioning stare.

"I hate to see her doing other people's laundry and sewing at night 'til she can hardly see. But people don't pay her a lot. She has to pay for the house and her food. She can't pay for us as well. I've got your back. Remember that!" And Percy chewed up the last piece of fat from the chicken, gnawed a bit on the bone, and then tossed it aside in the road. He lightly tapped Sam on the back to get them moving again.

"I don't remember Pa," Sam said. "I don't remember what he looked like. Do you?"

"Yeh. Sure. I remember. But I'm the man of the family now," Percy said.

"You're like my father. I don't know anyone else who's taken care of me like you have, Percy," Sam said, looking at the ground and shaking his head back and forth.

"Well don't get all choked up about it. I don't want responsibility for you. That's for sure. But I care about you," Percy said, putting his arm around Sam's shoulders, drawing him in a little too roughly. They looked into each other's eyes and Percy looked away quickly.

"Besides," he said, "it's easy to drag you along with me and we have fun together. Now let's get home and clean up before Ma sees us. I've got to get back over to the barn and help out today before they notice I skipped out. Maybe I can make some money so we can buy something to eat tomorrow."

All the way home, they jostled each other, smacking one another on the back and on their heads until they were both covered in sauce, chocolate and cream from Percy's dessert. They couldn't stop laughing. All in all, Percy thought it was a good day so far. No one had come looking for him, which meant they didn't notice that he never showed up at the barn to work. He had lifted Sam from his glum, hungry mood. They got to eat and didn't have to work for it. To get a meal this good, they'd have had to clean out the hogs and the horse stables for hours, a tough job especially for a bit of a boy like Sam.

The two figured they could run in back and wash off their guilt before Ma caught them. But as they approached home, they stopped short in their tracks. From what he saw, Percy was old enough to know that things were going to change big time and not necessarily for the better. Picking up on Percy's mood, Sam squeezed his big brother's hand.

THE WEDDING

In front of the house, Mamie, their mother, stood in her best dress. She was a creative seamstress and it looked like style and lace had been added to the sleeves. On her head was a small flat hat with a veil worn only on special occasions, and to her side stood a tall man with sideburn whiskers and a handlebar mustache that was pointed at the edges. He held a beaver hat with a wide brim and wore a long fitted coat like a riding jacket but nicer. His boots shined, and he had on a silky grey cravat. He looked at Ma with wolf eyes and a dangerous grin. She just looked down at her hands with a sheepish smile. Both boys thought the man had a stern look about him but there was hope for some kindness because Ma had that girlish look as they walked down the front path. She seemed happy.

The tall man's black attendant was wearing a suit that was nicer than any Percy ever owned. He was holding the reigns of the horse which had ribbons and feathers on it. Behind the horse was a carriage with a white shiny awning and white fringes hanging from it.

"Wow. Look at that fancy carriage. It's swell!" whispered Sam to Percy.

"Shut up. There's nothing 'swell' about it. Quiet!" Percy retorted under his breath.

Percy could tell that Sam had no idea what was going on, but he had seen this white-fringed carriage in front of the meeting house before. The boys watched the couple walk toward them. Then Sam looked up into the man's face and froze. It was half fear and half awe. Percy was disgusted but didn't show his feelings.

The man looked familiar. Early that morning, Percy saw him come off a boat in the harbor. The man spoke harshly to the black attendant. Nantucket was a free island. Black men worked on the whaling ships alongside the Quakers. They weren't always treated the best, but it was unusual for them to be treated as badly as they were by this man. Percy was appalled by what he saw. Now this same man took his mother's arm, helping her into the carriage. Percy barely caught his breath as his adrenaline surged. He watched in disbelief.

"Are these your boys, Mamie?" the man asked, as if they weren't even there.

"Why, yes, they are, and I know they look a bit a mess, Stewart, but they really are darling," she responded a bit apologetically.

Ma never criticized them to other people like this before, but the boys knew they were wearing their food.

"Boys, this is Mr. Castle," Ma said.

"Hello sir," the boys replied in unison, their frivolity gone.

"How old is the taller one?" the man asked, eyeing Percy up and down as if he were a horse for sale. "He looks to be old enough to marry or at least be at work. He looks like he's been running amok. He's a mess."

"Boys, run along and get cleaned up. And no more nonsense. We're on our way to the Meeting House. Follow us there and hurry up or you'll miss it," she called with authority in her voice that the boys were unaccustomed to.

"Yes ma'am," they echoed each other, looking up at her. Sam still didn't know what was going on, but his playfulness was gone. He was still clinging to Percy's hand.

Percy knew they couldn't get cleaned up that quickly. They'd have to run fast or get their own horse to do what Ma asked.

As they turned to go to the back of the house, he called back somewhat rudely, "What will we miss?"

"Mr. Castle and I are going to marry," she called back as they drove away.

Percy froze and went white. Sam had never seen him like this before. Percy dropped Sam's hand.

"Someone die? You gonna faint?" Sam asked.

Percy couldn't believe that his mother wouldn't give them any warning. It wasn't like her to leave them out of her life like this. He had friends whose mothers had remarried when their Captain's walks became "widow" walks, but his Ma loved them. He thought she'd include them in such a decision. Who was this stranger whose arms were around his mother and who treated people as slaves? He had to put a stop to this before their lives changed forever. He was all business now.

Percy grabbed Sam and they ran to the back of the house where a trough of water stood. Percy dunked Sam's head in the trough as he coughed and fought, and scrubbed him off brusquely as he tried to wiggle away. He wiped his hair down and plopped a felt hat on his head. Then he washed his own face and hands, wiping them off on his dress jacket, and high-tailed it to the Meeting House, Sam panting behind him.

"Hey wait!" Sam called out.

"Move it," Percy replied. There was no mercy in his voice this time.

As they arrived, Percy saw that he and Sam were late. The members of the local Quaker community were there and they could tell that the Quaker part of the ceremony was already done. Mr. Castle had insisted that a Pastor be present and that after they made their own promise to be married in the Quaker tradition, the Pastor would marry them legally as well. Percy was surprised that his Ma would agree to this, but it seemed that she just did as the man said.

Stewart and Mamie were standing in front of the community facing the Pastor, who asked if anyone objected to the marriage. Percy couldn't resist the opportunity and his hand shot up. The Pastor looked up quizzically at him and then over at Stewart, who swung around and scowled at Percy. The boy slowly lowered his hand and his head. Stewart would not be challenged by Percy. Ever. Refocusing attention on the Pastor, the groom straightened his jacket, lifted his chin and took his bride's hand decisively as the ceremony continued. Stewart was the master of his house and plantation, and now he was the master of Percy's mother and the boys.

Sam just stared as the man lifted her veil and kissed his mother. His mouth dropped open, and he tapped Percy on the arm, pointing. He never saw his Ma kiss anyone else before. He didn't even remember her kissing his father goodbye. She kissed him good night every evening. But that was different.

Percy never looked up. He just turned and walked out. Now they were Sam and Percy Castle, sons of Stewart and Mamie Castle. Randall, their father, was gone forever. Percy sensed that Sam would no longer need him to put food on his table. He knew his childhood was over, and vowed to begin a new adventurous life.

MAMIE'S RATIONALE

Stewart was sensitive to the fact that Mamie was leaving the only home she had ever known, and he wanted her to love him and not regret having to leave. He recognized how much having a photograph of Nantucket would mean to Mamie, and hired an exorbitant photographer to take a picture, creating both a memory of their wedding day, and of Mamie's beloved home. Mamie never had a picture taken before and had mixed feelings about having her image caught by a big black box, but as would happen so often in the future, she did what Stewart asked of her. When Stewart unloaded the packing trunks he gave Mamie, they all stood in front of the Nantucket home for the photo. Everyone smiled but Percy. He held desperately to Sam's arm, his last vestige of a time already gone, captured in the only photograph taken of him, Sam and their Ma.

After the picture was taken, Stewart turned to Mamie and took her hands. He smiled earnestly and said, "I'll send for you in a week's time. It will take you that long to pack your things. I want you to be happy with me and I don't want to rush you."

Then, the boys watched as Stewart gently brushed the veil from her face and kissed her cheek. He chided his attending slave for not moving fast enough, and left on a boat that went south, back down the east coast. Mamie was grateful to have this time alone with her boys and to prepare for her new life with a man who was a stranger to her. She did her best not to fret over it, and Percy admired her fortitude, while realizing that Stewart Castle would be a rift between them. He considered that she was probably doing this for Sam's benefit, and figured that although he had done his best to help around the house, and knew deep down she loved him, she was also probably tired of his shenanigans and wanted him to grow up.

Over the next week, his last on Nantucket, Percy reflected on his childhood. When his father, Randall, had died at sea, his mom struggled keeping her own head above water and left Percy to tend to Sam. Percy never took on a real job, though most of his friends were midway through an apprenticeship or at least had something steady. He thought about how he left his work and played pranks with Sam, like stealing food, or just going to the docks, or picking berries. In that respect, he figured that Mr. Castle was justified in criticizing him as immature. He winced at the thought of being jolted into adulthood, and felt squirmy inside at the thought of having to take on any sort of real responsibility.

Percy wondered how his mother met Mr. Castle, and why she didn't say anything to him or Sam about the betrothal. While they were packing, he sat down with his mother at the table and asked her to tell him about it.

Mamie explained, "I was lonely after your father died and I felt that you and Sam had no direction. You haven't had steady work and you need a man around the house to lead you. Sam is still impressionable, and I don't want him to spend his time running around town snatching chicken legs and whittling on the docks. Your father and I were never good at disciplining you and even though I know you try your best, Sam has no structure to his life."

Percy just slumped and said, "Oh."

Her words were a slap of reality across his face. He tried to keep Sam happy and fed and never truly thought of the future.

Mamie read his body language and continued, "I know you've been doing your best, and I don't want you to feel bad. Sam adores you and I can see that you would do anything for him. Loving and being loved are laudable qualities."

She lifted his chin in her hand and smiled reassuringly.

"Percy, there weren't any suitable men on Nantucket, and when I had tea with Mrs. Chase, she told me about Stewart's situation. He's Mrs. Chase's second cousin. His wife died in childbirth. He needs a woman to help care for his child and for his plantation home in Virginia. Mrs. Chase told me that Stewart is a good and kind man, and that he will take care of Sam and me, and I won't have to worry about Sam's future."

Percy nodded, showing his understanding of what she was saying, but secretly thinking, "How do I fit into this puzzle?"

"Ma," he said with urgency, "Mrs. Chase is mistaken. Mr. Castle is not kind and he is not a good person. He keeps slaves on his farm. Slaves! He doesn't pay them for their work, and he's not nice to them. I heard him being rude to his attendant on the docks when he arrived."

Mamie creased her forehead in concern but firmly placed her hand on the table in front of her, stopping him there. "Percy, I won't hear any more of this. Mr. Castle is now my husband and your new father. You'll have to do what he says if you wish to be a part of this family."

Percy shifted back in his chair. This was a severe affront from his mother and he was taken aback by it. Mamie loved Percy and she could see she upset him greatly.

She continued, "Percy, you're a free spirit and always have been. This marriage is as much about business as it is about love. I hope

Stewart and I will find love over time but having a future for Sam
is important to me, and I know it is to you as well."

Percy nodded but couldn't give her eye contact.

"Many people find a husband this way. Marriage isn't always
perfect. You have to work at it. Stewart might learn from me as
much as I do from him. He's not Quaker, but, by the same token, I don't intend to lose my mores and integrity and become a
slaver."

"But, still, why did you have to surprise us this way?" Percy asked.

"When Mrs. Chase told me about Stewart, he came to Nantucket
to meet me. That was about a month ago. You remember. I went
over to the Chase's house for tea one Sunday afternoon?"

Mamie hesitated, remembering the feel of the delicate bone
china cup in her hands out on Mrs. Chase's front porch.

"I wanted to be sure things would work out before saying anything. And actually, I figured you'd have lots to say to talk me out
of it, as you are trying to do now, even after the fact. This is a decision I had to make for myself." Her eyes looking downward, she
nodded, trying to reassure herself that what she was telling Percy
was truly in her heart.

"At the Chase's, on that first Sunday, I made an agreement with
Stewart. We said that on his next trip, we would marry. I had no
idea he would insist on having a Pastor present. I had in mind a
Quaker marriage. So, you and I were both surprised at that."

She glided the palms of her hands from her waist, down her lap
to her knees, primly smoothing out her apron over her skirt.

"I suspect that Stewart will continue to surprise us as time goes
on. I'll have to acclimate to a new way of life, and so will you. I
love you Percy and, as you say, you deserve to know the truth. I've
spoken very plainly and honestly to you. I'm sorry if I hurt your
feelings. Will you still help us make this change in our lives or will
you stay here?" She stopped, looked at Percy and reached her hand

across the table to him, like the lifeline she wished someone had thrown her husband at sea.

There was silence for a moment. Percy looked down at his hands clenched in his lap. He didn't realize that his mother had felt this way about him. He agreed that Sam needed direction. He wasn't ready to lose Sam or his mother from his life, so he opened his fist, took her hand, and simply replied, "I'll help you."

LEAVING NANTUCKET

The boys helped their mother pack up her dishes, some clothing and her quilt. She took one reminder of Randall, the boys' father, his original gold wedding band, an extravagance she had insisted on, which he never wore to sea. Looking at it and weighing it in her hand, she wondered how much she would have gotten for it had she sold it, but it was too late for that now. She hid it in her sewing box as she walked out of the house for the last time.

She and the boys turned, held hands and looked back, almost longingly, at the house. All three wished they could stay, but knew that they couldn't.

Sam scrolled his eyes up to the Captain's walk and down again, taking it in for the last time. The Captain's walk had the shape of a tall rectangle, over a large square cookie cutter of a house, like many others on Nantucket that were rebuilt after the 1846 fire. The white lace curtains looked like seagulls fluttering out of the open windows over the teal blue clapboard. Mamie had watered the flowers in the window boxes before coming outside. Sam memorized the lines and colorful façade of the house. He always admired the details on the Captain's walk- the little columns on the corners and the stained glass border on the windows. Mrs. Chase had promised to look after the house until it was sold.

Mamie glanced down the lane at other vacant houses, considering her neighborhood's history. Except for Mrs. Chase, almost all of her friends had left as well. By the early 1850s, fewer whaling ships came in to shore and the economy was not booming. Other families also found it difficult to live on the island, where everything had to be brought over from the mainland. Many of the young people were leaving in search of the west coast and the promise of gold and riches. It was her turn.

Percy had to tug at Sam to get him onto the buggy that Stewart had arranged for so that the three wouldn't have to lug the trunks by cart to the dock. Sam had loving memories of the fun times with Percy and the image of that seaman's house. Even in adulthood, these were the only things he remembered about Nantucket Island and his innocent childhood. He clung to Percy's hand as they rode over to the dock.

The ride was short and Percy wished it could last an eternity. He thought about his conversation with his mother and how his own life was about to change. Though he always took time for Sam and made sure he had food to eat, he never did have a real job, and was a bit of a dare-devil at heart. He didn't like to take responsibility for anything unless it was packaged with adventure. Sam was fun, his brother, and the last vestige of their father. There was a strong bond and loyalty between them, even though they were years apart. Percy looked over at Sam, whose small hand he still held. Who knew? Maybe Stewart could "make a man of him" yet! He was determined to help Sam and his Ma get settled in any event. Looking ahead to the dock, Percy saw the boat they would board, and watched as an osprey spread its wings and freely rode the breeze, gliding down from the mast to a nearby piling, circling the harbor before it landed. If only he could be that free! He felt his brother's small hand in his and decided that he would take on Stewart for the sake of Sam and Ma.

The buggy pulled up to the dock and some men lifted the trunks off and got them on the boat. As they walked over to the ship, Mamie held a handkerchief to her face to guard her emotions, but Percy could feel her anguish. Sam, she knew, would have a new home and a better future.

"Here's to a wonderful new adventure," she said to Sam as she kissed his forehead.

Percy, she figured, would leave behind his childhood and heritage, and become an adult the minute his feet touched the gang plank. She smiled at Percy as she held his chin.

"It will all be all right," she said, assuring herself as much as him, and she kissed his forehead.

She put her hands on their shoulders and turned them around to face the ship. Percy took Sam's hand and they walked onto the boat together. Mamie looked up to survey the boat they were boarding and then she put one foot in front of the other.

The boys explored the ship, half hoping the journey would last forever, and anxious about starting a new life. Mamie stood starboard-side, watching the ebb and sway of the tides as the shoreline came and went from view. Percy's words weighed heavily on her mind as the boat rounded Long Island. After a light rain on the third night, the morning bore a rainbow. It arched overhead, sinking into the ocean. From the cabin window, Sam could see the rows of colors, red, blue, green and yellow, as vibrant below the clear shimmering water as they were above. Focusing on the line where the rainbow dove into its own reflection, he considered that his life in Virginia might be as colorful as the life he left in Nantucket. Sam looked up at his mother and saw the rainbow reflected in her eyes.

"A good omen," Mamie assured the boys as she tied her bonnet and threw a heavy shawl over her shoulders preparing to go to breakfast.

As she stepped out of the cabin into the sunlight, she realized that she no longer needed her shawl. The wind was balmy and moist and unexpected warmth filled the air. Sam watched as his mother casually discarded her shawl. It drifted behind her to the floor, like so many days in the Quaker House. Forgetting about the rainbow, he longed for a view of the Captain's walk on Nantucket, with its colorful stained glass windows, and secretly hoped to see a passing ship with his father waving from the bow. Caught by habit, and a sudden fearful emptiness, he searched the horizon, for friendly sails, shuddering at the thought that if his father was magically alive somewhere and ever did get home, they would be gone, nowhere to be found. Sam blurted out his fears to Mamie who enveloped him in her arms as Percy swallowed his breath and studied the worn soles of his shoes. Grief filled the sails as they neared the Virginia coastline.

PART 2

The Castle Plantation and the Civil War

PLANTATION LIFE

Before long, they were on land, scooped up with their belongings into a buggy, and on their way to their new home. Sam's head nodded against Mamie's shoulder and he napped through the wooded countryside. There was a steep, long dirt road through a parallel row of tall trees, shading anyone who came to visit the Castle Plantation. As they got closer, Sam looked up at the swaying leaves crowning his head. When they arrived, Stewart's attendant helped them down from the buggy. Sam wandered around the front of the large plantation house. A veranda stretched across the facade with big rocking chairs. There was no Captain's walk.

Strolling over to a nearby garden, Sam sat on a large stone to admire his surroundings. He watched as Percy, carrying his own bag, and looking back at Sam, was spirited away by Stewart's attendant toward the slave quarters, more like a small bustling village. Sam felt the ground swaying beneath his feet, an unsettling feeling of the tides changing before him. He could see land all around him, yet the stone he sat on was lost at sea. He laid his hands on it to steady himself. There were no docks or ships or houses, other than the big house and some small shacks where Percy was headed. He watched waves of black men and women scurry around Stewart and Mamie, carting trunks and bags toward the veranda, taking directions curtly shouted by Stewart. For the remainder of the day, Sam was left to his own devices.

Stewart took Mamie for a tour of his property while the house slaves brought in Mamie's things. The big home overlooked a large green square with a colorful array of beautiful flowers. There were rolling hills of greenery in the distance.

"So you can see I have at least 500 acres of land and more than 30 slaves," he said proudly extending his arm out gracefully, to show the expanse of his plantation. Mamie's hand was linked in the elbow of his other arm as they strolled across the lawn. She noticed a round spot of sweat under his arm that grew steadily as they walked.

"You certainly are ambitious," she replied, fanning herself with a silk fan that Stewart had given her as a gift when she arrived. They were looking past the slaves' quarters, near where Percy would have a shack that Stewart provided. There were fields extending as far as the eye could see, and slaves coming and going. Having land was so new to Mamie that she didn't quite understand the organization of it or how everyone knew where to go or what to do.

"You have to have big dreams to make big money. I'm so happy you've come, Mamie," he said, turning to face her and taking both of her hands in his.

"We'll have such a rich life together."

Mamie looked up at him self-consciously. "Uh-huh," she smiled, and then looked again, over at the slave quarters. "What are they like, the slaves? Is it safe for Percy to be over there?" She nodded her head in the direction of Percy's new home. "Your house is so big. Can't he just live with us?"

Stewart took them a bit closer to the slaves' village and they walked along its perimeter. It was as if he were admiring animals in a zoo. "Look at them, Mamie." With some disdain in his voice, he nodded toward them. "Why would you fear them? Percy will be busy and out of trouble."

"Oh my," she said, pointing to each person they passed. "That man has such huge, strong arms and such a stern, lined, serious face! Why he's as black as night and his shirt is torn. And, that girl, she is as white as I am. Why is she here? I thought all of the slaves had dark skin."

"Her father was white and her mother was black. Oh honestly," Stewart said. He shook his head as if he was changing his mind and his story. "She just has lighter skin, but she could have black children. Best to stay here where she belongs."

Mamie smiled and nodded at the girl as Stewart extended his open hand toward the girl's face. Mamie discerned some tenderness in his gesture, but then noticed his eyes were stern, his brow creased, and his chin was turned down. The girl looked worried, cast her eyes to the ground, and hurried on her way, avoiding his touch. Mamie was confused by this interaction but figured things were different in Virginia, and she'd have to give it time. She changed the subject.

"How do the children do in the fields? Do they go to school or play?" Mamie wondered out loud.

Stewart snorted a laugh. "They don't need time to play. They need to bring me some cotton. And their mothers make sure that they do."

Mamie could hear the menace in his voice. "Oh, they're just children, Stewart, really." She mocked him.

"There's a pregnant woman and a man who's as old as my grandfather would be, if he were alive. Don't tell me they pick cotton too. You don't make them go into the fields in this heat, do you, really, Stewart? They're God's children too."

"I doubt it," he replied, tiring of her judgments. "They all bring in their weight in cotton before they get to rest at night. That's how we do so well. They're committed to me," he lied, forming a fist with his hand and dropping her elbow. "They love their work and they're a happy group." He relaxed his hand and forced a smile in Mamie's direction, remembering his purpose in taking her around.

But Mamie could see that none of the workers smiled very often; most not at all. When they were near Stewart, they avoided eye contact. Sometimes Mamie wondered what she had gotten herself into. She decided she would talk to Stewart again about the slaves, to know his thoughts better. One evening, when they sat together on the large veranda in front of the main house, she struck up a conversation.

"Why do you treat them so harshly, Stewart? They work so hard for us," Mamie was rocking in a wooden chair that Stewart had commissioned from the carpenter in town especially for her.

"Just look at them, Mamie." Stewart took the pipe out of his mouth and waved it toward the slave quarters. He filled it with tobacco as he continued. "They only know how to work or sleep. They work if they fear me and they sleep because they're lazy or exhausted. I want them to be happy. I'm lenient and charitable. That's why I give them time off on Sunday evenings," he said, lighting his pipe.

"They only have those three hours off all week, and they work so hard they can hardly walk back to their quarters. That's charitable? What about the poor little ones?"

"Oh please, Mamie. On Sundays they can sing or dance after dinner. Some of our neighbors don't let them ever congregate at all."

"They can sing and dance if they are so inclined and have the energy to do so." Now Mamie was sarcastic. "I only hear them singing laments and prayers. And what they sing doesn't sound joyful to me. Isn't there any way to lift their spirits, to give them time to rest? To give them hope in life?"

"Hope? Hum. What would they hope for?" He said out of the corner of his mouth, puffing his pipe as he considered that as an idea. "I'm not sure what you're so concerned about, Mamie. On Christmas and Thanksgiving, I let them celebrate. I give them a chicken and extra flour and beans. Some of the plantation owners never give them anything extra, but leave them to the mush they get once or twice a day. And some of them aren't even grateful for what they get." He looked at his pipe as if he were considering its virtues.

"They're like animals," he continued. "They eat what you give them and do what they're told. They're lazy or angry if you give them too much time to sit around." Stewart continued to draw on his pipe as he rocked his matching chair slowly next to Mamie. "I'll have to let Mr. Smith know that we are enjoying these chairs," he said.

Periodically, Mamie would bring up the topic of how Stewart treated the slaves. It didn't seem to make any difference what she said. He was always polite to her, but just waved off her views. He drove them hard when they worked, and they had to be grateful for every crumb he allowed them or his happiness waned, and then his belt did more than hold up his riding britches.

Mamie couldn't bare it when he abused them. She had never seen such cruelty. But Stewart treated them as property, not people, and didn't think they felt the pain the same way white people did. He drove them harder if the crops dried up or they didn't feel well and brought in smaller bags of cotton from the field.

Stewart told her, "Mamie, they'll just sit around all day or lash out at us if I don't keep them in line."

"Of course, they'll hurt us, Stewart. You're killing them."

"Mind me, Mamie. I know how to keep food on our table and they should be grateful to me for putting food on theirs."

Mamie could see her pleas were useless and only upset him more. If she got him angry, he'd take it out on the first slave who walked by the front porch, by lashing at him with his belt. To avoid these sorts of outbursts, she took to minding her own business and ignoring what went on. She tried to set an example instead, by treating her attendant well and showing that the attendant responded in kind. When Mamie approached Stewart with this example, Stewart said that she was only behaving well because her skin was lighter. Mamie never heard of such nonsense and soon she just stopped trying.

"I don't know why you always bother me about our helpers, Mamie," he said one day while he was dressing for an evening party.

"They're not our helpers, Stewart. They're our slaves." Her voice was hard and she was gritting her teeth, anticipating a new argument.

"Slaves. Helpers. Call them what you want. If we didn't have them, we'd be poor."

"Like them?" she asked quizzically.

"Because of them you have someone to cook and clean and even sew your clothing. I can give you beautiful cloth to wear and hang on our windows. You'll be one of the richest women in Virginia. All because of our *slaaaves*," he slithered past her with a satanic grin, his palm petting her chin and popping his eyebrows up and down as he took in her narrow waistline.

"Oh stop it, Stewart. You're like a little boy." She swatted him away.

As he danced over to the doorway, he leaned back in. "Tonight, I'm going to let all of our friends know how well I'm doing. My slaves are the hardest workers, and I'm the richest man!" He waved his arms in the air arching over his head, with a silk scarf in each hand that he plucked up from a basket by the doorway. He danced back over to Mamie and stole a kiss on her cheek, dropping the scarves onto a glass tray on her bureau. She picked them off in annoyance, being careful not to knock over the atomizers.

She could smell his greed. "You have too much pride, Stewart." She playfully pushed him away. "Move back. You'll wrinkle my dress."

"I suppose that next you'll tell me that it's not the Lord's way for us to show our pride," he scoffed.

In her opinion, he was just a naughty child. Her eyes pleaded with him.

"Okay, okay. I'll tone it down when you're in the room," he waved her off and walked out curtly to supervise Sadie and the other house slaves who were getting the house in order for a grand dinner.

The house was large by any standard. The house slaves came and went by the back door. There was a narrow back stairwell they used when they had to go upstairs to the bedrooms. Mamie and Stewart had a large bedroom and there were three others on the second floor. His toddler son from his first marriage slept in the first bedroom. Although she was under the impression that she would help raise the child, Mamie hardly saw him. He was cared for by a slave. Sam slept in one of the bedrooms, and the last one was used as a dressing and sewing room for Mamie, though she wished Percy could live there. A large outhouse stood in the yard behind the main house. Sadie made sure it was always clean for Mamie and also swept a path between the house and the outhouse so that Mamie would not soil her shoes or her dress when she walked over to use it.

Though Sam and Mamie sometimes felt they were prisoners to Stewart's whims, they were by no means his slaves.

On a sunny day, when the flowers were blooming in the garden by the front veranda, and the sky was the color of the Nantucket waters that Mamie would never see again, Stewart rode right up to where Mamie sat. He jumped off his horse and tied the animal to the post by a trough.

"At your service Madame," he smiled, bowing as to royalty. He could tell she was deep in thought.

Mamie laughed as she continued with her needlework. "Why, Mr. Castle, I'm going to lose my count on this hanky if I have to stop to look at you." A bluebird swooped by the porch.

"It's a lovely day, Mrs. Castle," he said, extending his hand to take hers from the wooden sewing frame. "Put aside your hanky, or whatever that is, and come walk with me," he coaxed.

Mamie sighed. She tucked the needle under her last stitch and put the frame down on her rocking chair. Smiling, she let him guide her down the steps and out to the gardens.

"Mamie, I had a wonderful time today with Sam. I promised you I'd bring him up properly and you would be proud if you saw him riding today." There was a spring in his step.

"Proud?" Mamie challenged him.

"Oh, excuse me. You would love him even more than you do," he corrected himself, not wanting to ruin the moment. "We rode to the western perimeter and all you could see were our fields." Stewart's hand swept the air as if to paint the picture. "For such a small boy, he's a good horseman on that new pony of his. He's thriving."

Stewart now had Mamie's arm in his. His back was straight, and his head high. She didn't remember seeing him this happy and excited since they met.

"He remembered the exact trail I showed him last week, and he knew to go around those ugly hovels and keep his distance. He's a smart one!" Stewart grabbed the air with his free hand, as if to grab the moment. "There's a big old tree by the river and he helped me tie up a rope swing so that he can swing out over the water and dive in. He said that Percy taught him to swim. I guess that Percy did one thing right," he said.

"Now, Stewart, don't," warned Mamie.

"Well anyway, I promised that tomorrow, I'll take him out on a skiff and show him how to get to town on the river. I think he'll like the water route so he can more easily bring back provisions when you need them. What do you think of that?" He turned. Looking in her eyes and taking both of her hands in his, he said, "I'm always thinking of you Mamie."

Mamie could feel the warmth in Stewart's hands.

"Two months ago, Sam was starving. Now he is thriving," her eyes met his. "It's all because of you, Stewart. I am forever grateful to you for your kindness. I'm so happy the two of you have gotten along so well. I'm so very, very happy."

Beyond Stewart, Mamie could see Percy's hovel in the distance and she could feel her heart squeeze with pain. For Sam's sake, her smile never wavered.

Over the next few years, Stewart taught Sam how to get to town on his own, and bring back provisions. People in town looked after Sam because he was so young and likeable. Unlike Percy, Sam kept his opinions to himself and Stewart trusted him.

Mamie and Stewart often spent the hot summer days on the veranda. Mamie sewed her needlepoint and Stewart smoked his pipe admiring his property. He told her of adventures he had with Sam on the skiff and at the river. Mamie noticed that Sam was nowhere to be found on afternoons when Stewart wasn't with him.

"Sam is still young. Your land borders the river and there's wilderness on the other side of it. I wonder where he goes when you're not with him. Do you know what he's doing on his own? Is it safe for him such a distance from the house?" Mamie asked Stewart.

"Oh, he's just a boy. He's doing 'boy-ish' things. He's swimming and having a good time exploring. I can't monitor his comings and goings all the time. The water is keeping him cool. He's not used to our southern climate. Why are you so worried about him? He's a kid. Why don't you ask him yourself when he comes in for dinner?"

Mamie thought that was a great idea and she started taking time to talk to Sam about his day while Stewart was off counting the slaves and the cotton intake in the evenings.

"What do you do all day when you're not at the house?" Mamie wanted to know.

"I hang out at the river," Sam said looking at her sideways, making it clear that he wasn't sure why, all of a sudden, she was interested.

"Mr. Castle tells me that you and he have some fun times to-gether," Mamie continued.

"Oh. Is that what this is about? Yeh. We're getting along just fine."

"Yes, mam, would be better than 'yeh'. You're growing up in a polite place. You should begin to use polite manners."

"Are you going to tell Stewart everything I say, or will we really have some privacy—a heart-to-heart?" asked Sam.

"Why do you ask such a thing? Are you hiding something from him? He is your father now and you should respect him so he trusts you."

"He trusts me. I'm just asking. Can I talk to you and you alone?" Now Sam looked her straight in the eyes.

Mamie sat back and knew that something was amiss. "What's going on? I won't tell, but you have to be honest with me at least. You're my son—and a child—don't forget that! I want to know that you are safe." She looked around to be sure none of the house slaves were listening.

"I don't want to be around the house. I can't stand how Stewart behaves."

"Mr. Castle," she corrected.

"Mr. Castle," Sam repeated with a sarcastic tone. "He is cruel and nasty and I can't believe you would love him."

Mamie's eyes opened wide and then began to water. She searched his face for any remorse, wondering if this was a child-ish response to something negative Stewart said or did directly to Sam. She knew Stewart behaved dastardly and was unforgivingly harsh to the slaves. Could he do something hurtful to her son? Now she whispered.

"He hasn't hurt you has he? Did he ever ask you to hide any-thing from me—something he did or said to you?"

"No. He takes me on outings and seems to have as much fun as I do. But he's just not a nice man. He says and does horrible things to the people who are doing the work around here. And, he does nothing but hate and smoke his pipe. He treats his horse better than some of the slaves." Now Sam stopped and seemed to realize that he might have said too much. He looked around to be sure no one was listening to their conversation.

"I'm sorry ma. You had trouble feeding us back in Nantucket but you've always been good and kind and never hurt anyone the way he does. I know we depend on him. He doesn't know I feel this way and I won't let him know. I'm a good boy when I'm out with him. You don't have to worry about that. But....do you at least agree with me about how he treats the slaves? And, let's not forget how he treats Percy."

Mamie's face was red and blotchy, holding back tears and anger. She married Stewart to give Sam a better life, never considering that Stewart would disdain Percy as he did. Even hating the cruelty that plantation life enabled, she told herself that it would be difficult, no, impossible, for her to return to doing laundry and sewing for others just to have her next meal. She caught herself saying, "That would be like my being a slave." Then she stopped and realized how she was beginning to think. She was never a slave. She was free to work and earn wages, even if they were meager. And she was free to marry Stewart or not, and she chose to marry.

"I'm proud of you, Sam. We are here now and we will make the most of it. Learn farming from the slaves and business dealings from your step-father. But, never-ever give up the values that your real father and I have instilled in you," she said.

"And what of Percy? He taught me to be brave and to question everything. He's not like Stewart. I'm strong and confident even when things are stressful and challenging because Percy is a good role model. He lives his own life. I want to live my own life, not the one Stewart has in store for me."

Mamie brushed his hair away from his eyes and kissed him on his forehead.

"I hate to say it but having these talks was Stewart's idea and it was a good one, though he won't know what we talk about. I promise."

"Thanks ma."

For Sam, the river was a relief from the stuffiness of Stewart's rules and his harshness around the workers. Because he was still young and above suspicion, Sam soon had other business there as well. Underground-railroad "smugglers" convinced him to help bring slaves to safe houses in town, from where they stole off at night. As his role model, Percy taught Sam to be smug and confident even in the toughest situations. Sam was old beyond his years and understood that what he was doing would have worse consequences than stealing chicken legs. It would also have better outcomes for those he helped if he succeeded. Because he was small, it was easy for him to hide. People in town thought he was just a cute little boy who would grow up privileged and inherit Stewart's land. It was worth the risk, and he sensed that his mother would support him if Stewart caught him. Besides, even at his young age, he promised himself that, as a Quaker, he would never become proud or impervious to the cruelty just outside his door.

Stewart tried to loosen Sam's strong relationship with Percy by being there to separate them whenever he saw that they were spending time together. One day when he rode down to the river to find Sam for an outing he planned, he saw the two having a serious talk under the tree where the swing was. He curtly broke off their conversation.

"What are you doing off the plantation, Percy? Get back to work now and don't be a slacker!" He admonished Percy while waving his horse whip in the air.

Percy swung his hat from his head and bowed low to Stewart. "Yes sir, right away." Then, he ran away toward the slave quarters quickly, so Stewart couldn't swat at him for being rude.

Sam hated to see Percy treated that way but knew his own advantage would only last as long as he could hide his feelings. So he kept his tongue.

"I don't understand why a grown man would want to play with a child," Stewart said out loud to himself. "Tsk, tsk, tsk."

"Aw. He just misses me," Sam said. "Remember, we used to hang out all the time. He doesn't mean anything by it. He's just checking up on me."

"Well he should check up on the field workers to be sure they're pulling their weight. One went missing just yesterday and hasn't shown up anywhere. That's a loss Percy is responsible for. It's his job to be sure they all show up at night. I don't understand why he can't keep on top of things!" Stewart shook his head in disappointment. Then he looked up at Sam and smiled. "I'm sure glad I have time with you." But just as quickly, he changed his tone. "You stay away from that Percy," he said wagging his index finger in Sam's face. "Don't you go copying his ways. You don't want to end up with his life style." Stewart chuckled to himself after that remark.

Sam just looked at him with no expression on his face. He swallowed hard. "So what do you have planned for me today?" he finally managed to say and forced a smile.

MAMIE'S INFLUENCE ON THE PLANTATION

Mamie brought New England charm and grace to the plantation. As promised, Stewart gave her a slave to help her dress, sew and redecorate the house. Mamie said she always did everything for herself and didn't need a slave, but Stewart insisted. As always, Mamie did what Stewart wanted. She treated her attendant well, for she was just a girl, a few years younger than Percy, and she let her keep her name which was "Saida." Stewart thought it foolish to let a slave keep her African name.

"Why in the world would someone want to be called a name like that? What kind of a name is Saida?" he mocked. "Anyway, her mother gave her that name, just to be difficult. She didn't ask me." But then Stewart stopped abruptly, as if rethinking what he was about to say. Steeling his emotions, he continued, "She belongs to us, and she is almost white. She should have a white name if she's going to be in our house."

"I see what you're saying, Stewart," Mamie said, but she really didn't understand at all the message Stewart almost imparted.

"Saida is her name and the name she is used to. I want her to feel happy so that she'll help me out."

"Her job is to help you out. If she's rude or does anything you don't want her to do, I'll tend to her," replied Stewart.

"No! No," Mamie said emphatically. "She'll be my attendant. She won't be a problem, and I want her to have a name she's happy with."

"Okay. Okay, my dear. So what name might that be," Stewart smiled down at Mamie trying to appease her. "I gave her to you to make you happy. I don't want to argue about her. Can we compromise?"

"Thank you Stewart." Mamie looked up at him with a coy smile, although she hated playing these games with him. "How about we call her 'Sadie'. It's close to her African name but is Americanized as well."

Stewart nodded, gave her cheek a peck, and waved her off, muttering to himself, "who really cares what you call her." And Sadie, it was.

When Mamie told Sadie about her new name, Sadie smiled. She had found an advocate in Mamie, but only as far as Stewart would allow. Stewart could sense that Mamie's Quaker upbringing made it difficult for her to take on his Southern ways. He was fond of her and could tolerate a little flexibility.

Stewart remembered that Mamie's Nantucket house was teal blue and he bought her several yards of teal satin as a gift for a new dress. Sadie sewed it with a wide skirt supported by wooden hoops, a ruffled fitted bodice and soft white crocheted gloves up over Mamie's elbows. Mamie's old dresses were much simpler. She never owned anything like this before but she could tell from the look on Stewart's face that it made him happy to see her in it.

Stewart wanted to show off his new wife to his friends so he invited ten land owners and their wives from the neighboring plantations. He planned a dinner party the likes of which Mamie would not have been able to imagine while back in Nantucket. The men went on wild turkey hunts, and roasted two pigs on spits in the yard while they drank and argued about politics, the economy, and slavery. They came on beautiful ponies with hand-worked leather saddles. Some came in surreys and wagons decorated with cushions and canopies with fringes, as fancy as the one that Stewart used for their wedding. The men brought their wives and Mamie saw their velvet and satin gowns with wide petticoats and elaborate shawls. Their hair was rolled upward and pinned under fringed or flowered caps tied under their chins. Some carried colorful umbrellas that matched their dresses and shaded them from the sun. Each brought a bag with knitting or needlework to keep them busy while the men hunted and the slaves cooked side dishes.

The head cook made all sorts of pies and pastries and there was enough food to feed everyone in the house plus the 20 or so people whom Stewart invited.

Mamie met her neighbors this way and started to cultivate friends. The Castles were invited to other plantations for parties, and Mamie got to see how the other wives decorated their living and dining areas and how they treated their house slaves. While the men talked in the dining room, Mamie and the other women sat in the parlor room off to the side. Sometimes they sewed to keep busy and sometimes they just gossiped.

After several such parties, Mamie approached Stewart.

"I see that your friends let their wives decorate the main floors of the houses with style and purpose. Every one of them has a different look to it. I'm impressed by their artistry and creative ways."

Stewart was thoughtful as if remembering his last wife. "Yes, Susan began to decorate our dining area before she became pregnant and....." His voice trailed off.

"I'm sorry, Stewart, that's probably a sad memory for you."

"It's okay, dear. Now I have you and things are brighter." His palm brushed her cheek.

"I'm wondering if it would be okay if I put my own touches on the house now that I'm here. Would you mind that? I have some ideas and maybe I could bring some Nantucket to Virginia," she smiled.

"Why that's a splendid idea, Mamie. I have only one request that I want you to follow."

"Sure. What is it?" Mamie was curious.

"I want you to leave the picture of me where it is, between the windows at the head of the table. It shows prominently there, especially when dinner is served. When people come to visit, I want them to see that I'm the master of this house," he said with too much pride in his voice.

"Oh," said Mamie. "You mean the one with you wearing your long grey coat, the one you wore at our wedding?"

"Yes. I wore that at both of my weddings and I want people to see my fashionable beaver hat. The saber makes me look like an army man. It never hurts to have people admire you, you know." He puffed out his chest, looking too full of himself for Mamie's taste.

"Don't you think it might look better upstairs or in the side parlor? I'm not sure the dining room is the best place for such a proud, presumptuous display," Mamie suggested.

"Nonsense," said Stewart, waving her off, as he always did when he got his way.

When Mamie spoke with Stewart, she didn't have a set idea about the changes she would make. She just wanted to see what he would say. Now that he was amenable to change, she figured she could soften the room with some new curtains. She took Sadie with her to the local general store and ordered yards of calico cloth dyed grey to match Stewart's coat in the dining room portrait. The cloth would have small pastel yellow and pale pink flowers with green stems printed on the grey background. She also ordered white lace for ruffling.

Stewart laughed at her when she told him what she planned.

"In Nantucket, the ruffles fluttered in the breeze from the ocean." Stewart fluttered his hands in the air like the blowing ruffles. "Here in Virginia, they'll hang limp from the humidity and heat." He frowned with arms hanging limply and palms down, mimicking his impression of the curtains.

Mamie smirked and just said, "Wait and see." This time, she waved him off.

When the cloth arrived, Mamie told Sadie to take down the heavy grey velvet draperies that Stewart's first wife had put up. Sadie made the new draperies. The dining area looked open, airy and more cheerful this way and it reminded Mamie of her Nantucket home. When Stewart saw them for the first time, he paced back and forth with his hands clasped behind his back. He was looking them up and down, and back and forth from the curtains to his portrait. Then he kissed her on the forehead and told her, "This will do."

Mamie and Sadie chuckled behind his back at his self-centeredness. Making small changes such as this helped Mamie feel more at home. She needed to be useful and creative. Sadie had the good sense to find out from Sam and Percy what Mamie liked and then recommended it to her so that she would feel reinforced in her decisions. Mamie took Sadie's advice to heart when she added her own decorating opinions. She saw that Sadie tried hard to please her, and she was more of a friend than a house slave when Stewart wasn't around. Living in such a big house so far from her neighbors could be lonely, and Mamie was grateful to have Sadie around.

Mamie gave Sadie the old curtain material so she could make herself a skirt. She also gave her the leftover scraps from making the new curtains. Sadie fashioned a bed for herself that she kept folded up during the day and put outside of Mamie's door at night so she could sleep better on the hard floor near her mistress in case she was needed. Mamie encouraged her to make rag dolls for the slave children. When Stewart heard about this, he was livid.

"I'm letting her stay under my roof so she can make clothes and toys for slaves? What could you possibly be thinking about! She needs to work for us. Why do slaves need toys? It will keep them from their work and slow them down, and why in heaven's name can't she sleep on the floor?" Stewart ranted.

But he saw that, in fact, the toddlers took their dolls to the fields with them and played, while their mothers worked without being interrupted. Having a toy actually freed the mother to work harder. Stewart approved and let Sadie continue to make the dolls. Sadie felt she lifted the other slaves' spirits a bit by doing these little things that Mamie would encourage and Stewart would allow. Once in a while, Sadie would smile at Stewart for this small kindness. But Mamie soon saw that Stewart could take advantage of a smile, and apart from being angry at Stewart, she worried about Sadie, since she was really still a teenager, and didn't know any better, yet.

STEWART AND PERCY

Percy lived in a modest shanty by himself just inside the edge of the slave village, and had to work for his keep. The only belongings he had, he brought in a bag from Nantucket. Even at that, he was better off than some of the slaves who were new to the plantation.

Mamie was concerned for his well-being and wanted to check on him, but knew Stewart wouldn't take her over to see her son. One day, when Stewart was in town, she went over by herself to the slave quarters to find Percy. She wasn't aware of the work schedule and when she got to the village line, all of the workers were out in the fields. She wandered aimlessly, hoping to pick out her son's hut, and was appalled at the squalor and lack of amenities. There were no visible outhouses. The shacks had dirt floors, a few tree stumps as chairs, doors swinging unsecured, and windows open to the elements. The whole area had a stench about it. It was much worse than she imagined. Stewart's slaves were barely existing. A stark contrast to the life she was living. How did Percy survive?

It was late afternoon, the sun was still hot, and Stewart was riding home from town. He saw Mamie out by the slave quarters and rode over to her.

"My dear. What on earth are you doing here! This is no place for you to be walking. I hope no one has seen you out here." He looked around to see if anyone was nearby.

"Hello Stewart. I'm looking for Percy's hut. I just wanted to see how he is doing and maybe visit a few minutes. I brought him some cupcakes that Sadie baked for him." She held up a basket covered with a calico cloth to keep the flies away. "But it is further from the house than I realized. I'm afraid, I'm quite lost and my feet are already aching."

"I'll take one of those," he said as he pulled a small cake from under the cover, ignoring that they were not meant for him. "Now, go home, Mamie." This was a stern command. "This is not a proper place for you." He stuffed the cake in his mouth, "Yummm," and rode away, leaving her there to walk back on her own.

Mamie looked around at the group of hovels. She hung her head in shame and walked slowly back to the house, following Stewart's horse. It wasn't like Stewart to treat her this way. "His demeanor must be evidence of how he feels about Percy, not me," she thought. She realized that she would have to find another way to reach out to her son.

When Sadie made curtains for the Castle plantation house, Mamie purchased a few extra yards of cloth and instructed her to make curtains for Percy's hut as well. The curtains would be tacked firmly to the wall at the top and have a loop and hook at the bottom. This way, they could be secured to keep out the dust, wind and rain, but opened to let the breeze in on hot evenings. She also made him bedding so he wouldn't have to sleep on the dirt floor. Sadie snuck over to Percy's hut to install the curtains and bedding while all the workers were in the fields, and Stewart was at the river with Sam.

Coming home from a hot day's work, Percy noticed Sadie coming out of his doorway. He saw that his windows had curtains. He grinned and tipped his hat in gratitude, and she smiled, shyly nodding her head. He wasn't sure if this kindness was from his mother or from Sadie but he was grateful for the privacy and protection the curtains provided, and the comfort of a soft bed. From time to time, Sadie left muffins or biscuits that Percy found at the end of the day. Often, he shared them with friends he made amongst the slaves.

Percy learned how to take care of himself by spending time with his slave-neighbors when Stewart wasn't around. He had people skills and paid attention when field hands whispered or spoke to him. The field workers saw that Percy looked out for them and they trusted him in turn. Even so, the transition to this hard way of life was more difficult than he had anticipated.

On the flip side, Percy had no real job skills. He was young when his father left for his last sailing and no one had ever established an apprenticeship for him. Stewart provided him with work he could do, and responsibility that he abhorred.

"Your job will be to keep an eye out that none of the slaves slips out at night. If they do, catch them and bring them to me. If you can't catch them, then tell me immediately so I can send out the senior foreman on horseback to find them," Stewart explained.

"Why would they want to run away?" Percy asked, although by now, he knew the answer.

"Seriously! Okay, well, now…" Stewart stammered. "Sometimes a slave has a family member at the next plantation over. Sometimes it's a child or a wife or a husband. They want to visit. But they can't. They belong here."

"I'm sorry. I don't understand. Why are their kids at another place if they're here? Why aren't they together?" Percy was incredulous. He had heard of such things but could hardly believe his mother would marry someone who would do that.

"Percy, we own our slaves. They belong to us. If a slave is on another plantation, they belong there. They can't be here and there. If my neighbor wants to use my labor, he has to pay me for it. I don't want my workers to wander off and leave me without a way to run my land. Don't you cross me on this or anything else. Just do your job." Stewart was adamant.

"But if I was here and Sam was at our neighbor's farm, I'd miss him. I'd be tempted to run over and visit him. Why can't they have time to visit?"

"I said don't cross me. Do you understand? You'll live on my land and eat my food if you do your job. Otherwise you're on your own."

"Yes sir. I understand," Percy said. But he really didn't understand at all.

Percy wasn't happy about this arrangement but he knew he had no choice if he was to stay on at the plantation, so he did his best for a few years. Putting his fear aside, he just couldn't stand idly by and let people be so mistreated. He was generally sick over what went on, and did whatever he could to ease the burden of at least one or two workers each day. Regardless of his new familial relationship to Stewart, he knew Stewart would beat him silly if he found out, so anything he did was done in a clandestine way. Most of what he did was warn the slaves when Stewart was around, or make excuses that kept them out of trouble. Percy used the same "street smarts" that he had used to get food in Nantucket, to protect the workers on the plantation. It worked for a while.

One day, Stewart took Sam to the river and they took a boat to town to buy some sugar and flour that Mamie wanted so she could teach Sadie how to make her favorite Nantucket muffins. While Stewart was gone, Percy and Max, the slave who groomed Stewart's horse, crept over to the chicken coup. Max kept watch while Percy snuck in and took two eggs. Then Percy kept watch while Max chatted with Sadie, who passed him some leeks and potatoes that she had put in her apron pocket from the storage bin. Max and

Percy cooked a nice soup for dinner and Stewart was none the wiser. Max's family ate well that evening.

Percy remembered the days when he and Sam had to scrounge for food and basic comforts. He had compassion, especially for the children. Unbeknownst to Stewart, Sam sometimes came back from a day at the river with pails of cold water that Percy took over to the slave quarters to help cool off the smaller children after a hot day in the fields.

Stewart soon caught on, but never caught Percy in action, and started to keep a strong watch on Percy. Mamie would never let him whip Percy like one of the slaves, but Stewart had a few strong threatening words with him that Percy never forgot. Percy was more careful after that, and soon had an idea. He came up to the main house, and asked permission to come in. Sadie let him in.

"What on earth are you doing in here?" Stewart challenged him.

"Leave him alone, Stewart. He just wants to see me," said Mamie.

"Then go outside and visit with him. He smells like one of my horses," Stewart said in disgust.

"I'm sorry sir," Percy said. "I'll go over to the lake and wash up after we talk."

"Yes, I guess that would be a good thing to do more often," Stewart said.

"Anyway. I just want to say. I got a job helping in the apothecary store in town. It's kind of like an apprenticeship," Percy lied. He just stood there in front of Mamie and Stewart holding his hat in his hands, like one of the slaves, not daring to look Stewart in the eyes.

Stewart stood up tall and smiled.

"What does this mean exactly," said Mamie, wanting more information.

"Uh. Well. Uh," Percy stammered. "It means I'm moving to town. I'll have to live at the store to keep it secure while I learn about what to do."

"Move to town?" Stewart repeated, nodding his head. Stewart clapped him on the back, "That a boy!" he proclaimed. Then he wiped his hand off on his britches as if Percy had a contagious disease he didn't want to catch.

Stewart couldn't imagine how Percy arranged such a thing but also couldn't wait for him to leave. It would be one less mouth to feed, and he really wasn't much help around the plantation anyway. He noticed that some of the slaves exhibited an air of entitlement when Percy was nearby. He wanted to squelch that as soon as he could. It would be easier with Percy out of the way.

Mamie knew when Percy wasn't telling the truth, and she wondered where he was really off to. Percy was "high maintenance" but she loved him just the same. She pulled Percy aside and gave him a sack of rolls and a clean shirt before he left. Then, she ran up to her boudoir and, being careful that neither Sadie nor Stewart was near, she took out the gold wedding band that she brought from Nantucket in her sewing box. Back at the door, she slipped it into Percy's hand. "You may need food and clothing. Put it on. The people in town will consider you more respectable if they think you have a wife. Sell it if you're desperate."

Percy looked at the valuable gold band and grasped his fingers around it, considering it a gift from his father. He put it on and thanked her.

"Watch your back and stay safe," Mamie told him. "I'm not sure you should keep in touch, at least out in the open. I don't know what Stewart will do if you show up here again. He got word that you are making friends with some of the slaves."

Mamie kissed Percy on his forehead, a symbol of a new beginning. He kissed her back for the old times. He held her at arms' length to give her a serious once over. He wanted to remember her in a loving moment in case they didn't see each other for a while.

THE CIVIL WAR BEGINS

S tewart's carriage driver heard rumors in town that some of the slaves might go free or that slaving might be stopped altogether. Slaves were forbidden to talk about it but the message crept through the plantation just the same. Slave-masters were concerned that the slaves might rise up and fight or kill them as revenge for how they were treated. Some were harsher in the hopes of keeping their slaves in tow. But some said that slave owners would free their slaves if they promised to stay and work on the farms.

Stewart's neighbors held wild meetings in town. Men rode recklessly, shooting in the air, beating anyone with dark skin if they saw them out at night, and sometimes even hanging them "for good measure."

"Teach 'em a lesson," they shouted.

What that lesson might be, Percy could never figure out. It seemed to him that the men who hung them needed a lesson. But he kept his mouth shut and soon crept out of town, away from the dialogue. He was not one to be swept up in a cause he didn't understand or believe in. He needed time to discover his own way. He had fabricated the apprenticeship job, so leaving was easy.

As he walked the back streets, he could hear the men shouting.
"Secede from the Union!"
"Keep your slaves. Kill all abolitionists."
"The Union will starve."
"This is a big mistake. We'll show 'em."
Some even feigned concern while being disrespectful, saying slaves were like children. "What will they do and where will they go if we don't take care of them?"
Many feared they might even take over their land.
News came to Virginia that Northern soldiers were held up in Fort Sumter and surrounded by Confederate forces ready to attack. After that attack occurred, the North gave up the Fort and more states, including Virginia, rallied for secession from the Union. The Civil War began.

PART 3

Westward

PERCY'S TRANSITION

Percy was confused and afraid. He had always called the shots and was proactive about adventures in his life. Since Mamie married Stewart, his choices became narrower. Now he was making a life for himself as a hermit-woodsman in the forested area outside of town and away from the plantation, but he could see that things had to change. Living on the plantation taught him to be resourceful, so he held onto his father's gold ring.

The war marched closer and the slaves were treated very severely. Plantation owners were angry, and more than once Percy saw a black body swinging from a tree as he walked through the woods toward the river. He hid on these occasions, not wanting anyone to know where he was or what he saw. He had slipped out of sight once the war started. For as long as he could, he would live in the woods and not express which side he was on. He had no intentions of joining the fight on either side. His primary aim was to stay alive and out of harm's way. He didn't believe in killing to settle disputes.

When he went into town for provisions, he saw men and boys lined up in front of long wooden tables. They were signing up as

Confederate soldiers. Some just put an X as their name and some were so young, Sam might have passed to be old enough. Percy had seen so much of the brutality on the plantation that he could only imagine what a battlefield would be like. He hoped Sam had enough sense to stay out of it and that Stewart wouldn't influence him otherwise. Percy always just slipped by, got what he needed and disappeared from town as quickly as he could without being pulled onto the line.

Mamie didn't get involved because she knew she and Sam depended on Stewart and had to do whatever he said. They had nowhere else to go. Because Sam was interested in primping himself in the mirror, and going to school and sitting near the girls, Mamie thought he didn't really care about politics. He was too young to fight a war. He knew he was good looking and didn't want to lose an arm or a leg just because Stewart was afraid of losing his slaves.

Sam knew it was prudent to keep his mouth shut on the topic, and he also felt what Stewart did was wrong. He didn't know what would happen on the plantation if a war got this close or where the slaves would go or what side they would be on.

One day, on his way to the lake, Sam saw Percy out in the woods.

"Psst, psst," Percy hissed from behind a tree.

Sam ran over to where Percy was hiding. He looked around to be sure no one saw them.

"What are you doing here? You want to get yourself killed? Stewart has everyone on the plantation on the lookout for you. He was humiliated when he heard you lied to him. He won't stand for it," whispered Sam as he kept nervously surveying the area to be sure they were alone.

"I've been in the woods nearby. They're signing up everyone for the army. Stay out of town and away from the recruitment tables. Things are going to get bloody and horrible," Percy warned.

"I can take care of myself," Sam said defiantly. "You can't imagine what I've been doing, and getting away with." Sam sounded sure of himself. "Stewart has no idea how many slaves he's got on this property and how many are already gone. He just cares about what people think of him. And right now, his mind is set on getting ahold of you. So go. Get lost. We'll be fine. Stewart trusts me. He won't hurt Ma. You've got to get going," Sam urged Percy as he kept peering around the tree anxiously.

Percy ducked down and ran quickly back to where the tree-line was thicker and more protective. Sam waved him away. He was smarter than Percy could imagine and was already helping abolitionists secretly, and had been for several months. He imagined that he was probably the youngest abolitionist 'soldier' in Virginia.

One night, by his lean-to in the woods, Percy saw what he thought was an Indian, maybe a scout, hiding between the trees. The scout disappeared for a few minutes and then suddenly, came running through the woods with three runaway slaves. They hid again, looking around nervously. They weren't there in the morning. Percy figured they slid off into the night when most people were asleep. He had no idea where they were going or where they ended up, whether they were safe, or if he would find them swinging from a tree the next day.

Percy didn't know his way around the surrounding areas. He thought about what he might do. The only places he had ever been to were Nantucket, the plantation, and the nearby town. Nantucket was far away. He couldn't go back to the plantation or the town. He couldn't live in the woods forever, especially with the war moving closer. He had to find his way to a place where he could make a life for himself. Maybe he could do this if he followed the runaways. He kept track of this 'underground' movement, which he observed again, a few nights later, and watched from afar. If he was correct, they always moved toward a northwesterly direction. He didn't want to secretly track them, since he sensed that they might all pay dearly for it were he to make a mistake and attract the wrong kind of attention to their movements.

Now that the war was in full swing, in addition to runaways, he saw deserters. They ran quickly through the woods. One had a gun and wore grey pants. They were much too big for him, and were held up with suspenders. He still had on his night shirt but it was blotched with something brown and oddly shaped. Percy realized it was dried blood. The man's eyes were wide and there were streaks down his face, maybe from crying. He could hear the man sobbing and breathing hard as he ran. At closer look, Percy thought this man looked too young to be a soldier. Wherever he was coming from, it didn't look like he was going back. Back in Nantucket, Percy's dogs had caught a rabbit in the brush. One of them pranced out of the bushes all proud about her catch. The rabbit was still alive. This man's face and eyes reminded Percy of the rabbit right before Bowser ripped it open. Percy ducked out of sight and watched as the man ran by.

Another night, a man came running, and suddenly bumped into Percy grabbing him so tight he thought he'd break his arms.

"Hide me quick," he wheezed between his teeth, shaking Percy hard.

Percy was startled, and not thinking, pushed the man away, hiding himself, instead of helping the man. Percy lay flat next to a tree limb that had fallen nearby. A minute later, he heard a loud crack. He peeked out from behind the log to watch the same man fall dead across his path near his hiding place. Men shouted from where the shot had come. Percy rolled closer to the log, hastily covering himself with leaves. Footsteps ran toward him. He held his breath. He heard the man's body being moved; maybe being turned over. There was silence. Then, more footsteps, running away from Percy into the woods. Then, "crack, crack, crack!" Gunshot in the distance.

Percy stayed hidden until the next morning when it was quiet again and the deserter's blood had run under the log and dried onto his own leg. Percy got up and backed away in fear and disgust.

He wildly swatted at the blood on his leg, trying to get it off. Maybe he'd go to hell for not helping that man. He rationalized, "Who's to say what side he was on." But then he thought, "What side am I on?"

Percy went to the river and washed the blood off of his leg, carefully surveying the area around the clearing where he was. He calmed down after a bit and sat quietly contemplating what he hadn't done, and how he might escape the madness that was surrounding him. He heard the popping of guns in the distance and wondered how far the shooting was from the Castle plantation. He went back to the dead man and dragged the body closer to where he had been, near the river. He buried it in a shallow make-shift grave and covered it with leaves and fallen tree branches. He piled on as many stones as he could find around the shore of the river, to discourage animals from digging up the body. He removed his hat and bowed his head and begged God to forgive him for not hiding the man. He looked around realizing that standing out in the open, the way he was, made him a target for any trigger-happy soldiers. He took off down the riverside to get as far away as he could from the sound of war.

As he ran, his thoughts buzzed loudly in his head, and he tried to reassure himself of his own intentions.

"This wasn't what I had in mind when I left town. I am not a coward. Not a coward! If I had a gun, I would fight to defend myself or Sam or Ma. I would have hidden that man if I wasn't so surprised. I was just caught off guard."

He sobbed as he ran. He had never touched a dead man before. He had never even seen one up close.

"I couldn't have protected him anyway. There were more of them than just the two of us. I didn't have a gun. I am not a coward. I am not a coward," he repeated to himself.

He decided that maybe he had made a terrible mistake regarding the dead man, or maybe not.

"Maybe the man had slaves whom he beat and mistreated, like Stewart," he considered. "I won't feel so badly if that's the case," he rationalized as he ran.

He shook his head to try to throw off his feelings of inadequacy. He had to clear his mind. He had to get away. He would think about all of this later.

For now, Sam would have to depend on Mamie and Stewart, and his good looks, charm and stealth. Percy hoped he wasn't deserting Sam to danger. He was personally humiliated and felt deep shame and guilt about running, but also had no idea who was shooting at whom or which side was which. He calmed his confusion by convincing himself that it was better to get away alive and have time to think, than to stay and be shot. He ran the perimeter of the town line keeping out of sight, and staying in a thicker part of the woods. He wanted to get a feel for which direction the soldiers were moving toward.

Overnight, he hid deep in the trees, but was still only a mile or so from town. He reasoned that to escape the fighting he would need more than berries and squirrels to eat. He would need provisions such as food, a blanket and maybe a gun or a knife, but he had to be careful if he was going to slip into town. He was still confused and didn't know if he needed some "creature" comforts, or was just feeling so guilty that he would risk being caught. If someone did see him, it would look odd that he wasn't in uniform, carrying a rifle or just plain off in the war. He wished he had taken the uniform from the dead man, but what if he was on the wrong side? He had also told a lie that the apothecary and Stewart knew about. He had to lay low.

Percy wanted news of where the war was and where it wasn't. He needed to find a way out. He remembered how he and Sam had drifted into that Quaker party years ago and made off with their dinner. He figured he might just slip into town, pick up what he needed and slip out again. But he was older and bigger and more noticeable now. He'd end up in jail or in the army by force if he wasn't careful. He thought of the scout he had seen. If he saw him again, maybe he would track his route this time. He decided to take a chance and go into town. He would see what he could do about getting information and supplies. He'd be careful but he'd get what he needed.

Percy felt those old flutters in his chest as he pulled his hat over his eyes, bent over and walked crookedly down the main road to hide his identity. He purposefully bumped into people so they would think he was sick or too drunk to watch out for them. They pushed him away and didn't have a second look or thought about it. He was repugnant because he smelled from living out in the woods, and running, and they didn't want him near them.

"Ugh. You're disgusting. Get away from us, you awful man," one woman said indignantly, and she gave him a shove, pulling her child close to her side.

After a while, he realized that most people on the street were women and children and that they didn't care at all about him. They were glancing in the direction of where the shooting was coming from and shuffling through the streets as quickly as they could with their own provisions in hand. Mothers held their children's hands tightly and kids went bug eyed every time the cracking and popping of guns could be heard again.

When he walked by the blacksmith's barn, someone reached out and grabbed him, pulling him into the stables. He nearly lost his balance. He was shocked. It was Sam. He was smaller than Percy but had an authoritative air about him, and was dressed like a miniature Stewart. As he was opening his mouth in surprise, Sam slapped his hand over it.

"Quiet stupid. You want them to know you're in here?" Sam pulled him around behind the door.

It was dark in the room and it took Percy's eyes a minute to adjust. Then he saw her. Just in back of Sam against the wall and breathing hard, with a tiny girl at her side, was Mamie's dressing maid, Sadie, the one who tied her corsets and lowered her dresses over her head for parties; the one who had helped her decorate the dining room and brought cakes out to Percy's hut. Her forehead was creased with worry and fear, and she held her sister's hand too tightly. He thought he saw the little girl shaking. She backed into the darkness as Percy approached.

Sam was helping Sadie escape Stewart's lewd advances. The child was her younger sister whom Sam swiped from the neighboring plantation as it was raided by some abolitionists. The group was riding with long wooden stakes on fire. They yelled obscenities and started setting fire to the main house, ignoring everyone in their path. The little girl escaped, crying, into the yard where Sam was picking up some borrowed seeds and flour for Mamie. He grabbed the little girl instead and ran back to the Castle Plantation out of sight of the perpetrators.

Sam snuck her into the wood shed on the Castle plantation early in the morning. He dared to tell Mamie that Sadie and the child were hiding, before he went back to his usual routine, so as not to be noticed out of place. Mamie took them some food. Then, keeping their hiding place secret, she begged Stewart to let Sadie go with the child.

"They burned our neighbor's house. The child got away with only her life. They'll come here too! They say they're abolitionists, but they're killing slaves and landowners alike. Sadie and the child will be freed anyway when the blue coats come," Mamie argued. "Just let them go! They're just young'uns," she said.

Stewart slapped Mamie and she fell back against the wall. He had never touched her like that before, and she was astonished as her hand held her flaming cheek and ear.

"I want that Sadie girl. I like her. She's mine," he rudely admitted. "But I'll hang Sadie and that child if I catch them trying to run," he snarled at her. "And, I'll hang anyone who tries to help them!" He added, drilling his eyes through her.

Mamie sank to the floor holding her battered face in her hands and wept. She realized then that her satin dresses, calico curtains and fancy dishes were not going to save her from the violent storm shattering the south, or from her husband, crazed, about to lose all that he worked for. She had to protect Sam and keep her wits about her. She vowed to do so.

Mamie knew that Stewart had no idea that Sam was involved and still trusted him. She kept all sorts of secrets to protect Sam as Stewart was on the rampage. She knew she'd kill Stewart before she'd let him hang Sam. She found a gun that Stewart had hidden in a drawer in the parlor. She took it and hid it in her boudoir, where she knew he would never look.

The fighting was drawing closer by the hour, and Mamie hoped that Stewart would leave to join the fray before he found Sadie, and, as luck had it, he did. The shooting grew louder, closer. Stewart left Sam and Mamie at home and rode off to see if the armies were crossing his property line. He never came home.

Sam and Mamie decided to help whichever army approached them first, in the hopes of keeping a roof over their heads. They would offer food, water and shelter for the wounded if it came to that, anything, not to be shot or sent off into the woods to starve. To keep them safe, they told the house slaves to hide until they knew which army would approach first.

Sam took off with Sadie and her sister before the sun came up the next day. He left word that he was going into town for food in case of attack and would be back later in the day. He often went into town alone by taking a boat on the river, as Stewart had taught him, so no one thought anything of it. Sadie and her sister lied down in the boat and Sam covered them with some cotton sacks, as he had several times before, with others. They weren't missed until late in the day when Sam was already back in the house. No one ever suspected him. Mamie was just happy to see him alive, safe and back home. No one missed Stewart. They held their breath and waited to see who would ride up the pathway to the veranda.

Once in town, Sam knew that the blacksmith had connections with a scout who helped runaways, and that the scout would arrive soon. Sam wasn't sure what he'd do with Percy, but wanted to get him off the street. Percy told Sam that he'd be sure they were safe if he could go along. Sam laughed to himself. He was off the hook on this transfer. Percy had his back again and was principled enough to take on this huge responsibility. Sam smacked Percy on the cheek, but while doing so, stopped and looked at him hard in the eyes, knowing he might never see him alive again, remembering the Nantucket house and the rainbow on the ocean. Percy's face softened as they caught each other in a brotherly embrace. Sam noticed his father's gold band as Percy released him. He took Percy's hand in his own and ran his thumb across the smooth, shiny gold. "I still don't remember dad's face. There's only you. Be careful," Sam said.

"With all of the opportunities that Ma and Stewart gave you, I'm so impressed that you are growing up as a young man with principles," Percy said.

"Don't give me that, Percy. I know how much you want to stay clear of the war. Thank you for helping with these two." Sam nodded in the direction of Sadie and her sister, hiding in the darkness of the blacksmith's barn. "You've always got my back." Sam continued, "A man wearing a red shirt will come by and ask if you have any oxen for sale. Tell him you have two but one's a young'un. Do whatever he tells you and bring them along," Sam said as he motioned at the two who were hiding in the dark. "Keep the door open until he comes. That way the light's too bright to see inside and it doesn't look like you're hiding anything."

Percy marveled at how smart Sam was at such a young age. But then, under the circumstances, he knew his brother would have it no other way. He remembered how Sam worried over a stolen chicken leg. If stealing food bothered him when he was just seven years old and starving, how could he consider leaving Sadie behind now? He hoped Sam's luck would hold out.

"Godspeed," Sam said then, and whistled Dixie as he strolled past Percy into the street, a miniature of a man, dressed like a southern dandy. Ten and twelve year olds were grabbed and handed guns to fight. Because of his slight figure, and short stature, Sam looked too young to enlist and the recruiters left him alone.

Percy had the chills for a moment. He suddenly realized what he was about to do. This was a dangerous deed that he didn't have to take on. But he promised Sam he would. He remembered the man who was shot in the woods. He looked at Sadie and her sister looking back at him with a mixture of hope and fear. He didn't owe them anything. But he would do this for them and for himself. He imagined that if they could survive leaving with just the clothes on their backs, surely he'd be okay as well. He inhaled and struck a feigned relaxed pose against the door jam, mimicking Sam's style with his hands in his pockets, pulling back his jacket. It would be like one of their childhood pranks. Instead of making off with a chicken bone, they made off with Sadie and her kin. Leaving his face covered with his felt hat and looking down at his feet, he whistled Dixie back at Sam, and he couldn't wipe the grin off of his face. The pick- up went off without a hitch.

Almost four weeks later, the three of them and their scout, maybe the same one Percy had seen in the woods about a month earlier, were at a roadside post, hundreds of miles from Stewart Castle's Virginia plantation. They could still hear shooting creeping toward them. While traveling, they had kept off of the main roads, and used waterways and canals whenever possible. They barely rested. Now, they could hear the popping in the distance, but they stopped seeing running soldiers the previous day.

Sadie and her sister were spirited off by another guide so quickly from the roadside post that Percy didn't see them go or have a chance to say goodbye. He couldn't imagine how they had the energy to continue their journey. Sadie's sister didn't look well, but fear and adrenaline kept her going. Percy didn't know if he would see them again. He wasn't sure where he was and had no idea where any of them would go from here.

PERCY MEETS JACK

At the post, there was a small wooden tavern with an outhouse in the back. The tavern was so well hidden that Percy didn't see it when they first arrived. It had vines clinging to the walls and was tucked in between the trees. Horses were tied to tree trunks, and wooden posts created fencing around them. Farm wagons and carts were lined up near the outhouse as well and covered with branches and other foliage. Some men worked on creating covers for the wagons so that they would be protected from the weather as they continued on their journey. The whole scene looked to Percy like a natural outdoor barn. No land was cleared around the buildings so, as long as they were quiet, they were hidden. The structures looked as if they grew up in the woods like trees or bushes with ivy and wild flowers crawling up their sides. There was a makeshift jail the size of a slave's shanty that was rotting off to the side, unused for months or possibly years.

The place was well secluded, and Percy finally relaxed. He needed a plan. There were several horses out back so he figured that many people came and went from here. Maybe someone could give him ideas or even take him along. He went inside to test the waters.

As he walked closer to the tavern, Percy noticed that posters were tagged all over the front of it, intertwined with leaves and vines.

"Wanted dead or alive!"

"Wagon masters needed."

"Wipe your shoes off before you come in...."

There were wet leaves and mud everywhere. It must be a joke.

"Oops. I'd better do that one," Percy chuckled.

His interest was captured by one in particular that was written in a shaky hand.

It said, "Get Rich Fast! GOLD!" Was this a joke as well?

Percy thought, "Sounds easy. Sounds fun. Sounds right up my alley." The rest of the sign said the gold was in Montana, Colorado and California and that you could join a wagon train by asking for information inside the tavern. The posting looked new.

Percy thought, "What a strange place to put such information. Who was looking at these signs anyway and how many people had gone by here? Was it always this crowded?"

He realized that runaways must have been coming through this area for a while and that some of the slaves must have gone north and west looking for a more open, freer place to live; North to Canada maybe, or even west to Colorado or the Black Hills, for gold. Maybe this was his way "out" as well.

Percy was essentially fresh off the plantation and had no idea where or how far away California was, but he had heard stories of Montana Indians, the Colorado River and the Black Hills that were haunted with spirits and holy men. He really had nothing to lose. Sadie was gone and presumably safer than she had been before. He did what he had promised Sam. He wanted more information about the gold.

He wandered into the Tavern, noticing that it was different from the saloons in town. There were no women or soldiers. No bedrooms. You ate. You drank. You sat to rest and left. Everyone sported traveling clothes, and worn ones at that. There was no distinction between rich men or poor men, black men or white men. They all wore the dust of the road on their hats and clothes, and sat on logs that stood on end around tables that were cut from wooden slabs. They whispered to one another. The buzz was quiet and respectful and all heard the shooting approach from a distance. By the time the war arrived here, the room would be empty, and the brush would cover their trails.

On the other side of the room, there was a tiny make shift bar. Percy approached a log next to a man wearing leather boots with spurs and a big leather hat. He had on a deerskin jacket with fringes hanging from the elbows down past his hips. The man and his jacket were so big that the fringes touched the floor as he sat on the wooden seat. He had an unkempt beard and a dark suntan. Or maybe he was just dark. It was hard to say in the dim light. Above his beard, his eyes were small but lively, moving quickly around the room taking it all in. Behind that beard, you could see his face was carved with deep enough creases to hold a penny in them and his huge hands hugged a tin beer mug as he turned to nod at Percy, who believed the man was there waiting for him. His destiny. This man was the only one at ease in this precarious situation.

Percy looked around tentatively. He was on new ground and had no idea how to address this formidable person. Percy looked at him out of the corner of his eyes while surveying the rest of the room.

"So, what's a wagon master?" he naively whispered out of the corner of his mouth, cringing at his own words due to his embarrassment.

Breaking into a mischievous grin, the man slurred, "Have a seat, young man."

He grabbed Percy's arm and dragged him onto the log-stool next to his.

"My name's Jack. What's yours?" he said, followed by, "Another beer Milly."

Milly was wearing men's clothing and Percy hadn't noticed her before.

"Name's Percy. Percy Castle." Percy extended his right hand.

Jack smiled and took Percy's hand, a bit roughly. "Polite one, aren't you?"

Percy didn't know if he was being teased or complimented. No one ever said that to him before. He just grinned and said, "Thank you," when his beer arrived. They toasted and Jack explained how the wagon trains were gathering to go westward.

By the end of the day, Percy was working for Jack. It was his first real job. Jack saw that Percy was excited by the notion of traveling west to open land and the prospect of gold, that he had no fear of leaving the familiar behind, and what he lacked in knowledge, he made up for in ambition and shear guts. He would thrive. Percy reminded Jack of himself when he was just starting out. He was naïve and it was easy for him to be drawn in.

Jack was one of the best-known scouts in the Black Hills. He had come east on leave from the Laramie stationed cavalry, to visit his family, and to help a new group of travelers venture out of Ohio with some Mormons on their way to Colorado. None of the travelers had any idea what lay ahead as they left civilization and started on the slow potentially fatal ride westward. Jack taught Percy everything he knew, and from then on, Percy's life was shaped by what he learned from Jack.

MASSACRE ON THE PRAIRIE

Jack and Percy hung out in the woodland tavern. They agreed on Percy's pay. As darkness fell, the shooting in the distance died down. The tavern emptied out. People who napped during the day at the tables now gravitated wearily, but with purpose, to their wagons and horses, quietly heading out.

Percy liked traveling at night. He heard the owls in the woods swooping for their prey. Here and there, looking up, there were openings in the woods where the clouds parted and the stars shown through. On the ground, it was pitch black, but he imagined shapes of animals in the clouds above.

Percy walked in front of Jack's wagons to locate potholes. Jack hoped he had a keen eye since it took hours to fix a wagon's wheels if they hit a hole, and the darkness would hide the bumps and snags in the road. As they started out, Jack tested Percy's skills, and was soon confident that in the wilderness, when it mattered most, Percy would notice if anyone was hiding in the hills to attack.

Soon the wagons stopped. Percy found a hole in their path. He unhitched a horse, taking it around the hole first. Then, a group of men helped to push the wagon around to avoid breaking the wheels which were so valuable to them on the long dirt trails to come. Finally, they hitched up the horse again. It was slow going but faster than changing a broken wheel. They had to get out of the wooded areas and reach the main trail well before daybreak to get ahead of the fighting. They also still had some runaway slaves with them which made it all the more important to leave the area before daybreak. If they were caught, they might all hang, depending on who found them. Percy thought of Stewart. He watched the road very carefully and didn't make any mistakes that evening. Jack was impressed and grateful.

The trip was long and arduous. Percy and Jack[1] became close friends. Gradually, over the weeks, people joined them. By the time they were on the trail to Nebraska, there were 80 people in the group. A few were runaways, who continued north and eventually broke away, heading toward Canada. Many were Mormons. They traveled until late Fall. They spent the cold weather near the old Winter Quarters in Omaha, Nebraska, a common stopover, years earlier, for those going west.

By the springtime, seven emigrants had died from the bitter cold and fevers that, coupled with scurvy, ravaged the very young and the old. A handful left for Canada.

The snows waned. When Jack made rounds through the camp-grounds, he found that only sixty wanted to continue on, now that they saw how difficult it would be.

"I'm not sure the Mrs. will want to continue." Mr. Smith scratched his rough beard, which had sprouted during the colder months. "She's heard some scary stories from some settlers going back east," he added, shaking his head, trying to weigh his decision. "They said there are tribes warring on settlers and travelers. Massacres! They call them."

"You can't live on rumor," said Jack. He put his hand on Mr. Smith's shoulder in reassurance. "Women are skittish sometimes."

"Yah, uh-huh. I've got kids with me," Mr. Smith considered.

"I've seen the Bozeman trail first hand. Last time I saw it, it was just about ready for wagons to roll. By now, it should be smooth going. As far as those rumors are concerned, I know some of the tribal chieftains. They are civilized and just want to keep their land. If we stay together, we'll be all right. They'll see us just rolling through and not stopping on their territory," Jack said, trying to give Mr. Smith confidence and some information he could pass along.[2]

The snows melted. Jack and Percy helped the group of sixty pack up their belongings and prepare for their journey. The Oatmans, the Ramseys, and the Smiths were among them. They were Mormons, committed to going to Colorado. They joined Percy and Jack and helped repair broken and rotting wagons and carts, and collected tools, flour and deer skins in anticipation of the next winter. Jack spoke to these three families and convinced them to talk to others. They added extra provisions to their hand carts and wagons to help the cavalry stationed at Laramie. Although this slowed them down, it gave their journey a new mission of importance especially for those travelers who were not Mormon.[3]

Jack and Percy encouraged their group as they got them in line.

"You come up here, young lady," Jack took Abigail Smith by the hand. Her mother and younger sister came along as well. Jack put the other women and children up front. If they were at the back, they'd lag behind. If they were at the front, they would mingle with those behind them and stay within the group as their pace slowed. The men pulled the carts that would be used as a barrier to protect the rear of the group, should an attack occur.

"I want to walk with my dad," Johnny said.

"It's a very long walk, young man. You'll have to keep up if you stay in the back with your dad."

"I'm almost a man," said Johnny, puffing up his chest to look bigger. "I'll keep up."

"I'll be sure he stays with the group," Johnny's dad assured Jack.

"Okay, young man." Jack ruffled Johnny's hair, hoping he was strong and that his feet would hold out.

With that, the trek began. The road was muddy from the melting snows and early spring showers. Soon, the green hills were rolling in the distance.

"Look how the land is changing over there." Mrs. Oatman tried to distract her children from their sore legs by pointing to the beautiful landscape in the distance. There were green hills and a hint of mountainous terrain as far as the eye could see. "We'll be there in a week or so," she added.

"Is it muddy there too?" Olive asked, wiggling her caked and blistered toes.

"By the time we get there, I think it might be hotter and maybe drier," her mother said. She really had no idea what it would be like.

Abigail's younger sister ran up to Mrs. Oatman, and listened to her description of what the future held. She pulled on Mrs. Oatman's hand and continued sucking her thumb as she half waddled and half hopped, her feet hurt so badly. Mrs. Oatman picked her up and nodded to Mrs. Smith, who nodded back. The child was deposited in Mr. Smith's handcart for a nap. She burrowed into the blankets piled high on the cart and fell asleep right away.

A minute later, Mrs. Smith shrieked, "Oh my Lord!" A small skeleton lay twisted by the roadside. Mrs. Smith covered her mouth with a white bandana, holding back her breakfast, breathing heavily.

Mrs. Oatman ran over and put her arms around her, drawing her away. She then took Abigail and put her hand in her mother's and told her to walk ahead quickly. Abigail walked, her forehead crinkled and her mouth tightly drawn closed.

Scraps of clothing and pieces of bones were spread across the trail in layers of dust and dried mud. The women kept their eyes pegged on the hills in front of them, knowing they didn't want to catch a glimpse of what the road under their feet held. Some hugged others in their arms as they quietly sobbed or prayed, walking so as to avoid the debris.

This leg of the trail was the worst regarding wagon litter, scraps of clothing and bones of cattle, as well as those of people left behind. It appeared as if human remains were buried right under the trail so that animals would not dig them up as they returned to the earth.

"I heard they take the women and scalp the men," one woman whispered. Her two-year-old son began to cry. "Hush," she said, shaking his hand to keep him quiet.

"I don't think they would do that to us," another said. "We're on the Lord's mission, after all," she whispered. "Aren't they human? Do they think they own this land? Look at it! It never ends. It's a wasteland." She began to panic as she looked around, feeling how small and alone they were. "What value could it possibly have for them....or for us. Lord, why have you brought us here?"

"Hush, woman," her husband scolded. "The Lord will punish us for sure if you go on like that!"

Jack rode up to Percy and they talked quietly for a few minutes. Then they both rode down the line of travelers, encouraging them on.

"It's okay Mrs. Oatman. These are old things. They've been here for months. It's over."

"We're okay. Just move on ahead, there, Mrs. Smith. Keep moving kids."

"Look at the beautiful hills ahead. Let's get there."

"There, there now."

Percy smiled and pulled a child up on his horse's back and gave him a ride as he rode to the back and then up front again. When it looked like they were past the worst of the bones and litter, Percy took up the front and Jack followed the carts at the rear. Both kept their eyes on the vast prairies around them.

To give the travelers a break, Jack encouraged some men who had guns and spears to hunt some prairie dogs and other smaller wild life, while the women rested. They cheered if there was success since this meant meat for their dinners.

Jack heard stories of Apache and Sioux attacks in the area but he believed that if they stayed together while traveling and formed defensive circles with the wagons when they camped, the natives would leave them alone since they were just passing through.

The landscape was new to Percy, and he kept his eyes peeled for landmarks and any sign of Fort Laramie. He depended on Jack for directions as he went.

Whenever they saw the remains of previous travelers, Jack reminded the group that the military stationed at Forts Laramie and Kearny were there to help the wagon trains reach their destinations safely and to deter Indian attacks.

Percy's mind was racing after passing the ruins of past wagon trains.

"It's been days. How far could it be? What was I thinking to trust a stranger? What sort of journey is this? Gold indeed!" His mouth felt like cotton and his tongue was dry. His canteen held an inch of muddy water—"almost gone." He sipped just enough to wet his teeth and gums. He thought of his mother and Sam, and remembered the ring. He checked his hand to be sure he hadn't lost it. It was caked onto his finger with dirt and dried mud, and his hands were swollen from the dry heat and hard work. It would be hard to get it off but, for now, at least it was safe. Percy scanned the vast grassy plains. Dust bunnies of sage rolled around the caravan and there was no sign of life.

"Was carrying these extra goods such a good idea?" Percy mused to himself. "If Indians are out there, I can't see them. Are they invisible? How come that wagon train had no time to protect itself? Where is the cavalry they said would protect us? I thought there were treaties with the tribes. Why would they attack innocent people?" Percy realized there was a lot he didn't know.

Jack and Percy kept the group moving. Jack knew it was just a few more miles and the Fort would be in sight. He planned to stop when the group could find solace in seeing humanity within reach. He rode ahead to Percy.

"It is disconcerting to be in the middle of nowhere," Percy confided in Jack.

"It's comforting to be away from civilization," retorted Jack, smirking at Percy's timidity. "If you stay away from the Fort, you can pretty much do what you like out here. The hills are full of wildlife and plants and gold…you'll see. It's okay. Don't go coward on me. It's not far now. I have friends in the Sioux and Apache tribes. They're the toughest bunch. They'll remember me."

"Uh-huh." Percy glanced over at Jack out of the corner of his eyes. "He is nuts," he thought to himself. "I used to be afraid of spiders," he said out loud.

Jack spouted a ghoulish laugh, turned and rode back through the line. "I hope they remember me," Jack sighed to himself. He looked at the well-worn path ahead of them and recalled the disaster they passed. He hadn't heard about the recent militia attacks in Sand Creek where innocent women and children in a Cheyenne village were murdered.

"Oh my Lord, not again!" Mrs. Smith cried. "It's a child." She pointed wildly to skeletal remains on the road.

"Move ahead, move ahead," Jack prodded.

"No. No!" Mrs. Smith and Mrs. Oatman joined in chorus. They ran back in the line to their husbands. "Please, please. Turn back. Save our babies, our family! Please. Please." They were panicked and crying now, shaking their husbands.

"Shush," Mr. Smith looked around wearily. "We'll stop soon. We'll be okay. Quiet woman! The Indians will hear us. They'll see we are weak. God is with us. We are fine. Be still."

"Please. Now. Please. Go back to your children. Get back in line." Jack was off his horse, holding them by the shoulders and moving them back to the front of the line.

Still up front, Percy could hear one of the children wailing in fear behind him. He turned back and could see the group moving again. "Lord help us," he said.

The Fort was still not in sight but it was clear the group needed to rest. Jack found a spot where there was a stream and a lone stubby tree for shelter. The group settled in for the evening forming a circle around the tree, near the stream. There was disagreement and arguing amongst the travelers that evening. Even some of the Mormons began to question their path as the dangers became more apparent to them. Commitment was tested.

The next day, the weather did not cooperate and they waited for torrential rain storms to pass by. They moved the carts and wagons back from the stream as it swelled from the rains. They filled their buckets and deerskin sacks with water. Some even took advantage of the deepening stream to bathe.

"We'll have to keep our eyes on the soil between the grasses. There will be mud and that's trouble for the wagon wheels," Jack told Percy, who nodded in understanding.

Late in the evening as the rain lessened and the women and children withdrew to their wagons and blankets, Mr. Oatman approached Jack.

"We may want to go on alone in the morning. We can't stay here forever. It could rain for days and my wife is shaken by what we saw today. I don't want her to get the children upset. It's easier to go on than to sit here out in the open," he suggested to Jack.

"I have to warn you, Mr. Oatman. A single family on its own out on this land is a sure target. No Indian's going to think twice about grabbing your wife and killing you and the kids. You've got provisions in that cart as well. We're okay as long as we're all together. Please don't do anything hasty," Jack counseled.

"Thanks for your opinion. I'll have to think on it." Mr. Oatman slowly walked back to his family, now huddled together in blankets near the cart.

He sat down near his wife and whispered to her. "He says to stay close and have patience."

"The Lord forgive you, Mr. Oatman, if you don't get me and your children out of here alive," his wife answered. "We'll talk again in the morning."

Jack saw dark clouds rolling down the prairie toward them. He hoped everyone was together in the morning. Two more days passed. Eventually, the weather lifted and they went on.[4]

There were no more human remains on the trail and the clutter and trash lightened up a bit as well. The children seemed more at ease and the women joked about new recipes for prairie dog and potatoes. Even as their feet were blistered and swollen, they made good progress because their spirits lifted. The women helped each other with the children and the men lightened their carts to help them keep pace with the wagons.

In another day, the wagon train made camp within sight of Fort Laramie.

"Now see here, my dear. There's the Fort. The Lord is on our side. He wants us to get through this trial."

"Yes dear."

"Mommy, can I go and see the horses while they're being fed?"

"Go ahead Johnny. But come back soon. Daddy wants to fix your shoes."

There was a sigh of relief around the camp. The wagons drew in a circle and hand carts, cattle and horses were stowed in the middle as the exhausted travelers settled in and prepared for their evening meals.

The women and children brought potatoes and roots from the wagons as the men started up the cooking pits. The men spitted the prairie dogs for roasting. As they worked, they sang songs describing their journey and purpose, grateful for having made it this far.

As Percy settled in for the night, he heard the women and children's voices mixing with the men's in the Handcart Song.

"....with the faithful make a start
To cross the plains with your handcart.
For some must push and some must pull.
As we go marching up the hill...." 5

The voices started quietly, as the women, especially, were timid about making any noise that might attract attention from warriors hiding in the wilderness.

"...And long before the valley's gained,
We will be met upon the plains...." 5

The men realized that noise wouldn't make any difference. If the warriors were coming, they'd come. They picked up the volume and sang strong with conviction:

"....Obedient be and you'll be blessed...." 5

Soon they joined in unison. Percy didn't know the words but he hummed along on the choruses. The sound was strong and confident and people began to relax as they prepared a modest meal and tried to calm their nerves.

Many had bleeding feet from walking the long miles over grasses, rocks and streams. Repairing shoes and taking care of their feet was essential before striking camp in the morning. Stopping now gave them an opportunity to tear strips from petticoats and old bedding to wrap their feet and rest. Those who had shoes, padded them with rags and what paper they could find on the trails they crossed.

Stuffing his own shoes with rags and placing them on his son's feet, Johnny's dad pointed to the fort in the distance.

"Look there Johnny. We'll be safe now. See? The army can see us. They're on their way. Wave, son," he said as he alternated squinting to see if anyone was really watching out for them, and pushing the rags into the shoes to sooth Johnny's blistered feet. Johnny looked up and waved in the direction of the Fort.

"Abigail. Bring me those dried beef strips. I'll heat them with the potatoes on this fire, here," Mrs. Smith called to her daughter. She moved quickly, as if ready to run at any sudden intrusion to the camp. Abigail took her younger sister's hand and they ran together, over to their mother with the dried meat. The younger girl stood with her thumb in her mouth, sucking with anxious movements of her jaw. Abigail looked over her shoulder at the Fort as if, by some magic, it protected her as she moved from her safe hiding place in the wagon, to her mother out in the open cooking field. Mrs. Smith hugged them close, and they leaned in against her as she placed the meat onto a pan and put it near the fire.

Jack was watching the fort and noticed a small band of militia riding their way. It took about thirty minutes for them to reach the worn out campers. A soldier who looked like he led the group, jumped from his horse and handed his reins to the militia man next to him. He entered the camp on foot and approached Jack. They offered each other a curt slap on the back, recognizing each other, and the soldier sat near Jack's fire to talk. They spoke softly so as not to arouse the curiosity of the others in the camp, who briefly glanced over but, ravished by their traveling, went back to their meager dinners.

"Jack, we're off on a scouting trip. There's talk of Indians in the hills. Warriors from different tribes are banding together. They're coming for revenge. A group of militia men massacred an Indian camp over in Sand Creek at the start of winter. The village was burnt to the ground. Several squaws, kids and elders were killed just at dawn with no hope of defending themselves. It was a horrible, bloody massacre according to some witnesses."

Jack looked around to be sure no one was overhearing their conversation. "What kind of crazy man is running the Fort! Who does things like that!"

"You'd better keep your voice down and keep your thoughts to yourself when you get to the Fort. No one will tolerate dissension. The politics of it are bad enough and the incident is being reviewed. These are generals from the Union army. They'll tolerate slaves, but won't care how many Indians they kill if they're in the way of the railroad."

Jack nodded his head, only half understanding the situation.

"For now, just keep your eyes open and your gun handy. The men from the Indian camp will be strategic. Red Cloud is one of the leaders and he plans ahead. Make no mistake. They'll be cunning and dangerous if they appear. Remember, some had family members massacred."

"Thanks for the tip. Maybe you should stay nearby in case we need your help," Jack said.

"Can't do that. Sorry. We have strict orders to scan the hills over there," he pointed northwest. The general will have my hide if I disobey. We have to keep the Fort safe first; then your group," he said pointing his chin toward the campers.

"But, most are just families and some have kids with them."

"Sorry, Jack. Watch your back. Take care." And the soldier quietly left the camp and rejoined the militia group that rode off to the northwest.

The members of Jack's group who saw the militia come and go also saw the fort on the hill in the distance. They thought the militia was there to protect them and, with a false sense of security, went back to what they were doing. Jack thought they were but a few miles away from this safe haven, but now he saw how long it took the riders to reach the camp. The distance was deceptive with the glare from the sun. The soldiers in the Fort would be able to see them where they were, but it would take too long for militia men to reach them if there was trouble. They were on their own.

Percy felt uneasy about camping outside the Fort. Even as the group was settling in, he confided to Jack as he poked the embers in the campfire.

"Is it too soon to camp? Shouldn't we push to the Fort before night? I'd feel better if the women and children were within the Fort walls once it's sundown."

Jack looked around and considered Percy's view in light of what he knew.

"If we ask them to pack up now, they're liable to panic. We'll never get that far. Look over there at those people with their bleeding feet. They've been hobbling along, just keeping up. I doubt if they could take another step. They're not the only ones. I say we sit tight and keep a sharp eye out for trouble. There's a scout at the Fort that will be watching us in case we need help," Jack replied, trying to keep his voice even. "The militia is out. That means that the Indians are close-by. They will cut us down if we make a run for the fort."

"They may cut us down if we don't. How long will it take them to reach us if there's an attack? It took that group of militia men quite a while to reach us. At least thirty minutes," whispered Percy.

"Too long," said Jack, chewing on a piece of dried grass. "But we have no choice. We can't leave anyone behind. We're stronger if we hold the circle tight and look like we're confident."

Percy nodded in tentative agreement and settled down like the rest of the group but kept his eyes on the surrounding hills. He had an uneasy feeling of being watched from afar.

Up in the hills above the Fort, Red Cloud and his warriors had a good vantage point to watch the emigrants making their way across the prairie. Some grieved the loss of their loved ones, wives and children, who were massacred by the militia. For the first time Cheyenne, Apache and Sioux banded together in a War Counsel. They argued about what to do.

"If women and children are traveling with the men, these white Americans plan to settle on our sacred land."

"It's already littered with the refuse they leave behind."

"The Railroads are cutting through the hills, and Buffalo herds are pushed northward. We will have to follow them."

Crazy Horse argued about unfair and broken treaties as well as stolen sacred land.

Another warrior spoke harshly as well.

"No one cares about us. They murdered our families. They disregard us. We are not alive to them."

All agreed, these behaviors were not something they could tolerate. They prepared for war to avenge their losses.

Wolves sang in the distance. It was as if they echoed the 'handcart' song. A lone eagle swooped across the camp casting a dark feathered shadow. The horses and cattle stirred, but soon were quiet, exhausted from the long trek. Each wagon had a leader who took a turn at guarding the campsites. Some families camped out in tents next to their handcarts within the wagon circle. They had no protection but their blankets and the stars overhead.

As dusk descended, one leader shouted a warning, "Indian sited." Children grabbed the nearest adult, shaking. Some women and children hid in the wagons or under blankets.

Johnny ran to be with his dad.

Mrs. Smith searched for Abigail and her sister so they could go into a nearby wagon to hide. "Come Abigail," her voice quivered. But Abigail was already running way ahead of her, dropping her sister's hand.

Several men took up their guns and clubs and went over to the side of the circle where the visiting warriors approached. There were only two and they had no weapons. But they wore feathers in their hair -- platted and black, their faces painted bright colors. Jack was concerned at their garb but he didn't say anything. He knew that the feathers were a sign that these individuals belonged to a war counsel. These could be chieftains checking out the train for useful goods before a larger group attacked, but he didn't want to prejudge them, or incite panic. The Indians held up their hands to show that they were empty and smiled their friendliness. Soon, even Jack was drawn in by their relaxed demeanor.

One spoke to Jack in a language that the others did not understand. Jack relayed their message.

"They only want to see if we have anything they can trade."

Johnny's father spoke up. "They have their eyes on our horses and cattle. Can they be trusted?"

Jack motioned with his hand for him to be quiet. He said softly, "They didn't mention them at all. Be still."

Because it seemed they were alone, Jack and the others invited them to have a bite to eat. Percy didn't join them. He kept a keen watch on one side to the horizon and on the other side for any warning the Fort might afford.

Jack explained to the warriors that the group was peaceful and was on a long journey and could not spare much to trade since some of their provisions were for the fort on the hill. He said they would leave the area the next day. The Indians nodded, glancing at one another. Soon they politely got up, left the circle, and rode away. Because they were friendly, people relaxed and some of the guards even went to sleep as night fell.

"See? They were friendly. It's okay, Abigail. Go to sleep now." Abigail's sister cuddled up between Abigail and her mother, sucking harder on her thumb, and opening her sleepy eyes intermittently to be sure their mother was still beside them in the wagon.

The weather was forgiving and the starlight show shining down in the pitch blackness was almost worth the dirt and dust under their heads.

The two warriors who had come earlier snuck back into camp. Anyone who might have seen them didn't look twice because they had been there before, and were peaceful and familiar looking, and strolled right by with a smile and an air of confidence as if they belonged. But suddenly, they were poking and spooking the cattle and horses, and a stampede began in the inner corral circle.

"Yah!" they shouted as the animals kicked up the dust.

The horses pushed right into the closest wagon, toppling it, spilling its contents on the ground, including a woman and her child who were sleeping in it, and opening a passageway for fifty warriors on horseback painted in horrifying technicolor, yelling in fierce voices, waving axes and clubs, with flint knives in the waiting, for scalps and other unspeakable atrocities as they took their revenge. The toppled wagon and its contents, including the woman and her child, were trampled. The warriors were whooping and screeching and everyone in the camp awoke in a panic and a flurry, running every which way. There had been no plan for fighting back as a community. It was every family for itself.

"Come on Johnny." Johnny's father grabbed the boy and ran. He had no idea which way to go in the chaos or where his wife had gone. Soon Johnny was alone and his father was nowhere to be seen.

Abigail, her mother and sister huddled in the wagon under a blanket. Her mother held a rifle under her arm, ready to protect her girls with her own life, if need be.

Percy watched as a horseman grabbed two little girls who had been hidden in another wagon. The warrior let out a piercing whoop and rode away with them. Percy scrambled to stay out of his way. He couldn't remember if the Oatmans had left the formation earlier or if these were their two little girls, but there was no time to consider who they were. Others rode on ponies and ran on foot around the camp setting fires to anything they touched, destroying everything in their wake.

A little girl was standing by a wagon all alone, shaking and holding herself in folded arms, her mouth open in a silent scream and her eyes bulging in absolute terror. A young warrior, wearing a single feathered headdress, rode past her and swooped her up by her pony tail. Before Percy could think about what was happening, the warrior lopped off the pony tail along with half of her skull. Her body fell from his hands and slumped on the ground lifeless, her face unrecognizable. The horseman turned a circle, holding up his prize. Then, he rode back, jumping off his horse with a knife, whooping loudly. He was cutting off her tiny hands as her crazed, tearful mother jumped screaming out of the wagon, "No! No! No! Let her go! Let her go!" He turned and stuffed a tiny hand into the mother's mouth, and Percy could see the knife run her through. A minute later, her blond hair was also in the warrior's hand as he reached with the other into the wagon for provisions, stuffing them into a bag on his pony.

Until now, Percy hid, thinking he could escape. He sat breathless, his heart beating like a desperate fox in the chase. Watching the ruthless attack on the girl and her mother jarred his memory of the blueberry patch on Nantucket. He recalled that his two dogs ran together into the brush. One came prancing out victorious, a rabbit dangling from her jaws. The other dog grabbed it from her, ripping its tail off and leaving its spine exposed. As the rabbit dropped to the ground, it morphed into the deserter whose blood soiled Percy's soul in the Virginia woods.

Percy snapped alive. He ran to protect Johnny who was running from an assailant. Johnny reminded him of Sam when they were kids. This time, a warrior jumped off his pony, went right past the boy, pushing him to the ground and aiming for Percy. Out of nowhere, Jack was suddenly in front of Percy, shielding him and pushing him away. Percy saw a long knife protrude from Jack's chest. It must have entered from behind. Percy could see the blood drain from Jack's face as he fell to his knees. The warrior pulled the knife from Jack's body leaving him limp on the ground, like the rabbit in the brush. He ripped off Jack's jacket and mockingly pulled it over his own shoulders as he proceeded to scalp him. A man's scalp was very valuable to young Indian fighters and this warrior thought Percy's scalp would be next. Two scalps would give him honor on the war counsel.

But Percy was fast. He scooped up Johnny, and ran under the nearest wagon. The pursuer, back on his pony, rocked the wagon back and forth until the top cracked and fell from its base. Inside were two children and their mother who was aiming a rifle. The warrior screamed at them and they froze in profound terror. As the assailant attacked them, the rifle fell over the side of the wagon and was never shot. In a minute, they were dead, huddled together in a bloody mess.

The warrior jumped from his horse and onto the wagon. He looked over the other side to find Percy, who by now had let Johnny go. In the pandemonium, the boy was nowhere to be seen. Percy grabbed the rifle that had fallen off the wagon. He had never fired one before but aimed and pulled the trigger. A red mass bubbled out of the warrior's chest as he looked down at it startled. He looked questioningly at Percy and then fell over on the wagon, senseless. Percy ran out from under the side of the wagon, and was hit in the head. Everything went black.

Gradually, Percy opened his eyes. His head hurt and when he ran his hand across his forehead, his hair was gone on one side. His hand was bloodied and his scalp burned. He looked around and saw nothing but broken wagons, body parts and partially naked men with feathers on their heads bent over him. A warrior had torn off Percy's shirt and was studying his tattooed arm. Percy followed his gaze and, going in and out of consciousness, thought back to the day he was tattooed.

PERCY'S SALVATION (1850S)

Percy was sitting on the docks whittling what he hoped would be a duck, when he saw a whaling ship anchoring in the outer harbor. He dropped his whittling, and ran up the beach to catch a better look.

From the beach he could see the ship lowering a boat into the waters. It looked like some of the men would come ashore while the rest of the crew waited for high tide and permission to sail the larger ship into port. Percy sat down and watched as the men rowed. It was slow going. They must have been tired. The tide was still going out and they were rowing against it. The ship would definitely wait for morning before pulling in.

As they got closer, he saw that one man had pictures painted on his arms. The man jumped from the boat and helped pull it near to the rocks and sand. The others jumped out into the water and splashed around like birds in a bath. They were relieved to be on land. They laughed and played around in the surf like children. They must have been at sea for at least a year, maybe two. It was probably their first bath in months!

"How could they tolerate it?" Percy thought.

He remembered his father returning from a tour on the whaler. He was saturated with a fishy odor. "Phew!" But Ma would draw him a bath, and soon he'd be his old self, smiling, and scooping up his young son to share his seafaring adventures. Percy missed his father's strong, gentle arms and loud voice. "How come these men get to come home, but not my dad," he thought as he grabbed a handful of sand and tossed it into the water hoping to dissolve his bitterness.

In the low tide, two men waded out to clam, while two more ran up the beach to find wood for a fire as well as some berries. Percy ran along with them. They didn't seem to mind having him along, but didn't pay much attention to him either. There were thorny bushes along the way and they picked the berries as they went. He started up a conversation.

"Once I was here picking berries with my brother Sam and we saw a bear. I chased him away," boasted Percy.

The men barely looked at him.

"Over there are the best berry bushes. You'll see—over there." This time, the men looked up, and he ushered them along. They nodded, thanking him. Percy saw that if he helped them, they would pay attention to him. Maybe they were just tired.

"How long have you been away?" he said to the man with the pictures on his arms.

The man with the painted arms stopped and looked Percy over before he answered.

Then he said, "It'll be fourteen months. Long enough to learn English."

He had only a slight accent but Percy couldn't figure out where it was from.

"You sound okay to me," said Percy.

The man continued. "Went down to the Galapagos and 'round the Cape. We got lucky and got in the middle of a family of whales. They were friendly."

He laughed and slapped his friend's back who was also laughing.

"Too friendly," he said. "One of them rammed our boat and we had to stopover to fix it. Caught her on the way back though. A tit for a tat, you know." They laughed again.

"Now she's riding in the belly of our schooner," he said pointing out at the whaling ship.

"How did you get yourself painted like that?" Percy asked, but he stopped short, hoping he wasn't being too forward.

"Ah. You like 'em pictures? Aren't they special?" he said, now facing Percy. "There was an island man from New Guinea covered with tattoos and he showed us how to use some wooden needles and charcoal dust, and we was so bored waiting for the boat to be ready that we just sat there with him, and he went to town on my arms. Like 'em?" he said proudly, pulling up his shirt sleeve all the way to show them off. "Cause I can do one for you if you do. I've tattooed something on almost everyone on the boat at this point," waving his arms around at his companions and smiling a toothless smile.

Percy looked at the man seriously and took the man's arm in his hands, looking up at him to be sure that was okay. The man nodded for him to go ahead.

Percy surveyed that painted arm as if the man's life's story was written all over it.

"Yeh," he said, nodding his head in deep concentration and awe. The pictures were magical. "That would be real fine. But how much you going to charge me for it?" he said, springing back into reality, letting go of the man's arm, and backing up just a bit.

"Aw. It'd be my pleasure," the man said. "The islander who tattooed me said these pictures tell my story and carry my spirit in them. They gave me power and good fortune to survive the trip. To tattoo someone else brings more power to my arms and will help me hone my skills. So, I'm tattooing anyone who wants it so I get stronger and better at it. This is my last whaling trip. When we dock, I'm taking my share and going to New York. Maybe I'll open a tattoo shop there."

"What's your name?" Percy asked.

"Martin," the man said. [6]

The man picked up the pieces of wood he had collected and Percy carried some berries in his shirt, which became stained with an odd blue-ish color. Martin's artwork was superb and when the needling healed, Percy had a beautiful black sperm whale riding his shoulder....

PERCY SURVIVES (1864-1866)

The warriors had seen tattoos on Mohaves, who used them to signify kinship. Percy's great black sperm whale was a bold, angry sea-monster that Sioux warriors had never seen before. They considered that he must have special power to warrant his having such a beast on his body. Perhaps he was some sort of leader. Maybe he was even a member of a Native tribe.

They noticed he was moving and shook him awake. They asked him what power he had, but he didn't understand them, and his head was throbbing. He didn't remember much after that. They threw him over a pony and took him back to their village, hoping to learn more about the markings on his body.

As the tribal warriors rode off, one lone Indian—a chief named Red Cloud—stopped on the hill to face the mass destruction. He sat tall on his horse, stern, serious, strong, no regret, scalps tied to his blanket which was caught up in the battering wind. Yet his right hand covered his heart over his bone and feathered vest. His warriors avenged their people. His eyes reflected the pain he could not hide as he surveyed the results of the attack. 'Nothing lasts forever. Not this wagon train. Not my freedom. Not this life.' He whispered a line that he remembered from a religious man who passed by his settlement when he was a young boy.

"Each person's origin is dust, and each person will return to the earth having spent life seeking sustenance. ....human beings [are like]

A broken shard,
Withering grass,
A shriveled flower,
A passing shadow,
A fading cloud,
A fleeting breeze,
Scattered dust,
A vanishing dream." [7]

Then, he spoke defiantly, proudly, extending his arm from his chest as if to bless those who had fallen, but he blessed the sacred land instead. "You, the Land, are ever-present." He turned to join his war party.

The scouting exposition that had stopped at the camp had caught sight of the Native warriors in a valley waiting to attack. They approached them but never made it back to the Fort or the wagon train to alert anyone. The Fort officers watched the attacks in horror from the ramparts and later sent a second exposition to see if there were survivors. Jack's body was found by a reconnaissance scouting group. He was in pieces and they hoped he was dead before the various "souvenirs" were taken from his body. A militia man found his buckskin jacket on the ground and brought it back to the Fort for positive identification.

No one at the Fort knew about Percy, so no one knew to look for him. The report to the central office in Washington D.C. indicated a total massacre, all 60 dead, although they only found 57 bodies. Revenge was sought by the military. But Red Cloud's warriors outfought the military time and again.[8] The militia's biggest "victories" were over innocent women and children asleep in tribal villages supposedly mistaken for the warriors' hideouts.

PART 4

(1860s-1880)

YOU CAN'T FOOL US!

The warriors who had picked up Percy brought him back to a Lakota camp where he was nursed back to health. His tattoo held strong superstitious powers over the assemblage. The plains' grasses turned brown and the hills were the color of burning autumn flames by the time he was up and about. By then, he had to pull his own weight in deer skin, pemmican, and dried venison as the tribe was moving further into North Dakota to find a winter camp. Having been with the Sioux for several months, Percy had picked up some of the language of the Lakotas. One day, he asked to speak with the assembly of chieftains in his village.

"This terrible monster (pointing to his tattoo) gives me great strength and knowledge. Take me to the Black Hills, your spiritual grounds, to make me more powerful. I'll help you overcome the settlers," he lied to the assemblage.

Percy thought this was a way he might survive his captivity, and even get to dig for gold. But he miscalculated.

"Do you think we are so easily taken by your stories and your lies? Go. Get out of this assembly." The Chieftain waved him away. "We've had enough of the blue coats' lies and enough of you, as well."

The Lakotas wanted Percy far from the sacred grounds and out of their camps. The next day, as the tribe mobilized, two members tied Percy's travois to their own horses and took him to Fort Laramie instead of following the others. They wanted to see if they could trade him for provisions, needed to survive the winter. They figured the soldiers would negotiate for a white man.

Outside the fort gates, they waited while Percy called to be let in. The tribal representatives kept him on the horse so that he couldn't run from their control. Because there were only a few Sioux with Percy and he was riding with one of them, the cavalry look-out understood that Percy was in a precarious situation. The gates were opened. Once inside the fort, Percy implored the general to negotiate his freedom and to let the Indians go because they had helped him survive.

Percy was valued at two rifles, two handguns and one large sac of flour, all of which the Indians carried away, leaving Percy in the Fort. The warriors felt they made a good deal; one less mouth to feed for the winter, for flour and guns. The military also felt they made a good deal.

"What's your name," the general asked.

"Percy Castle."

"Can you find your way back to the Indian camp?"

"Yes sir. But they move every day," Percy replied honestly.

"They'll be back." The general looked out at the Natives riding away. "They'll be back. Which way are they moving?"

"Northward," replied Percy.

"We'll get a rider to notify Fort Kearny and take care of them good! We need a new scout. If you plan to stay here, that'll be your job."

Percy thought, 'What choice do I have?' He said, "Thank you. I'll be your scout as long as I am free to come and go as I like. I'm just happy the Lakotas didn't kill me."

PERCY AND SADIE

Fort Laramie had a good view over the valley. But up above it, the Native American tribes had their own vantage point of the fort and could see when the men came and went to do their work. As the tribal Natives began to realize that they were being squeezed off of the land, and that the militia was helping this happen, they decided to defend themselves. As a result, scouts, leading men from the Fort to the milling worksites, had to watch vigilantly for war parties. [8]

Percy hung around the trading post and knew where most provisions were stored. When looking for some flour and corn one day, he came across a package shoved deep in the back of a shelf. He was curious and pulled it out. More than a year after his friend had died, Percy found Jack's deerskin jacket wrapped in cloth and shoved behind some beans, forgotten. Percy unwrapped it and held it up to the light. He could see the hole where the knife penetrated the jacket, killing his friend. The jacket was stiff, crusty and brown, and Percy shook it out. He remembered the first day he met Jack, sitting on the tree stump in the hidden tavern in the woods. He could still smell his friend's tobacco and liquor in the coat as he held it tight. He could hear Jack's booming voice and his infectious laugh. His thoughts took hold of him and soon Percy was sobbing into the jacket in the store's back room.

"He gave his life for mine," Percy thought.

Percy looked around and returned to reality. Someone might discover him sitting in the back room this way. Slowly he composed himself. He rewrapped the jacket and took it under his arm out to the bunk house, slipping it into a box under his bed. Percy turned the gold ring, still on his finger. He saw Sam's smile and remembered his young voice, "I've got your back." Percy kept the morbid memento, hoping never again to take love or friendship for granted.

Because of the time he had spent with the Lakotas, Percy had a sense of their habits and knew bits and pieces of their language. This was helpful in the trading post when Natives came around to do business. Percy would mingle with them when they came to trade, trying to extract information about the whereabouts of the rest of their group, and claiming that he missed those who had kept him alive after the massacre. In this way, he learned about their future targets. One day he warned the general of an impending attack.

"This warrior says they'll buy what they want now but come back later with others to attack and take what they need."

Because Percy alerted them, lookouts on the ramparts watched for the warriors who were on horseback in the distance. Soon, they sounded an alarm, alerting the people in the outlying area to come into the Fort, and locking it down in time to save lives before an attack began.

On this occasion, people were running into the fortified area bringing whatever they could salvage from their meager homes and stores. Percy noticed a familiar figure among them. A woman holding blankets and a bucket full of breads and some jelly jars, was holding the hand of another younger girl. The younger girl was darker, and Percy recognized the older one. It was Sadie, his mother's runaway slave whom he had helped escape, years ago. Her young sister was still with her. Out here in Laramie, Sadie was free, passing as white, and apparently helping at the trading post. People must have thought her sister was her black attendant and Sadie never said anything to dissuade them of that belief. Percy was surprised that he hadn't recognized her before.

She and her sister survived the move westward and had gotten this far. The trip was arduous for Sadie's young sister. They stopped at the Fort for medical care and to rest, and decided not to move on. With the help of a soldier from the fort, they put together a tiny shanty home for just the two of them. They worked for the trading post and soon had enough credit to get cloth and some chickens. They traded clothing and eggs with the Natives in exchange for buffalo hides for the winter.

Percy approached Sadie and gave her a friendly hug eliciting a warm questioning smile. Holding her at arm's length, he looked her over and she him.

"Look at you. How beautiful you are," he said.

Living in such natural and rugged surroundings made her tough yet soft and feminine. Her body was firm, even muscular, from doing hard work and she had grown into a mature woman. She looked at him in surprise, barely recognizing him. She fingered his newly grown red beard and commented on how he had become a man.

"Where is that skinny boy who moved to the Castle Plantation and caused such a ruckus with the Master?" she replied.

Soon they were laughing and telling stories of the times they remembered. They sadly recalled Stewart's brutality, but Sadie noted how kind Mamie had been to her.

"Look," she said, whirling around, "I'm still wearing my grey velvet skirt," and her sister held up a grey doll with tattered lace around the bottom of its dress.

Percy looked away, holding back a wave of emotion, fingering the gold ring, and remembering his parting from his mother. Only now did he understand what she had put up with in hopes of a better life for her children and how she had tried to help. Neither had seen Sam, Mamie or Stewart since that day more than two years ago, when Sam had spirited Sadie and her sister out of hiding and into town to escape. All three had been shaking with fear. Out here in Fort Laramie, although Percy was in his element, he was lonely. It seemed to him that, by Providence, Sadie was here to keep him company.

Sadie remembered how Percy seemed to save the day, and maintained an air of confidence. She admired how he seemed to thrive on adventure.

The attack on the fort was imminent. Time to reminisce was short.

Percy brought Sadie into the Fort's Chapel as the attack began. It was enclosed and would offer some shelter.

"You talk to the General all the time. Does he say anything about slavery or the war ending? I try to keep to myself. I'm worried about being found out and sent back to the plantation," she whispered to Percy once inside the Chapel.

Percy shook his head no and hushed her, looking around at others who had sought refuge in the stone building. Together they prayed for Sam, mostly, but also for Mamie and even a bit for Stewart, asking that he learn to be a better person. They also prayed for all of the people at the Fort, as well as themselves. They even put in a word for the Natives—that they would make peace with the settlers. But, given what the Tribes were losing, they knew that wasn't fair to ask.

Percy's responsibility was as a scout, not a soldier. He generally stepped back during conflicts and never fought. But soon the shooting was so furious, that he ran out to see how he could help. "You'll have to stay in here until the fighting stops," Percy shouted, covering his ears from the blasts of the guns just outside, as he opened the door.

"Be careful," she yelled.

Sadie realized how dire the situation must be if Percy was willing to endanger himself in this way. She remembered how he hid in the woods in Virginia instead of joining the army. She was grateful that he made a good decision. She was pretty sure how she would have felt had he joined the Confederate army instead of helping her escape. She wasn't sure if he was going outside now to help in order to impress her or if he really was concerned, but she was proud of him.

Outside of the Chapel, several of the men were hurt, but in half an hour, the warriors retreated into the hills and things were quiet again. Sadie and Percy helped to tend to the wounded.

After that attack, Percy's job was more dangerous. The militia never knew when warriors would attack workers on the road to the mill or the shacks around the fort's walls. Because of frequent attacks, Percy was kept close to the fort, and he and Sadie had lots of opportunities to spend time together. When he wasn't out on a mission, he helped in the trading post, where she worked.

"I can't believe we didn't meet before," said Sadie. "You're in here all the time. Didn't you see me?"

Percy really had no excuse. "I wasn't looking for companionship and never actually looked at you. I figured if there was a woman out here, she came out with her husband and that was no business of mine. But when you came running into the fort, we were face-to-face. How could I miss you then?"

"Oh. Uh-huh. How could you miss me in here?" she mused to herself out loud.

Percy felt embarrassed. She often wore men's overalls and a large hat. He just never looked and didn't want to admit it. But now that he had looked into her beautiful brown eyes, he couldn't help but notice her.

The two of them lived at the fort for years. The volunteer soldiers went home. After the Civil War ended, the government sent soldiers, who had tours of duty left, out to man the forts as the country expanded westward. Percy didn't like the dangers he faced but he had opportunities to go off on his own and dig for gold. He wasn't terribly successful but the thought that he might find some, someday, made him want to stay in the area. He was also excited about the changes he could foresee as more and more people emigrated.

Percy often went over to Sadie's small shanty. One evening when Sadie had made some dinner for him, she asked, "Do you ever find any gold out there?"

"Nah. Nothing big. I once found a nugget but it was just copper. A big let-down. It's exciting though, panning. You see those sparkly dustings and think—I just have to find one big nugget! One! And I'm out-ta here for good!" He looked out the window at the barren earth between them and the shadows of rolling foothills in the distance where gold was hidden in the streams. He enjoyed his freedom to roam, but missed the streets of New England.

"Oh." Sadie looked across the makeshift table at him. His beard looked redder in the candlelight and some grey touched its edges. "You're handsome," she said spontaneously, regretting it the minute it left her lips.

"You're beautiful," he replied without hesitation.

"I'll miss you if you find gold and leave." She got up suddenly, looking down, and took their dishes out the door to the trough outside where she rinsed them.

He followed her out and put his hands around her waist.

"You could come, you know. If I strike it rich."

"No. It's not possible for me." She turned in his arms to look at him. Her eyes followed the laces on his linen shirt down to his waistline where his britches were tied with a leather strap, then down to the ground.

"Have you ever thought about marriage?" he asked.

Sadie gasped. "To you? You want to marry me? In Virginia, they'd hang you...and me both!"

"We're not in Virginia and no one here knows you're not white. Who cares out here anyway? Do you think anyone will look twice? Maybe that squirrel we just had for dinner would care."

"It's not funny, Percy," she said. "I always had this dream that I might get married in a church, like white folk. When Stewart started coming after me, I lost that dream. I figured no one would ever look at me again."

Percy lifted her chin in his hand, eyes meeting eyes. "Well, I'm looking."

Their lips met softly. They smiled.

Because it wasn't legal for them to marry, Sadie didn't want to take a chance having a soldier oversee her wedding vows.

"How would we do this?" she asked Percy.

"When I was a kid, back in Nantucket, the Quakers said their own promises and a preacher wasn't needed. There was no legal contract. God oversaw a marriage. I can't imagine that out here on the prairie, where God is all around us, he wouldn't let us be man and wife. Let's do what my mother did with my dad, my real dad, Randall. We'll say our own vows." He took her hands in his. "Then God will help us survive," he said dramatically. "That is of course, as long as I don't find gold!" he joked.

She pushed him away and laughed, "Oh, that'll never happen."

PERCY'S GOLD

On the next Sunday, Sadie and Percy went to the Chapel after the regular service was over. Sadie wore her grey velvet skirt and a clean white cotton smock, symbolizing her life as a young girl, a life she would now leave as she became Percy's wife. Percy washed up and wore his usual buckskin jacket, cotton shirt and britches, the only clothing he had, feeling that funny flutter in his chest that he had had as a child when he was about to do something he wasn't fully sure of. He pushed the gold ring that his mother had given him in circles around his finger and considered his future. He had a surprise waiting for Sadie.

Alone in the Chapel, Sadie and Percy faced each other and took each other's hands. Sadie told Percy she loved him and would continue to love and obey him. Percy told Sadie that he loved her and would do his best to keep her safe. He took the ring from his finger and slipped it onto Sadie's. Looking at the unexpected ring, Sadie's eyes grew wide.

"Look inside," said Percy. Sadie slid off the ring and looked.

"It's inscribed," she said. "I can't believe you did this. It says, 'P and S'. That's so sweet!"

He gently helped her slide it back on her finger, never taking his eyes off of hers.

She smiled and kissed him. No minister or witnesses tended to their promises and no document certified that they were husband and wife. But Percy and Sadie trusted one another. Still holding hands, they went home to Sadie's shanty, content as they walked, man and wife on the prairie.

MARRIED LIFE AT LARAMIE

Sadie's sister moved in with one of the traders on the post whose wife passed away, to help take care of him. The next summer, Sadie and Percy were expecting a child.

"I'm not frightened about having the baby out here on the prairie," Sadie told Percy. "But what if the baby has dark skin?"

"Don't worry," Percy assured her. "I'll love it and will care for it, no matter what, just as I love you and take care of you."

"Back in Virginia, I saw plenty of girls give birth right out in the fields," Sadie reasoned. "I even helped some of the new mothers when their time came. I'm thin and my clothes are so baggy. Maybe we can keep this a secret until we know what the baby looks like."

Percy knew that even though there were few births out near Fort Laramie, there was a doctor in case of a dire emergency that he might convince to help. "I've seen a few women give birth at the Fort on their way westward. They came into the fort or the general's wife went out to them when they needed help through their labor. I'll help you or I'll get you help when the time comes."

"I know I can count on you… when the time comes," Sadie said. Percy kissed her hand.

When Sadie went into labor, she went inside the house and wanted Percy to provide her with some basic supplies and then to leave her alone. Percy wouldn't leave her side, but finally agreed to wait in the sitting room so he would be there if she called him. He didn't like the idea of Sadie being alone during such a risky time, and he wanted to help, although he had no idea what he could possibly do.

After two hours, he snuck out and brought back the general's wife. She poked her head in the bedroom door and Sadie said she could come in. The general's wife showed Sadie how to breathe deeply to help her relax. Sadie was strong and healthy, and she didn't have any problems during the birth. Percy was very proud to be a father of a screaming, squirming little boy, whom they named Rufus. Rufus was light skinned like his parents. Percy and Sadie were grateful for that since it would make Rufus' life and theirs easier as he grew up. Rufus was a tough western sounding name, appropriate for their tough prairie life. Percy's real father had been Randall, and Percy wanted a name that started with "R" so that he would remember his father. Randall didn't sound tough enough but Rufus had a solid western twang to it. Sadie nursed Rufus, and sometimes, Sadie's sister came over and helped out, especially when Percy was assigned to go out with the cavalry. Rufus did well and, as a toddler, seemed to have Percy's lust for adventure.

Percy kept Sadie and Rufus safe by living just outside the fort with them in a somewhat bigger home built of a combination of timber from the mill as well as adobe. He mostly built the house himself, but some of the mill workers helped him put on the roof. There was a loft upstairs where he and Sadie slept, with Rufus to the side. It had a slit for a window so that they could keep a lookout on the horizon. Percy ran with his son in his arms back to the fort, with Sadie behind them, whenever an attack alarm was sounded.

They did this for a year or two and it worked well for them, as the attacks decreased over time.

Percy had friends in the fort, some of whom couldn't imagine what Percy was thinking when he and Sadie had a child. He had a dangerous job as a scout and life on the prairie was treacherous at best. He was away frequently on assignment, and when he was, Sadie stayed home with Rufus, and worked at the Trading Post. As time went on, attacks were fewer and far between but Sadie was still worried for her safety and health, and that of their child. Typhus was rampant and took a great toll. Bad weather stole the only vegetables they could grow in their garden. What kind of a life was this for their son?

One day, knowing that Percy would leave soon on a cavalry scouting assignment, Sadie nervously began to express her concerns to Percy.

"While you're away, what am I going to do if I can't get Rufus out of the house in time to escape an attack? You know how he dawdles sometimes and doesn't listen. We'll be scalped before I can drag him out of here, and you won't be here to help us."

"Rufus may be young but he knows how important it is to get to the fort. And besides, it's been ages since the last attack. Most of the Indians are on reservations now," Percy tried to console her.

"Listen, Percy, I know you just can't wait to get away from this place, but we have to think about Rufus and his future. Sometimes, Indians take children. If Indians take him as a prisoner, he'll be their slave. I know well what that's like. We have to do something concrete and serious to protect him."

Percy could see that she would not drop the conversation. He considered her anxiety and was also concerned for their son.

"Okay. Okay. Here's what I'll do. I'm going to dig out a hiding place for you. I'll put it in back of the house so if warriors come in, they won't see you right away," he answered. "You can take Rufus there and tell him it's a game. Maybe he'll come more willingly then." He figured that would satisfy her and he could go on to his usual daily routines.

However, Sadie was not so easily sated. "How in the world will you do that!" she questioned. "It's going to have to be a big hole in the ground! He's not a baby anymore."

"There's a place as you go toward the fort where the land forms a small hill. I can carve out a cave with a small entrance way. I'll weave a grassy door that you can pull closed to hide when you go in. I think it will be safe. It's off to the side a bit. You can come with me and we'll have a look tomorrow," Percy planned out loud.

That seemed to satisfy Sadie and the spot turned out to be perfect for what Percy had in mind. Percy dug out a hiding place for them. Sadie felt much better about Percy's being away after that. She drew strength from the knowledge that she had survived escaping slavery against all odds, and Percy was looking after them, after all. However, lately, she wondered if her reliance on him was made more of her own fabrication than of Percy's actual doings, since he was away so often.

As Rufus grew into a young adolescent, Percy sometimes agreed that he was concerned about Sadie and Rufus' long term well-being. He wanted Rufus to learn a trade, meet girls and "have a life of his own." He wasn't sure how that would happen out on the prairie where his role models were gold-diggers, trappers and soldiers. He thought Sadie should go back east to a safer place in the north, such as Canada, or perhaps New York, but he loved hanging out with Rufus. Sadie wouldn't hear of leaving him alone or of leaving her son with him, so they just kept up as they were.

"Do you feel tied down, having to take care of us this way?" Sadie could tell that Percy was preoccupied, as he read his orders for the next week.

He looked up at her and smiled. "Not really," he said half-heartedly. "I want you to be happy. Now, taking care of Sam when he was a kid-that was being tied down!" He resumed his reading not looking up at her.

"I guess this business of marriage and parenting is a new thing for both of us," she sighed. "Rufus can be a handful."

Percy stopped what he was doing and looked at her.

"I'm not sure really what it's all about either. My dad was mostly absent while I grew up and he was gone when Sam was really young. I guess I was as close to a father as Sam ever had. Stewart couldn't wait for me to leave and he wasn't a great role model to learn from anyway. But I have fun with Rufus. I guess I love him. He'll settle down," he nodded his head, his orders still in his hand. He was thinking about how the needs of his family life were both a joy and a constraint.

"Raising Rufus is difficult at times, but he makes me feel grounded. I still cringe at the thought that someone might discover me and send me back to the plantation. But with Rufus, I know those times are gone. Laramie is my home and I feel as safe as anywhere here in the house that you built for us."

Percy kissed her gently on her forehead.

Yet, Sadie sensed that for Percy, her presence was mostly for comfort and convenience. Recently, his heart seemed to wander. She reached over to take the orders from his hand to see where he was off to next.

Percy's next assignment started the following day and was dangerous. As he led the cavalry through a mountain pass, watching for Indians, snakes, and falling rocks, he felt the blood rushing through his veins. Sadie and Rufus were the last thing on his mind as the bitter, cold air grazed his face. Once the cavalry was safely on its way back to Fort Laramie, Percy turned off toward the hills, and spent a few days on his own, gold digging. He loved his solitary time in the mountains when he could dream of being rich. He grew to understand the land and could easily fend for himself out in the wild, eating berries and catching squirrels for dinner. He could keep a fire going and ward off wolves. He had even brought home venison to Sadie one winter. Although this was prime time for him, he sometimes got confused about his circumstances. He could enjoy his solitude and, at the same time, yearn for a hot bath and the clean, crisp sunlight streaming into the windows of his childhood home on Nantucket.

When he returned home, Sadie could see that the prairie took its toll on Percy. Tired of the constant riding and tough conditions, Percy developed gold fever and began to daydream of when they'd be rich.

"Just imagine," he said to Sadie one day while they were stocking provisions on the shelves of the trading post.

"What?" she said, standing on a ladder and taking a bag of flour from him so that she could hoist it over to the adjacent shelf. Her back was getting stiff and her arms hurt. She wished that Rufus would help out more often.

"Imagine if this place was a big general store, and Laramie was a famous western town with rich people like "Stewart Castle" buying lots of different kinds of goods. We could own the store and have all we want to eat—fine foods and clean clothing. No catching squirrels, and washing in the river." He smiled at her as if it would happen any day now, the picture in his mind reflected in his eyes.

"Did you hit your head or lose something, like your brain? What's gotten into you?" Sadie stopped what she was doing and looked down at him. "Wipe that ridiculous, stupid smile off your face, Mr. Castle, and throw me the next sack of flour. We can't be dreamin' all day. I'm aching and Rufus needs his supper." She could see he was restless and conjuring up a bottomless wishing well.

"What if we moved to Deadwood? It's just up the road a bit, by the Black Hills. I could spend more time digging for gold and maybe we could be rich."

"You can't be serious. We've worked hard to make a living here. If we did that, maybe we could starve to death! Besides, I heard that Deadwood is a lawless, dirty town and not a place where you'd want Rufus to grow up. At least at the fort we have a life, a job. There's order and cleanliness. Provisions. The militia is right here to protect us if there's an attack."

"Uh huh," he said, and he passed the next sack up to her, his mind far away.

Rufus was almost a reincarnation of Sam for Percy. He could have fun with Rufus but he had to take care of Sadie, like taking care of his "Ma." Sadie still offered him her sweet beautiful smile but their passion had settled down to a platonic taking-each-other-for-granted relationship. Life was just too difficult to conjure up the energy for much more.

Percy saw that some people got very rich from the gold that was mined. He also saw first-hand, the results of failed mining in the form of scalped miners' bodies and skeletal remains on the sides of the hills near streams. Some miners were so stubborn that they wouldn't leave their claims to get provisions. Lives were claimed by bears, weather, warriors and just plain ignorance of knowing how to survive in the wilderness. Percy had this know-how. He also had responsibilities, but he felt that the longer he waited, the further away his dreams would drift.

PERCY'S GOLD

Percy saw that times were changing. Whereas the Cavalry previously had to protect settlers in wagon trains, now they had to defray fist fights over land ownership between railway companies as lines ran across narrow passes in the mountains and connected gold mining towns, with the ultimate goal of creating the transcontinental railroad. Negotiations took place even as trains stood on the tracks waiting to reach the next stop. When brawls broke out, the cavalry would be called to help calm the unrest.

On one of these calls, Percy rode ahead of the militia, helping them to reach the narrow pass where the altercation was in progress. As Percy arrived on the scene, he sized up the situation. There was an engine on either side of the pass. To the west, Percy saw a train on the tracks behind the engine, coming in from California, likely, he thought from the San Francisco area where gold was transferred before being loaded on the box cars. It looked like the men were being restrained by the railroads' owners. In front of those cars, gathered in rows, ready to go at it again, were 50 or 60 men with crowbars and clubs in hand. Some men were dressed in blue jeans with suspenders with white cotton smocks underneath. Percy had heard about this new fashion but had not seen it yet. The material was called denim, and was supposed to last forever. Percy chuckled to himself and he realized that he had been wearing the same buckskin britches for years. 'Why would anyone give that up for blue jeans that had to be washed?' he thought. Others had round straw hats protecting them from the sun.

To the northeastern side, the tracks were already laid down and at least 100 men stood at the ready, holding heavy square metal mallets, clubs and crow bars as weapons in front of those rails. You could see the mallets were well worn, the metal heads indented from having hammered thousands of spikes into the rails that ran this far west.

Neither engine was manned but smoke was still billowing out of the one coming from the west, which must have been running until just recently.

Something else that Percy noticed, from having been close to the Indian battles for so long, was that the northeastern group sported blood on their weapons, as well as wear and tear. They were serious fighters with experience. If another brawl broke out, this might not be a fair fight. He pulled his hat over his eyes and reminded himself to keep out of the way.

The train masters were dressed in city ware. They had coats and wide brim hats as well as fine leather boots, the likes of which Percy hadn't seen since his days on the plantation. They were obviously more well-to-do than their workers. Some smoked long pipes as they sat face to face at a makeshift table trying to resolve their dilemma without coming to a more violent physical confrontation. Each person in turn waved his arms or hammered his fists on the table as he made his point. Others nodded in agreement or looked over at the workmen who were clearly itching to fight.

As the track masters huddled over their negotiations, periodically, their workers yelled insulting remarks to one another but stood their ground. The cavalry rode in and cordoned off the men in an effort to avoid a bigger brawl than the one that led to their initial involvement. Their arrival only served to anger and inflame the men. Laying tracks was big business for the railroad companies and for the government. Everyone involved could see the importance of having transcontinental access. As hard as they tried, there were not enough cavalry men to hold back the workers who were paid by the foot of track that they laid. Their work was held up and they would not be paid for the time their bosses took to negotiate. Furthermore, one group of men might be laid off, right there and then, if their boss sold out to the other side. If this happened, the cavalry would likely be protecting that boss as well as curtailing the brawl. The situation was intense.

One of the men on the Union Pacific Line, coming from the Missouri River area, filled his pockets with large stones and climbed up on top of the engine. He threw a stone at the gang master of the Central Pacific Line and hit him hard on his head. The gang master fell to the ground and all hell broke loose. To get out of the way of the brawl, Percy quickly and silently stole aboard the train from San Francisco. He thought the train would protect him from the fighting. He planned to walk a few cars back, get off the train and call his horse. The two of them would wait a safe distance off and later lead the cavalry back to the fort.

The engine car was hot and dark and his tattooed shoulder hit a scalding key ring as he passed the engineer's station. Percy saw piles of coal on one side and lumber on the other. To the side was the biggest oven he had ever seen. There were embers still burning from the seams around the closed door. The air was thick with choking smoke and the floor had coal dust half an inch thick around the furnace. The door at the back of the engine car was locked tight with a key bolt lock. He would have to find the key to go any further. He wasn't used to snooping in other people's business and he hadn't stolen anything but food when he was a starving child back in Nantucket. No one was minding the store. No one would see him. No one would know if he found and stole the key until the engineer came back to move the train. His options were to go back out to where the brawl was, and risk being hurt, or to find the key and move on. He didn't want to leave the shelter of the engine. He could hear the noisy yelling, banging and shuffling from the brawl, and he knew the distraction would shelter his search for at least a few minutes.

It was dark and he couldn't see much. He ran his hands around the walls near the door where he had hit his shoulder. He lurched back suddenly as he burnt his hand on the corner of the furnace. As he leaped back, something stabbed his shoulder. It was the same key ring he had bumped upon entering the car. Percy turned and felt for the key. He grabbed it, unlocked the door and jumped into the next car. It was a few degrees cooler but still stifling. He wondered what would warrant such security on a train that was running through mountains where nothing lived other than a few defeated Native Americans and a mountain lion. He closed the door to the engine car behind him and looked around.

Percy froze and spit his chewing tobacco into a dark blob on the dusty floor. "Well I'll be," he muttered to himself, wiping his mouth with his sleeve. There were bags and boxes piled high along the sides of the car, and a metal safe in the corner. The bags were made of heavy cotton, not unlike the blue jean material that the workmen were wearing, except that they were white and tied closed with rope. If there was flour or other food in the bags, he might take a bag and it would not be missed. The soldiers at the fort were always desperate for additional provisions which were slow to arrive. It wouldn't hurt if he, Sadie and Rufus had some extra food around either. After all, *who would know?*

A gun was propped against a wooden chair near the rolling door. A guard must have jumped from the car to join the brawl. Percy was alone but heard the noisy fighting outside. After yanking the barn-like door shut to avoid being seen, he reached for one of the bags and was amazed at how heavy it was. He could barely lift it with one hand. It wasn't flour or any kind of food. He sat looking down at the coarse cotton bag with his beaver hat hanging from his neck, and his scraggly red beard resting on his deerskin jacket which was tied closed with a leather cord. He weighed his options. The scuffle continued outside and the rolling door was secured. The engine door was also still closed behind him. Percy took his knife from his buckskin boot to cut a line in one of the bags. His mouth dropped open. There wasn't much time to decide. His hands were itching to let the bounty flow through his fingers. He had killed one man before but that was self-defense and didn't count. He had stolen before. But that was food, as a starving child in Nantucket, so that didn't count either. "I'm a good man," he muttered, surveying the car. There were more cotton bags than he or anyone he knew could *ever* count. *No one would ever know.*

Percy untied a second bag and reached his hands inside, almost certain that there would be some grand prank of the Universe. But no. He felt them. Cold, hard nuggets...

He pulled his hat from his head and dropped it on the floor. This was going to be much easier than all the gold digging he had ever done. He figured it must be from mines in San Francisco or Montana and there were thousands of pounds of gold on the train. He couldn't believe his eyes as he realized how much was here at his fingertips. Even parts of one bag would make him and his family richer than Stewart Castle had ever dreamed of being. He stopped thinking.

Percy stuck his head out of the door and whistled. His horse came up to him. He filled his saddle bags and his pockets with nuggets, pushing some into his boots and filling his hat as well. His shirt was tied closed with narrow, but strong flax roping that Sadie had twined. He pulled his shirt out of his britches and made a pouch in front of his belly by tying the cloth with the twine, and filled the pouch with gold as well. He slid the door closed behind him, quickly securing his loaded hat to the back of his saddle, and rode away. The horse was young, strong and agile and barely felt the extra weight of the gold. With so much of a ruckus going on, Percy figured none of the cavalry men saw him leave or knew where he went. The militia took twice as long to find their way back to Fort Laramie and no one there had seen him come or go.

Percy wasn't sure what excuse he would give the general for having left the scene. To avoid having to make up a story, he decided not to stay. Instead, he snuck back to Sadie at night. He told her what he did and showed her some of the gold. He said he would have to leave and implored her to come with him.

"No one will know where we are. The gold isn't processed and could have come from anywhere. We can be rich just like I've dreamed."

Sadie was appalled.

"What are you thinking about," she cried. "We have a life here and a son. What lesson are you teaching him and what will you do? You'll be caught and we'll be disgraced forever. They might even kill you! If they figure out that I was a slave, they'll kill me too just for good measure!"

"They won't know where the gold came from," he shushed her with the palm of his hand in front of her face. "No one saw me take it and they'll think one of the track layers stole it. They can't possibly find me or blame me if they do. They can barely find their way back and forth to the railroad. Besides, the Wyoming and Montana hills are filled with gold. Who's to say I didn't dig it up on my own? Who can prove anything?"

"What kind of a bag are you holding? Did you get that on the train too? Will they recognize it?" Sadie asked, still agitated, her eyes wide.

"Oh. Oh. I should get rid of it. But what will I use instead?" Percy realized she was right. They'd know immediately that the gold came from the train if anyone saw the bag. He looked around wondering about a possible hiding place. Or, maybe he could burn it. But Sadie was increasingly upset and he ended up just taking the bag as it was.

"Percy, you are a good and kind man. You've never stolen like this before. We've always been happy living off the land. Why are you doing this to us?" she cried, clutching his shirt with increasingly white knuckles.

Percy took hold of her wrist and held it tightly. He got down on one knee as if proposing to her. "I came out here for a better life. Except for you and Rufus, all I've had is misery. I want more for all of us. Come with me, please. Come now," he begged. "We can't wait for morning. They'll be asking where I went, and why I left them there."

Sadie pulled her wrist free, now bruised from his tight hold, and put her hands on his shoulders, looking desperately down into his eyes pleading. Suddenly realizing the full impact of his actions, Percy sat back. He covered his eyes with his hands and, shaking his head back and forth, he moaned, "Oh god, oh god, they'll shoot me if they catch me with the gold. I have to go. I have to go. If you won't come, I'll have to leave you here."

A warrior could not have ripped Sadie's heart more abruptly from her breast. Rufus was in his early teens and decided to go with his dad on this new adventure. He was not mature enough to realize the full impact of his actions. As Percy brought a pony over for Rufus, Sadie put one hand to her mouth and one across her stomach in anguish and disbelief. She ran back into the house and brought out the doll her sister had brought from Virginia. She told him to keep it. It would remind him of his roots and of her. He was amused by the gift but took it to make his mother happy. He stuffed it in his saddle bag along with some bread and jerky. Rufus bent over from the saddle and kissed her goodbye, and, touching his face, she could barely breathe.

Back in the house, she sank to the floor and sat there in a daze. Percy promised to come back and get her once he was settled, and tried to kiss her goodbye again but she met his eyes and pushed him away. With a wrinkled brow, he turned to go. He had to move quickly if he was to escape safely with Rufus. They rode all night toward the mountains and took refuge there for a few days before continuing on.

Percy built a lean-to where he and Rufus could have shelter from the weather while he figured out what to do. They camped a few miles outside of Deadwood and went into town periodically for a bath and some home cooked food. When the weather flared up, they took a room in the Deadwood tavern for a night or two to warm up.

Rufus was amused by how people looked at their worn dirty buckskin clothing.

"They must think we're just lucky vagrants with some gold on our hands," he whispered to Percy.

"If we're careful, anyone we meet in Deadwood will think we're lucky gold diggers who found enough to stay alive. No one will know what's hidden in our shanty out there," Percy nodded his head toward the road out of town.

But, just to be certain, Percy never left Rufus' side, and the gold remained a well-kept secret.

Rumors spread that Sadie went along with a group of Mohave Indians who came to trade at the post. In reality, she moved in with her sister and only came out to work in the store. She was devastated and didn't trust anyone. Percy didn't go back to get her out of fear that he'd be caught or that Sadie had told someone what happened. He felt he had to protect Rufus now that they were together.

Sadie never told anyone what happened. Deep down, she loved Percy and wanted to protect him. The cavalry general asked her where he went. She replied, "That loser took my boy and went gold digging, and never came back."

Sadie's sister saw that she was heart-broken and devastated. She did her best to care for her, cooking her meals, waking her and pushing her out the door so she would meet her responsibilities. The winter came on quickly and more harshly than usual. Sadie was despondent and ignored her cough when she first was taken ill. The house was freezing but it at least shielded them from the howling prairie winds coming to steal their souls away. It was difficult keeping a fire going. The snow piled across the chimney and smoke filled the cabin each night. One evening, Sadie struggled with her cough and her fever soared. She shook violently, uncontrollably, desperately calling for Rufus. A spoon at her mouth was warm and wet and her tongue could sense a salty broth, but she couldn't stop shaking and most of the broth was on her chin. Her tears washed the mess away. She turned the gold ring on her finger and removed it. Her sister hugged her and rocked her in her arms, singing,

> "....We will march thro' the valley in peace.
>   If Jesus himself be our leader,
>   We will march thro' the valley in peace.

> "....We will march thro' the valley in peace.
>   When I'm dead and buried in the cold silent tomb..." [9]

Sadie's sister looked down into Sadie's eyes as she uttered her last words,

"I don't want you to grieve for me." [9]

The ring fell from Sadie's hand and rolled across the floor.

PART 5

(1880-1905)

"ON THE LAM" IN DENVER

In the spring, Percy heard that she died and he was, at first, bitter. He blamed everything but his own actions. 'She didn't care about making a richer life for us. If it was up to her, we would be slaves to Fort Laramie forever.' However, when he learned the details of how she died, he softened and was heartbroken, deeply regretting having left her.

He hugged Rufus and told him, "I will never marry again. This is all because of my own selfish greed and lack of foresight."

He was determined to make something good from his dastardly behavior, and soon figured out a way to do so.

"Where are we going?" asked Rufus as they saddled up early in the day.

"You'll see when we get there. It's a place called Denver. It's a small town now but it will soon be bustling. I heard it will be a crossroads for the railroad. It'll be a hub, with lots of people from many different places," Percy explained.

"Will we know anyone there?" asked Rufus. After seeing Deadwood, he realized how raw and lonely a town could be.

"Not likely," Percy said, "and that's a good thing. No one will know where we've been or that we have gold. We can get rich gradually. And, Rufus, take care. If anyone asks, you are white, not mulatto," he smiled and gave Rufus a thumbs up sign, which Rufus returned in kind.

"Got it. How long will we have to wait to start using the gold and be rich?" Rufus asked innocently.

"Not sure. But you can't tell anyone about the gold. We'll hide it outside of town in a safe place when we get there," Percy continued. "That way, even if I'm caught, you can benefit since you'll know where to find it when you need it. If we're careful, you'll still be rich long after I'm gone. And your kids will be rich. You can live in style."

When they got to Denver, they settled at an Inn in the middle of town and got their bearings. One night, they rode out of town loaded up with the gold. Percy found the perfect spot to hide it and they rode back to the Inn, without anyone knowing that they had even been gone. Percy kept a few small pieces of gold to trade so he could get a business started in town. When he went to trade it for money, he said he and his son had dug it up in the Black Hills. He even drew a fake map for the bank Teller explaining exactly where the gold had been. You could see people's eyes open when he pulled the nuggets from his bag. But all Percy saw was the anguish on Sadie's face when he left her.

Percy realized that he wouldn't be able to cash in all of the gold in town. Too many people already noticed that he had two beautiful, pure nuggets. They might suggest that he had more and then he and Rufus would never have any peace.

Having experience as a scout, and understanding what provisions traveling people would need on the prairie, Percy set up a goods store across from the railroad in Denver. He knew how to trade for goods and, by going to the reservations, he was able to keep his store stocked on a very small budget with Indian head dresses, turquoise jewelry and other novelties that travelers loved to buy as souvenirs. He developed a social conscience upon losing Sadie and recognized that the Native Americans got a short deal upon losing their lands. He established a sort of fair trade arrangement with the tribes and brought them a generous return. He bought the more serious staple goods from the eastward trains that came by.

As for Rufus, he took the doll that Sadie had given him and put it high on a shelf in the store where no one would look to buy it. When he was lonely, he knew where it was and it brought him warm memories of the past.

After selling the first two gold nuggets, Percy felt like he was under the constant scrutiny of the bank teller and anyone the teller told about the nuggets. People came into Percy's store just to see the man who "struck it rich." Percy didn't want their attention, but he did want their business. He didn't tell tall tales or lies, and he charged honest prices. He just smiled when they referred to the "gold find" and changed the subject by showing them some of the things they could buy. After a while, the novelty of a gold-find wore off and people just came to buy what they needed and to talk to Percy, and Rufus, who had inherited his father's winning ways. The store was frequented by many of the train passengers traveling through, as well as the people in town.

Percy couldn't shake the guilt he felt about having stolen. Now that things had settled down a bit, he wanted to stay out of sight long enough for Rufus to take over the secret stash. He taught Rufus how to negotiate with the tribes and the train masters. Percy never lost his fear of being captured but he knew he would deserve it if it happened. He even thought that he felt empathy for how Sadie must have felt when she feared being discovered as a runaway. Not wanting any trouble if it could be avoided, he hoped he and Rufus would fade into the background of this busy and growing town.

One day, at noon, Percy closed the store so that he and Rufus could have a quiet lunch. He wanted to have a heart to heart talk with his son. Percy grabbed a large chunk of hard white cheese from the ice box in the store room. With a sharp square chopping knife, he lopped off a big piece for Rufus and a smaller piece for himself. The baker had traded a loaf of soft white bread, a delicacy, for a bag of flour that Percy had gotten from that morning's railroad delivery. Father and son each broke off a piece of bread and sat down to eat.

"You know I always tell it like it is. And I hate to ruin this moment that we have to enjoy our meal together. But, someday you'll be alone, son. I want you to be prepared."

Rufus let the flavors of the cheese and the soft bread melt in his mouth as he looked over at his dad with a sour look on his face. "I hate these conversations. Can't it wait 'til we're done eating?"

"Well, no. 'Cause it'll be busy then, and I don't know when I'm going to get you to pay attention to me again. So just listen, okay?"

Rufus nodded and took another bite.

"I never told you this before, but I have a brother. A brother I cared about and still care about. But he stayed back in Virginia, and I'm not sure where he is or what he's doing or even if he's okay. He helped your mom get away from a plantation. I went along for the ride. Oh, I helped a bit too. But if it wasn't for him, she would have stayed on the plantation and who knows what would have become of her."

Now, Rufus stopped chewing and put his food down. He looked at his dad with a new respect and really listened carefully.

"Sam, that's my brother, and I were kids together on Nantucket Island. That's back east. I took care of him, a bit like I've taken care of you. Well," he hesitated, "maybe better. We didn't live on the lam so much."

Rufus could see this was hard for his dad to say.

"I miss Sam. I guess I love Sam. Almost as much as I love you. Do you understand, son?" Percy hadn't taken a bite of his food yet and was choosing his words carefully.

"You've been good to me, dad. I understand that you'd be close to your brother," Rufus replied.

"So, as I said, I don't want you to be alone if something happens to me."

Percy looked up at Rufus and then over to the window to be sure no one was waiting for them to open.

"This store is doing really well. You could easily live off of its profits," he began. "It would make me feel satisfied—like it was almost all worth it-- if I knew you would be generous to Sam."

Percy turned from Rufus, and stood up, with his head bent down. He ran his fingers through his hair and then plunged his hands in his pockets as he walked across the store floor. He stopped at the counter and turned back to face his son.

"It hasn't been a picnic for either of us, and I'm afraid you'll face the brunt of it, if anyone discovers the gold. Sam is resourceful. He'll find a way to get rid of it without anyone knowing. I just know he will." He paused. "If he's still alive."

"Dad. It's okay. I don't want it. Really. I couldn't touch it anymore. It's just too dangerous. We're fine. It's fine. Really, dad. I want to meet Sam. There's no one else. He's my family too. He can have it all, and I'm sure he'll be careful. It's okay. If there's an emergency we can always tap it. But we're happy here. I hope we never have to do that. It would be terrific if we could expand our little family and find your brother. It would help me feel connected."

Rufus got up and put his lunch down on the chair where he had been sitting. He walked over to Percy and took his hands. He nodded yes. Their foreheads touched in a moment of understanding. Percy looked at his son and saw Sadie at ease in his deep brown eyes. It was as if she was right there in her calico plantation dress with a bib apron and her braided hair, hands clasped in her lap, nodding approval.

"Sam is a good person. You'll like him, son."

Percy slapped Rufus on the back, and cleared his throat. Rufus watched as he opened the door to the store, letting the fresh air in. He could see the angst that the hidden gold caused his father. He felt it as well. Now, as an adult, he knew where to find the gold and was an accessory to the theft. He hoped the store would do so well that neither of them would ever retrieve the stolen bounty from its hiding place. He realized that it was the bane of their existence and hung as a pariah over their heads. It might never be in their hands again, but it would always afflict their hearts. He was determined to help his father's store succeed.

One day, when the Castle General Store had been open for a few years, a well-dressed man came into the store. He wore a fine fur-felt Stetson hat with a wide crown, and carried a shiny black cane with a metal tip. Rufus figured he came off the morning train. The stranger walked around looking at the goods and picking up jewelry to study it, as if he was interested in buying a piece for his girlfriend or wife. He asked Rufus all sorts of questions about where the items came from.

"So you say this is Zuni turquoise?" he asked.

"Actually, it's a Mohave heirloom. And this over here is Apache," Rufus pointed out.

Rufus knew about the various art forms each tribe exhibited and readily shared that information with customers. Mostly, however, this customer kept glancing across the room at Percy. There was something about him that looked familiar.

Percy saw that he was being scrutinized. His hands began to shake and he got up, turned away, and busied himself with some items on the far wall.

The man asked if he could trade for the turquoise. Rufus looked at what the man had and said, "Yes, of course." He figured the man probably didn't realize the value of a gold ring. When the man left, Rufus gave the ring to Percy who noticed its inscription.

Percy held it to his heart. "It's time." He gave it to Rufus. "It's Sadie's. It's ours. It was your grandfather's. My mother gave it to me. Now it's yours. Hide it. I don't know how that man got it from your mother. Put it away. Make it disappear and quickly!"

Rufus did as Percy asked.

An hour or so later, the customer returned with Denver's Sheriff who placed Percy under arrest for theft. The customer had been the train master for the Central Pacific railroad line and recognized that Percy had been the scout who disappeared the day of the brawl. How he did this, Percy didn't know. He had such a guilty conscience, he didn't argue, just going along and hoping that Rufus wouldn't say anything.

Rufus held his breath as Percy was led away. He knew he was an accomplice since he helped hide the gold. Percy looked at Rufus' face as he left, and hung his head. Rufus looked like an orphaned puppy. Percy promised himself that if he got out of this situation, he'd give the store to Rufus sooner rather than later, and stay near, but out of sight. He hoped that Rufus wouldn't have to lose both of his parents as well as his own freedom because of the gold.

The sheriff considered that the train master had clout with store owners in Denver because he brought in the town's provisions and special goods from the west coast. He didn't want to lose the support that the train gave the town. On the other hand, he wasn't interested in politics when it came to accusing a good, loyal citizen such as Percy. He reasoned that it would be a few weeks before a judge came through Denver and no one could present any concrete evidence that Percy had committed any crime. No judge would waste his time on an empty accusation. The train master couldn't prove anything, and he didn't live in Denver. As important as he was, he was just passing through, and it was his word against Percy and Rufus, both upstanding local citizens.

Neither Rufus nor Percy admitted that the gold was hidden and both denied having anything to do with the theft. In fact, they said they knew nothing about it. When questioned about the incident, Rufus replied to the sheriff, "How dare you suggest, on the word of a stranger, that such an upstanding citizen as my father had done such a thing."

Percy, in turn, said, "I ran away, afraid of the railroad brawl. I left my wife because we didn't love one another anymore. Besides, we were never legally married." Percy cringed at his own words, and hoped that Rufus didn't take them to heart. He nostalgically recalled the day he and Sadie lovingly said their own vows in the little chapel at Fort Laramie.

He continued. "It was disgraceful that I deserted Sadie, my son's mother. And it's not admirable that I left my post as a scout. On the other hand, Sadie had no legal rights and the army never formally enlisted me. I didn't commit a crime in doing either."

The sheriff decided to cut a deal with Percy's accuser. Percy was released.

The train master never believed what Percy said, and he thought that Rufus would know where the gold was hidden. He negotiated with the sheriff, who wasn't above earning a bit of extra money, to spy on the two in the hopes of discovering evidence. Because of this, the sheriff became a regular at the general goods store that Rufus subsequently took over. Rufus and Percy weren't happy to see him so often but they feigned friendship when he showed up, especially since he had argued to free Percy.

It became clear to them what the sheriff was up to, because he was always following Rufus around town, and when in the store, he asked meaningless questions just to be able to be there and watch them. Eventually, even the Sheriff got tired of bothering "Castle and Son" and left them alone.

Because of his experience with the sheriff, Rufus was always cautious when strangers came into the store. Percy sat in the back of the store, out of sight of customers. He took on the same persona he held in the woods of Virginia, hiding from anyone who might know his name. From the shadows of his chair in the corner, behind the store counter, he observed Rufus as he went about his business. He saw that his son took on a serious, pensive demeanor, and grew concerned about his future.

Percy again invited Rufus to sit and have lunch together. He asked Rufus how he felt about his life and what his plans were.

"I want to have a father-son talk," he began.

Rufus sat down and respectfully waited to hear what his father had to say.

"I'm concerned that you are holed up here in Denver because of me and what I did. I'll be okay on my own if you want to leave; if you're unhappy," Percy said. He looked into Rufus' face to see if he gave any hints of regret.

"I'm okay dad. I need you. I need family. I'm making an honest life for myself because of the trading and negotiating skills you've taught me. When I was a kid, I never could have imagined I'd be able to do all of this."

"But what of your future? Your happiness? Don't you want a wife and kids? You never go out and have fun."

At this Rufus looked down. He examined his hands and even picked at the dryness around his nails.

"What are you thinking, son? Tell me." Percy put his coffee mug on the table next to his chair, wondering what his son had in mind.

"I'll never marry and never have any kids because I'm afraid of what might happen to them if the gold is discovered. And frankly, dad, I'm even more afraid..." and here he hesitated. "I'm afraid that my children might be black. Mom and I were lucky. But what if my kids are not?"

"I would love my grandchildren, no matter what they look like."

"It's not up to you. Everything isn't up to you. Other people won't love them. Other people won't like them. I don't want to bring children into the world to suffer. I couldn't own this store if people knew I was black. How could I make a living for them?

I'm sorry. I've already come to terms with this. Let's not revisit it." Rufus got up, cleaned up the remains of his lunch and opened the store door, wanting the fresh air to rush in and wash away his loneliness.

He saw people walking by with sacks of goods; white women with parasols and ruffled dresses coming off the train that just pulled in; white men in leather boots leading their horses to the black-smith's; white boys running through the street with sticks clacking on round hoops, dogs at their heels. And a Native American and a black man hefting heavy bags of grain and flour out of the cargo portion of the train. His head down, he went back into the darker confines of the store. Dust floated in the air. He wondered how many working hands had touched the goods he sold.

Percy left his chair to help Rufus restock the store. He was already feeling like he was growing old quickly from worry. He watched Rufus, working beside him and thought about his son being alone. He missed growing old with Sadie and couldn't forgive himself for leaving her. Looking at Rufus, he remembered how he wanted more for himself and his family. He wanted real food and clean water to bathe in, no fear from attacks, and no more exhaust-ed nights in the wilderness. Now, he had those things. He realized that their most important assets were each other, and their biggest material asset was their biggest affliction.

"I love you," he said.

Rufus stopped what he was doing, turned to him and smiled.

When they weren't stocking the store, Percy sat in the corner. Sometimes he talked to himself. Sometimes, he just stared. Rufus remembered their conversation about Sam and how Percy's face lit up when he spoke of him.

Between customers, Rufus went behind the counter and whis-pered to Percy, "I want to meet my uncle Sam."

As if taking in his first breath, Percy inhaled, got up with new energy and left the store. He went to the telegraph office and sent a message to the town near the Castle plantation. Two weeks later, he received a message back.

"I'm alive stop busy stop married to Rosie stop
baby girl Ethel stop write to me Stone Ave NY stop
miss you stop"

Percy couldn't believe it.

"Rufus. Rufus. Look! He's alive and in New York. My little brother has a family. A girl. All these years. I never knew. He's alive." Percy stopped and realized he was sobbing.

Rufus read the telegram. It was hard to believe. How in the world did his father find Sam? And, in New York, of all places!

"It's okay. It's okay." He put his arms around Percy, and saw that his father was like a child. Hiding in his chair, he was losing touch. He just smoked and coughed most of the day, not talking to anyone.

"If he's busy, you have to go to him. He can't come here. Go. I'll be okay. Tell him about me, about the store. Maybe he'll come out later. You have to see him." He lifted his father's chin to read his eyes. Both yearning and fear looked back at him.

"I've only been on a train once," Percy said.

"It's okay," Rufus laughed. "This time you'll go as a passenger. Here, take some money from the store. We have plenty. Go see your brother and bring him back to me!"

"I'll just go for a short time. I'll wire him and go. People might notice I'm not here and start asking questions. Or maybe they already know, in New York, about the gold."

"No one knows, pop. It's okay. No one knows. You'll be fine. No one will ask you anything. You're just another passenger. Go see Sam." 'Before you run out of time,' Rufus thought. His father seemed unusually paranoid. Something he hadn't noticed before.

Rufus took the doll with the grey velvet skirt down from the shelf. He gave it to Percy so he could pass it along to his new cousin, Ethel, as a posthumous gift from Sadie. Percy wrapped Jack's deerskin jacket that he had kept for years, as a gift for Sam. Rufus thought that was a strange thing to do, but didn't wish to argue. He put some bread and cheese in a bag for Percy for the trip, hoping he would remember to eat it. It was a long trip to New York.

"Dad, people in New York dress nicely and the people who get off the trains here are clean and their clothing is pressed. Maybe you should take a bath and put on some new clothes for your trip. You haven't been out in a while."

"Sam won't care. He knows me too well. It'll take too much time to do all of that."

"Okay. Don't feel bad when I say this. You need a bath. You smell."

"Stewart Castle said that to me once. Don't ever say that to me, son!"

"I guess old habits stick. Okay. Don't expect anyone to sit next to you on the train."

"That's good. They won't sit near me. They won't notice me."

"Oh. They'll notice you all right. But go ahead. Maybe you can even catch the train this evening. I'll go across the street and see if there are any seats left."

Rufus bought a round trip ticket to be sure Percy would find his way home after his visit.

PERCY MEETS ROSIE

Percy got a seat on the train to New York to meet Rosie, Sam's wife, and Ethel, their new baby daughter. He was devastated that Sam was out of town on business when he arrived.

"He wrote that he was busy, but I figured he came home at night."

Rosie didn't respond to that.

"I have a present for little Ethel here." Percy took out the doll that Sadie made and handed it down to Ethel. Ethel hugged it and gave it a kiss. She went into the corner and sat on a blanket, rocking the doll and singing herself to sleep.

"Sam is lucky. She's sweet," Percy observed. "Sam will recognize that doll and explain about Sadie. Your husband helped her escape. I married her."

Rosie sat tolerantly across the room from this disheveled older man who smelled like he hadn't taken a bath in weeks, nodding her head. 'How could this man possibly be my Sam's brother,' she thought. 'I wonder if he's homeless. Maybe I should cook him a meal or offer him a hot bath.' But she sat frozen in her chair and let him go on.

"Jack was my friend. He taught me how to scout for the wagon trains and later I worked for the Fort in Laramie. But on the way out there, we were attacked and they killed Jack."

"Who killed him? Who was he exactly?"

"He was my friend. He saved my life and he knew everything about Indians and wagons and camping." He handed Rosie the package with Jack's bloodied buckskin jacket. She began to unwrap it.

"Oh no. No. Don't do that!" He reached across to stay her hands knowing she'd be very upset when she realized what she was holding.

"You should wait for Sam to be here. Don't you look at it. Let him see it. He'll understand what my life's been like when he sees it."

Rosie thought it was odd that he'd bring a gift but not let her see it without Sam. But, she put it on the floor in the corner of the room. "Okay. I won't touch it. I promise to give it to Sam when he gets back." She thought he was so odd that she didn't want to upset him. She just did what he said and then sat and listened.

"Good. Good. That's better." Percy sat back, relieved.

They looked at each other awkwardly and Percy smiled. Rosie didn't know quite what to do. Percy was a stranger and he was very strange. His clothing, his smells, his behavior. Sam was nothing like this man. She couldn't help but continue to wonder about their relationship.

"Well. Okay. Um. I can see this is uncomfortable for you. And I'm used to being alone back in the store. I'm going to go now before anyone figures out that I'm here or who I am," Percy said.

"I thought you said you're Sam's brother. Isn't that who you are?" Now Rosie was getting nervous.

"Yes, of course. That's who I am. But I have to keep moving. I'm going back on tonight's train."

"You just got here! You must have traveled for days just to get here. You're going back now?"

"Yes. My son Rufus is alone in the store and I have to get back."

Rosie couldn't wait for him to leave, although she knew Sam would be upset, if this truly was his brother. But, she didn't want him hanging around and certainly didn't want him in the house overnight unless Sam was there. He didn't look like he could pay for a hotel. She wasn't sure what to do. She went with the flow.

"Okay. Then. I guess you have to go. The train leaves in an hour, so you'd better run along." Now she just felt odd herself.

Percy reached over to kiss her good bye and she flinched.

"I'm sorry," he said. "I guess I feel you're family, but I am kind of filthy from all of the traveling. Bye-bye, little Ethel," he waved. "Goodbye Rosie. I'm glad we got to meet." Percy ran out the door and found his way to the train.

He slept on the train back to Denver and felt happy for the first time in years. When he got back to Denver, the old fears returned as did the Sheriff's watchful eyes. He hoped Sam would come out soon, but it wasn't for years that Sam returned his visit.

PERCY'S DEATH (APPROX. 1905)

Sam Castle's Diary, February 1905

I wish I had gone out sooner and maybe more than just once. I may as well have been dressed for a funeral. I was not used to wearing such a stiff collar and shiny shoes. I looked swell! I was pleased with myself. I wore my best suit to show Percy.

So, here I was. I was an old man compared to the rest of my family, Rosie being so young. But now that I knew where Percy was, I'd go anywhere to see him, although the idea of a sanatorium frightened me. I was not really sure who ends up in such a place. How did Percy get himself into this mess? He should be home playing with his grandchildren, for God's sake! I wondered if he had any grandchildren...for God's sake. Why didn't he keep in touch with me over the years? I never knew where he'd be next. Now I wish I had seen him more often.

The street from the station to the hospital wasn't paved and it was a long walk. It was just dirt and dust. Ugh! Who lives like this? Percy, I guess. It turned my shoes an awful grey color. I wondered if it would ever come off. Stomping them at the doorway didn't really help. I thought I'd make a bad impression on Percy. I had no idea what he would be like when I saw him.

I figured I'd stop at the shoe shine on my way back to the railroad station. Didn't want to go home like this. Little did I know how insignificant this all was in the big scheme of things.

The man at the front desk wore a blue uniform with an official patch on his sleeve. I stared at it closely, trying to decipher it.

He asked my name and when I didn't reply right away, he barked at me rudely, "You here to see someone or just passing time? What's yer name sir?"

"Sam," I answered.

"Sam what?"

"What? Oh, Castle, sir, uh, your honor, uh," I stammered.

I felt like a hick—me. Imagine! I ran a whole plantation as the South died and now, a shirt store of my own in a big city. And out there in the middle of nowhere, I felt out of place. I backed up a bit. He made me feel small.

He said, "Well this ain't no castle, but sign here," and he handed me a pen.

I wrote "Sam" in the box and asked where Percy Castle might be. He swung his arm out, both to show me and to get me to back up some more. It looked like he liked to keep people at a distance. Maybe that's how he kept healthy. He pointed down the hall, and I turned in that direction. "Not very friendly here," I considered.

The way stretched out before me like yellow taffy. I couldn't believe I was finally going to see Percy and Percy was so very, very sick...At first glance, the hall seemed clean enough. But I scrutinized it more carefully as I went. The walls were a mustard yellow and paint peeled from the corners of the ceiling. I noticed mouse turds in the corners by the doorway and traps behind the doors. Nurses wore white dresses and aprons, and stiff boarded hats, and some wore masks. They all just brushed past me, as their heavy, shiny black shoes thumped a rhythm. They also had an air of "I don't care much for the likes of you" about them, though shouldn't they have a godly air of compassion? I always thought that nurses did God's work, especially if they worked in a sanatorium. And, really, I looked sharp. I was in my Sunday best....no one noticed.

Just a bit further, I noticed another door with another guard sitting in a wooden spindle backed chair. It was quiet in the room beyond him. As I stretched a look into that room, he handed me a mask, and nodded politely to me, tipping his head toward the door, inviting me in. I put the mask in my pocket. I figured if Percy could be here without a mask, so could I. Now that I know what the problem was, I hope I don't regret doing that but I couldn't imagine having a mask on while I saw my brother for what was the first time since we were young and what became the last time forever. I took off my hat and slowly put one foot in front of the other.

My heart fluttered and I could feel the adrenaline flowing. I had a sick feeling in my gut. I could hardly breathe. Suddenly, I wasn't sure I belonged there. I hadn't seen Percy in years, though he always sent a card for the holidays and once sent a picture of Sadie. He labeled it, "The woman of my dreams." She was Ma's Sadie and had a sweet smile and saw something special in the camera lens for sure. She must have been looking at Percy. God! What he must have paid for that picture! From what I could make of it, Percy had had some crazy life! The jacket he left for me scared me to death. Yet, he had money to take that picture.

There were rows of beds on each side of the long room. I couldn't believe what I was seeing. Each bed held a zombie-like creature in its folds. Some literally tied to the bed with leather straps. I swear one was dead, his face cotton white, mouth open to the air and eyes gazing at nothing you'd care to see. A bit further on, I thought I saw Percy. The man in the bed just before Percy had one eye open. The other one was covered in a bloody gauze pad. His nose was swollen to the size of a cherry apple and he had no front teeth, though he smiled at me as I walked by. I hadn't seen anyone so beat up since the war. "Nice guy, that one," he said to me, and nodded over at Percy. His ankle was shackled. I wondered if he came in from a local prison, but I didn't stop to talk.

Percy. I hardly recognized him. He was just a young man when he left. He had a full head of hair and his eyes sparkled with mischief and impulsive energy. He said he would help "save Sadie," and then he "was goin' to make it rich… was goin' to make it big!" Now I saw that he was completely bald and his face was gaunt, frail and wrinkly thin. He had always been an outdoors kind-of guy with a ruddy complexion but now he looked like he hadn't seen the sun in years. He must have heard his neighbor, because he opened his eyes and caught sight of me.

"Hey," I said softly as I sat on his bed.

"Hey," he mouthed back. "Just in time," he rasped and then coughed.

Blood dripped from his lips and I picked up the rag next to his head. It had pink spots, some wet, and some dry, on it. I wiped his mouth for him, and I could feel the dampness of his blood on my hand. His arms were already lifeless next to him, and I could see in his eyes that he had surrendered to his destiny.

"Just in time? Is there a party?" I asked, settling my hand over his.

I recognized his wry smile even as he grimaced. When we were kids, we would hurry and get dressed in our Sunday best and go to church parties. We weren't invited but no one knew us, and no one seemed to care. It was the best way to get a fast meal for free. We'd grab a handful of our favorites and stuff our pockets. Percy would keep watch. I was so much younger that no one suspected me. They all thought I was cute. We'd run out the door before anyone noticed what we did and we'd laugh 'til our sides hurt. There was nothing funny about it though. We finished eating before we got home—there was never enough to share with Ma, and never enough at home to go around. Any meal was a good meal. It was good to feel full. Percy always had my back. He apparently had it now as well, though I had no idea. Yet.

Sam put his pen down and didn't write anything else in his diary. He just sat and thought about what happened next….

Percy didn't move but his eyes went from side to side watching to be sure no one heard. The man next to him had fallen asleep and the nurses left as soon as Sam walked in. Percy was dying but didn't look afraid, just resolved. He had an important task to complete before he was done with this world.

Percy told Sam a story. It was hard for Sam to believe. He thought maybe Percy was crazy from being ill for so long. Or maybe, well into his 70s, he was just demented. He told Sam he had a son named Rufus. Sam gave a loud guffaw!

"Ha! You? A son? I find that hard to believe. Where is he?" Sam challenged him looking around the room.

Percy tightened his lips with a worried look and scanned the room to see if anyone heard the commotion.

"A son," he whispered again. "… In Denver. Colorado. You know where that is?" he said.

Sam could see Percy was struggling and confused. He was right there in Denver, now. He grew more serious and just nodded his head for Percy to go on. Percy coughed again. More blood. He choked and made an awful face. Sam lifted his head and felt its full weight in his arms. He wiped Percy's mouth and forehead with the same cloth he had used before. He held him close in his arms.

"You're my big brother, Percy. I love you. Hang on, please!" Sam's heart beat hard and fast.

"Nurse!" Sam called with an urgency in his voice, but Percy smiled and shook his head ever so slightly.

Percy had a warmth in his eyes that Sam had never seen before, like he was sincere and really cared about him. Or, he thought, was death teasing them both?

"I'm so glad you're here. He'll give you the gold," Percy said. "Go find him."

"What? What gold? What are you talking about? Are you nuts? Percy! Percy! Nurse!"

But he was gone. Right there, in Sam's arms. Sam kissed Percy and gently laid him back down, half expecting him to wake up and laugh. It's all a joke, right? He couldn't take his eyes off of him.

"That's it?" he said.

Sam sat for a long time. No one came in. His own heart pounded in his ears. It was hot. He loosened his collar. He couldn't breathe. He was alone with Percy. Percy, who stole 'party' food with him. Percy, who taught him to swim and who jumped off the docks right next to the big ships filled with whale blubber in Nantucket harbor. Percy, who was both brother and man of the house for Ma in Nantucket so Pa could go off to sea and have work; who ran through the streets holding Sam's hand so he'd be safe. His big brother, Percy.

Sam thought, "He was so big and I was so little. He was old enough to be my young father. He made sure I didn't starve and that I went to school. He got me my first girl; that was sweet. And this is how Percy goes out? That's it?"

He knew so little about Percy's adult life.

Sam couldn't tell how long he sat with his head in his hands but the sunrise was startling as a masked nurse touched his shoulders.

"Sir? Sir? Are you all right?"

"Rufus," he said to her, dropping his hands and looking up slowly.

"What? Sir you've been sleeping a long time. Are you okay?" she said.

Percy was gone. His bed was empty. Sam looked at her wondering where they took him but all he could say, half to himself and half to her, was "What did he say about Rufus?"

She thought Sam was a bit off kilter and shook her head. "You'd better go home and get some rest, Sir, and get that mask on!" She went on to the next patient.

Sam remembered that Percy said he had a son named Rufus. He'd be Rufus Castle in Denver, Colorado. Gold? Really? In that case, Sam figured that while he was out there, he might as well meet Rufus and let him know his dad was gone; be there for him at the funeral. And it wouldn't hurt to find out about the gold that Percy mentioned.

First, Sam went to the Chapel in the sanatorium.

Just inside the doorway, on a round table, there were several thin pamphlets. Each had the name of a religion printed on its cover. He read, "Christian, Catholic, Jewish, Moslem, Hindu…..hum…..ah, Quaker."

He picked up the Quaker booklet and flipped through its pages. He found a page that said, "Prayer for a deceased relative." In bold letters, it said,

"The following extract, written in 1693 by William Penn, is a favourite reading at Quaker funerals...." [10]

Sam remembered going to the Meeting House as a child. That was one place where he and Percy were respectful and behaved as their Ma told them. Ma told them to think of everything they had done the week before and to talk to God about what they could do better the next week. Percy got them into so much trouble during the week that it usually took them the full half hour to "talk to God," hoping for forgiveness and inspiration for the next week. Sam often wondered what sort of inspiration God had given Percy. But he never asked about it. He always went along for the ride.

Sam hadn't gone to a Meeting House since his mother married Stewart. But his fond memories of Percy went back to their childhood in Nantucket, not Virginia. No one else was in the Chapel so he just stood and faced the stained glass window at the front of the room, and in Quaker style, he read out loud as if he were talking to God:

"And this is the Comfort of the Good,
    that the grave cannot hold them....
    ... Death is no more
    than a turning of us over from time to eternity....
    Death cannot kill what never dies.
    Nor can Spirits ever be divided
    that love and live in the same Divine Principle...."
(William Penn 1693) [10]

Sam closed the pamphlet and continued, "Thank you for Percy."

He placed the pamphlet back on the table, wiped his eyes dry, and left the sanatorium.

He next stopped at the shoe shine at the station. He wanted to look good for Rufus. He had his shoes shined but didn't get on the train. Instead, he went into the Post Office near the train station.

"Can you tell me where the Castle General Store is?" Sam asked.

"Why, it's right there, across the street! Has been for years!" answered the man, pointing for Sam to turn around.

Rufus was happy to meet Sam and devastated to hear his message. They attended Percy's funeral together and, afterward, Rufus kept his promise. When he returned to New York, Sam was a very rich man.

PART 6

(1900's)

PART 6

(1900's)

SAM AND ROSIE

On the train ride back to New York, Sam had lots of time to think. He wasn't sure he wanted Rosie to know about the gold. After all, it was stolen. He didn't know if he'd be in trouble for taking it and definitely didn't want Rosie to suffer from it. She had a tough enough life before she met him, and she was so much younger than he. He thought about using it to make her happy. The train rocked as it moved and soon he drifted off to sleep, dreaming about Rosie's life...

Back in the late 1880s Rosie left her mother and brother in Kiev to go to America with her father. Mirabelle, Rosie's friend, came along, and the three settled in Manhattan. Rosie's father was well educated and believed that women should read and write and Rosie learned English as a child. Rosie and Mirabelle were very independent and became somewhat high-strung young women for the times. They were able to help other immigrants learn English and bartered their teaching skills for a roof over their heads and food to eat. Sometimes, to the chagrin of Rosie's father, who was very religious and conservative, they lived like there was no tomorrow. They had no fears of being in a new place. Over the years, the three of them became citizens. Rosie also had sewing skills and was able to bring in some money beyond the teaching stipends they earned. The work was tedious and hard on the fingers and the eyes, but the money put food on their table. She recognized that New York was growing and that a smart woman could do well there. But the winters were brutally cold and Mirabelle was always ill.

One day, when Mirabelle was too ill to go to work, Rosie decided to stay home to take care of her.

"I feel so guilty that you keep getting sick. We came so far to get here to America, and you haven't been able to benefit at all. Maybe coming here wasn't such a good idea," Rosie said as she put a cold compress on Mirabelle's head.

Mirabelle's face was white and clammy. Her head was burning up from yet another cold and a nagging, chronic cough. "I'll be fine. Besides, you didn't force me to come here, and I'd probably be just as sick in my mother's house as I am in yours. Ours."

Rosie sat in a chair next to Mirabelle's bed and picked up the newspaper that her father had left on the table for Mirabelle. She flipped through a section about travel and vacationing.

"Imagine if we could go on a holiday. Just the two of us. Having fun. Finding friends. Maybe a boyfriend," Rosie dreamed as she slowly turned the pages.

"You'll probably lose your job now that you've stayed home," Mirabelle began. "How on earth would you pay for a holiday?"

"I can still sew and tutor. I'm not a helpless woman."

"Hum. Well I can't stand the winter cold. I'm always shaking when I sit at the sewing machine. What does it say in the paper about warm places to visit?" Mirabelle asked as she closed her eyes, wishing that Rosie would put the paper down and change her compress.

"It says that Georgia, Florida and Alabama are having a heat wave and that northerners should holiday there to escape the bitter cold." Rosie kept reading out loud.

"Where's Alabama? That's a funny name. Does it say where to go exactly?"

"*It says that a good spot is Mobile, Alabama. It has places to go to. Restaurants, music houses and bars. Imagine us in a music house or bar,*" Rosie mused.

Mirabelle took the compress from her head and leaned over on one elbow, chuckling.

"*We came all the way over here and we're cramped into this tiny apartment, the three of us. Maybe some adventure would do me good.*" She fell back onto the mattress which was soggy with her sweat.

Rosie changed her compress and gave her a sponge bath with vinegar. The next morning, Mirabelle's fever broke and she sat up in bed. Rosie stayed home again and fed her sick friend some watery broth she concocted from parsnips and potatoes. That evening Rosie's father came home and sat at the small wooden table. He looked over at Mirabelle.

"*Feeling better I see,*" he nodded, grateful for her returning health.

"*So, Rosie, my dear. I hear you've lost your job again. You'll have to do some extra tutoring or sewing this week so we can put food on the table.*" He sensed that something was up between the girls and looked from one to the other waiting to hear what it was.

"*Well. Papa, I have something to tell you,*" Rosie looked at her hands and began slowly.

"*Mirabelle and I are going to leave.*"

"*What's this? What do you mean? You can't just go off somewhere! Have you met a man? What will you do? Where will you go?*" He stood up, gesturing with his hands as he spoke. He began to pace the room, waiting for his daughter to continue.

"*It's me,*" said Mirabelle. "*I'm too sick. I can't stay here. The winters are killing me.*"

Rosie's father eyed Mirabelle with suspicion. "*So you want to go home? Do you think it's any warmer there? There's no food there and no jobs for women. Your parents will marry you off to the first eligible man who has a pulse. Is that what you want? I thought you want to get an education and to be independent, although I really don't understand why you want this….. but that's what you said you wanted. What now?*"

"No, papa," Rosie intervened. "That's not it. We hear there are places in the south where we can go and find work and where it's warm. Maybe Mirabelle can get better there."

"And, of course, you have to go along," he said bitterly, while, at the same time, considering the situation.

"I heard I have a distant cousin, or maybe he's a second cousin," Mirabelle said.

Rosie's father cocked his head and raised his eyebrows at this announcement.

"He's been living in Virginia but is moving to Mobile, Alabama soon. We can stay with him. He's older and he can take care of us and help us along."

"Papa, please," said Rosie.

Rosie's father threw his hands up in the air in concession. "I'm staying here. If your mother makes it across, she'll be looking for me here. I guess there's no harm in your doing some traveling. But you must let me know where you are at all times. Send me word by telegraph, if you can find the money for it. Or send a postal letter. Promise me you won't go astray."

"We promise," the girls said at once, grabbing each other by the hands. Mirabelle jumped out of bed with new found energy and the two went swinging around in circles until Rosie's father, with hands to his head, had to yell, "Enough already. Be still." The girls laughed, Mirabelle collapsed back on the bed, and Rosie set to getting their dinner ready.

Rosie's father sighed. He could hardly believe he had just given permission for his young daughter to go off with a friend in this foreign country to God knows where to do God knows what. They were "young ladies" now and eventually would have to fend for themselves. He knew this day would come but it came too quickly. He had hoped they would both be married before leaving him to go off on their own. For the next two days, while the girls made plans, he just sat at the table by himself when he came home from work, shaking his head from side to side, as if talking it over with an unseen advisor. "What woman goes off on her own?"

As the train neared New York State, Sam woke up. He still wasn't certain whether to approach Rosie about the gold. Rufus told him what happened when Percy told Sadie about it. Sam wasn't sure how Rosie would react. He thought back to when he first left Virginia for Alabama, set up his shirt store, and met Rosie. What was she like then? Were there clues that might help him decide what to do?

Stewart had disappeared one day while checking the perimeter of the plantation to see how close the fighting was. Sam learned sewing skills during the war when he and Mamie fixed uniforms for the Confederate soldiers who streamed across their plantation. Later, when the Union soldiers came, they did the same for them, but first, they took down the portrait of Stewart that hung over the dining room table, and made up a story about freeing their slaves. Sam sold the Castle plantation after Mamie was enticed away by adventure and a carpet bagging traveling man. Sam moved into a two room apartment over a shirt store in Mobile, Alabama with the money he made from the plantation sale. He took Stewart's portrait with him as a souvenir of the plantation, and had it in his apartment in Mobile, wrapped in heavy paper in the back of a closet. Soon afterward, Rosie and Mirabelle arrived.

Sam had enough money to live without finding work, but didn't want anyone to know what his situation was. Times were desperate and he feared being robbed. Because of his skills, it was easy for him to land a job as a tailor in a shirt store in Mobile, Alabama.

Sam was Mirabelle's second cousin, and he took her and Rosie in. He was several years older than they were, but in those days, because he was related to Mirabelle, he was considered their chaperone. He was happy to care for them since Percy and Mamie were gone and Mirabelle was family. He made sure they were safe, and he knew the right places to tell them to go when they went out. Because of his unique situation, feeding them was not a problem. The three had fun times together in the evenings and on Sundays, when Sam had off from work.

Sam was dapper. Even though he was almost twenty years older, the girls loved him and he had more than one female friend coming around the apartment. He was slight, with thinning hair but a winning smile. He wore fancy, expensive clothing and kept his appearances up far beyond a shirt maker's pay. Because he sewed, he tailored his own suits and they fit impeccably. He wore high collared shirts with cravats of silk and shiny buttoned up shoes. Rosie didn't understand where he got his money, but she loved how he doted on her, buying her flowers and elaborate dinners. She ignored the other girls who came around because he always came back to her.

Rosie and Sam fell in love and were soon married. Sam placed the gold ring that Rufus gave him on Rosie's finger. She never asked who 'P and S' were. Gold was gold and she loved Sam. It didn't take long for Rosie to get pregnant. She wanted Sam to have his own shirt store to make a reliable, good living.

"Sam, darling, I'm going to have this baby very soon." She couldn't look him in the eyes as she began, afraid of what he might say. She self-consciously looked down at her ever expanding belly.

"I want our children to be New Yorkers. That's where things are changing and happening. New York is such a big, great place," she said glancing up at him.

"But Rosie, I've been here in Virginia and now Alabama almost all my life. I like it here," replied Sam, not wanting to leave his friends and fun times. "It's so cold in New York. It's nice here in the winter time."

Rosie sensed that his "fun times" were a bit too much fun and she wanted him to make a stronger commitment to her and their unborn child so that she and the child would have a secure future, so she continued her quest.

"My father is back in New York. Alone. He'll want to see his grandchild." She massaged her growing belly in wide gentle strokes as she spoke.

"Oh. Hum," Sam furrowed his forehead, his eyes traveling down to where she massaged their progeny. Finally, she said what was really on her mind.

"Besides, I hate how people treat people of color here. The words they say! The names they call them! Even your friends partake in such hurtful nonsense!" she argued. "I believe the English for that is 'prejudice'. People were prejudiced against us, where we come from. We had to leave and come here to be safe. I don't want my children to grow up in this environment."

Sam was humble and never told Rosie about Sadie and her sister, or the other runaway slaves, and how he had helped. All of that was from a time of his youth, too long ago to conjure up for his new young bride. He wasn't crazy about the idea of moving north but he understood her concerns.

Sam went over to Rosie and traced her hands as she moved them across her body. He kissed her face and smiled his winning grin.

"I'll never take on those discriminatory ways, Rosie. I promise. If this is really what you want, we can arrange a move. But let's wait for the baby to be born first."

As soon as Rosie had her baby, a girl whom they named Ethel after Rosie's mother, they moved back north to New York. Sam got an apartment for them on Stone Avenue with a store front on the main street. From money left over from the sale of the plantation, and what he made at his southern shirt store, he opened his own shirt store on the ground floor of their home, and did very well. He also made clothing for Rosie who was very slim even after she had the baby. Rosie was able to help him with the sewing, as her father babysat Ethel. The work was not taxing. It was the perfect situation for Sam since he was already advancing through middle age.

Sam realized that one of the things he loved about Rosie was that she was principled. She was independent for a woman of her times. She moved hundreds of miles to help a friend and then hundreds of miles back again to try to shield her child from prejudice and discrimination. She might react in a similar manner to Sadie. On the other hand, she liked going out to eat and 'party' before they married. She took things for granted and apparently trusted him to handle the finances. She never asked where the money came from before. If he didn't tell, she probably wouldn't ask now, as long as she saw him working. He decided not to tell her about the gold.

Rosie was happy when Sam got home from his first trip to Denver, and sad, for Sam's sake, that Percy had died. Sam told her about Percy's son Rufus and about the general store. Shortly afterward, he received a telegram from someone in the Denver

Post Office. Rufus died of typhoid, and left the general store to Sam, his only living relative. Sam did not share this information with Rosie.

Instead, he approached Rosie with a new idea.

"I've heard that trains come in to Denver from San Francisco and carry goods from China. I can get nicer cloth and even silks for cravats cheaper out west. Rufus gets shipments all the time. I'm going to take the train from New York through Chicago and out to Colorado so that I can take advantage of the business people Rufus knows. We can upgrade our tailoring store with better material and goods. And, while I'm out there, I can check up on Rufus to be sure he's doing okay."

"Well, you just got back, but I guess that's okay. I can make due here for a few weeks while you're gone. Family's important and Rufus has been through a lot, what with Percy dying in a sanatorium and he being alone all the time." Rosie gave Ethel a spoonful of mashed potatoes as she spoke.

So Sam left again and Rosie didn't complain, though Sam took this trip many times over the years, leaving her alone to fend for Ethel and their New York store.

Sam always came home with an extra bolt of beautifully colored material for Rosie to use to make blouses and dresses for herself and Ethel, as well as a piece of pottery or jewelry for her. Rosie trusted Sam and never questioned his sincerity, although she and Ethel missed him terribly whenever he was gone.

"Are you sure you have to go out to that god forsaken place again? Is it safe to be there?" Rosie argued after he had taken the trip four or five times in one year.

Sam assured her, "It's fine. And, besides, I'll be with Rufus and he really knows his way around. He'll watch over me, and I'll bring back the most beautiful flowered calico you've ever seen. You can make blouses for both you and Ethel, some hankies or a skirt," he said, cupping her chin in his hand.

"You're such a sweet talker, you," she said and smiled and gave his hand a kiss. "I love you and we'll miss you while you're gone. Tell Rufus we love him and we'd like it if he'd come to visit some time."

"I'll tell him," Sam said.

He took her hand from his face where she had been stroking his cheek and kissed her palm in turn. He smiled that broad, mischievous, Castle smile, grabbed his bag and ran for the train.

The next 25 years of marriage rolled by. Even as Sam became quite elderly, he continued to travel to Colorado periodically. In 1906, Sam lied to Rosie about going to Denver. Instead, the Nassau County office logged a survey showing that Sam bought a large piece of property on Long Island. He spent his next three "trips to Denver" out on Long Island preparing a special surprise for Rosie and Ethel.

When Rosie found out that he lied to her and bought Long Island property, she was livid.

"How could you waste our hard earned money on such nonsense. There's nothing on Long Island but potato farms and wild animals." But she changed her tune when he took her for "a holiday ride" one July afternoon.

Rosie, Sam and Ethel caught an old steamboat in Manhattan and got off in Oyster Bay harbor. They walked into town along a dirt and stone path. There wasn't much around but they had heard stories of Long Island Revolutionary War heroes that had lived there. Mostly, there were woods and, scattered far apart, near the waterways, there were a few rectangular wooden houses with rows of small square windows toward the tops, bricked areas forming gardens out front, and white picket fences. On a narrow street in town, they caught an historic coach, horses and all, that Sam had arranged for in advance. Rosie was charmed but kept looking at Sam with bewilderment.

He just smiled at her and said, "Wait. You'll see."

"You're not taking me off to the woods to leave me there, because I was angry, are you? I can't imagine what sorts of animals live here." The undeveloped woodlands frightened her. He just smiled and patted her on her knee.

"No, sweetheart. You might see some deer or box turtles but no bears or tigers. I'm here with you. You'll see the surprise soon enough. Don't worry. It's a long ride. Relax and enjoy the beautiful trees."

He kissed her lightly on the cheek. They rode a bit further south and eastward. Rosie thought they would have to spend the night in a tent or a deserted cabin. She was worried they'd see coyotes. She kept a watchful eye between the trees.

As they came up what was later called Route 25, they turned off the road and back into the woods. A small path, just big enough for the coach stretched for about a quarter of a mile before a large clearing. The clearing was apparently an old potato farm, and before that an ancient Matinnecock Indian burial ground. It was squared off by tall trees and, except for the burial mound off to the left, it appeared to be flat.

The carriage drove up facing the mound, with trees blocking the view off to the right. Sam had planned it this way. Rosie's eyes took in the landscape slowly from left to right and finally, around the trees. As she turned, she gasped out loud, her hand covering her mouth. There, perched on another mound behind the trees, was a big blue house. It sat all alone overlooking the entire area. It was made of teal blue clapboard, the color of the ocean, and had a funny looking parabola at its top where windows ran around a rooftop room. There was a stained glass trim of red, blue and green on the windows of the parabola and window boxes with flowers in them on the windows below. Tiny Corinthian columns cornered off that rooftop space like a miniature, but grand, Roman forum. Sam announced that this was their new vacation home and that he built it especially for Rosie. Rosie thought for sure he had gone mad and she started to cry and smile all at once.

"But how will we live, now that you've gone and gotten us into debt? What will we eat? What are we going to do? We're in the middle of nowhere! Where in God's name did you get the money?"

Sam put his arms around her and told her not to worry. He said they owned it and no one would ever take it from them, although secretly, he wondered about that part of the story. He was always concerned about what would happen if anyone put two and two together and discovered where the money had come from. He decided not to think about it.

Rosie was so taken by the house and the beauty of the surroundings that she decided not to challenge him.

"I always trust you to do the right thing. I'm sure you figured out the finances before doing this." She looked at Sam with hope in her eyes that he had thought it through. He smiled and nodded his head. She returned his smile.

They rode right up to the front door and Sam helped her out of the buggy. He took her hand and they walked together to the threshold. He gently lifted her and carried her into the family home as if they were newlyweds all over again. They spent their summers in the house and Ethel spent most of her childhood in the countryside. Rosie grew to love being on Long Island and, sometimes stayed there with Ethel while Sam went into the city to work.

Sam had boxes of his belongings that he had never opened after leaving the plantation. In the Manhattan apartment, they were stored in a dark attic above their bedroom. On the next trip out to Long Island, Sam brought the boxes along. Rosie unpacked them in the house, putting up old pictures, and unpacking the other odd things she found. One picture was of a Confederate soldier. She found it distasteful but the colors in it matched her furniture, so she put it in the dining room. Sam laughed when he saw it but waved Rosie off when she asked about it.

"No matter," he grinned. "That's just the place for it. Leave it right there. Someday, I'll tell you about it." But he never did.

Over the years, the city stretched its tentacles out along the shoreline of Long Island and the suburbs grew up around the blue house, like the ocean around Nantucket Island. In fact, houses slowly appeared on every side of the family home's horizon. Before they knew it, the Castles had neighbors, since Sam sold some of the land to distract Rosie from wondering where his money came from. They ended up with a yard they could care for but mostly never did. They had a neighbor right next door who thought the Castles were rich because they had owned all of the surrounding land and had gotten paid handsomely to sell it to developers. Sam thought that was just fine. Let them think what they would.

World War I came and went. Sam was too old and ill to fight. His bouts of bronchitis became serious and he began to travel to Colorado regularly, saying the weather there helped his cough. His visits grew longer. Ultimately, he learned that he had contracted tuberculosis, maybe from Percy, or maybe from the women he had fun with in Mobile before he met Rosie. He realized he would meet the same fate as his brother and hoped he didn't infect Rosie and Ethel. At first, he didn't tell Rosie he was ill. He just started to keep his distance from her when they were together. She figured it was due to the difference in their ages, or maybe he didn't want her to catch bronchitis. He stopped hugging Ethel and as an adult, she never remembered him ever having kissed her. But he always looked at her with love in his eyes and a bit of regret. They had a special father-daughter understanding and relationship.

Sam kept the bulk of the "Trust Fund," as he called the gold, hidden in the hills outside of Denver near the cemetery where Percy was buried, and cashed out parts of the stash every few years so as not to attract attention. He made the transactions under different names and aliases and no one ever knew the difference. He was always paranoid that someone would recognize him or the name "Castle" while he was trading the gold, so he took it out of Denver when he traded it and had to go further away each time, thus making his trips longer. The train gold heist in the Black Hills in the late 1870s had been big news back then. Parents told their kids about it and Percy Castle was a legend, even though no one ever proved he was involved.

Although he used aliases to cash in the gold, Sam never changed his real name, so he and Percy were both Castles. He was sure someone would remember Castle since it was a catchy name. If someone did, he might end up in jail for not turning in the gold. Sam figured, 'you don't live forever' and decided to enjoy using it, but always had an unsettled feeling about being caught with it in his possession. Sam felt that the gold carried an uncomfortable aura, but hoped that Rosie and Ethel would benefit from having it. If they didn't know where it came from, they might have fun with it, and it kept a roof overhead and food on the table during the depression years. So, Sam never told Rosie. But there was lots of gold left and he had to pass it on to someone….

Whenever Sam returned home from a trip out west, it always took him a week or two to recuperate from the stress and strain of the trip. He would putter around the house when he got back; in the garden, fixing tiling or leaks and wall boards in the old vacation home he had built so many years ago. At these times, Rosie left him to himself. Eventually, he and Rosie permanently moved into the house, away from the hustle and bustle of city life. She could see that he was feeling his age, even though she thought he did pretty well. She knew his habits and accepted them. By then, she loved the family home and enjoyed living in it so she ignored the fact that he was almost twenty years her elder and a bit stand-offish.

Rosie noticed that Sam coughed a lot and looked fragile. He always seemed sicker when he came home from one of his long trips out to Colorado.

"Sam, I just don't understand why you have to go out to Denver anymore. You should be retired now and enjoying our home. You say it helps your cough but you're always so ill when you get back,"

Rosie implored him as he coughed incessantly upon returning from one of the trips.

"Oh Rosie, it's nothing. The train was smoky. I must have caught some bronchitis from the man sitting next to me. He kept coughing all the way home."

Sam always made excuses. He never mentioned gold dust or digging or his girlfriend or anything that might arouse Rosie's suspicions regarding what he did when he was in Denver. As the saying goes, Rosie's ignorance was also her bliss. Although Sam was cultivating a new love in Denver, Rosie always had a special place in his heart, and he wanted her to be happy whether or not they were together. So, he kept secrets.

When Sam was approaching his 80s, he made his last trip by train to Denver in a newly invented sleeping car. He never returned home. He wired Rosie that he was sick in a sanatorium and had to stay there for care. Rosie was in her mid-60s, and was tired of caring for the house alone, as well as of his comings and goings. She began to suspect that he had another woman in his life.

"What do you mean you're not coming home anymore? You live here! I'm your wife. What's going on? I've had a lot of patience with you and your shenanigans over the years," Rosie demanded.

"Well…it's not so easy for me to say," Sam lamented.

"Okay. Get it out, and now!" Rosie half yelled into the phone, although afraid of how he might answer.

"It's like this. When I came out to visit Percy, he was very sick. He had tuberculosis and I used some soiled towels to wipe up some stuff he was coughing up. The towels were already wet with his sputum and blood and I didn't wear a mask or wash my hands. I caught it, Rosie. I have TB. I'm too sick to be with you and Ethel. I'm afraid you'll catch it too," he said.

The line was silent. "Rosie?"

"I'm so sorry, Sam. I can't believe this. You were sick, but not *that* sick all these years, and you were going back and forth and back and forth. What does Rufus have to say about all of this? Is he taking care of you? Is he okay or did he get sick too?" Rosie asked worriedly.

"Well, the truth is that there is no Rufus. At least, not anymore. Rufus died years ago. I was afraid to tell you because I thought you wouldn't want me to come out here anymore. There was a store to tend to and eventually, I sold it. There was money in it," Sam explained.

"Wait a minute. What did you say? Did you say Rufus is dead? Sam, how could you lie to me all these years about something so important! He's really dead?"

"Yes. I'm afraid so. There's something else as well Rosie. Rosie, you there?"

"Yes, Sam. I'm here. What else?" she said resigned to whatever he would come up with now.

"Rosie. I have a girlfriend," Sam said.

"You what?! What! What the hell are you talking about! We're married. How long has this been going on?" Rosie was yelling into the phone.

"A while. I'm sorry, Rosie. Really, really sorry. It's just that I was lonely when I came out here, and…," Sam began.

But Rosie had already hung up.

Rosie wrote to him that she didn't believe that he was that ill, and then wired him again that she was tired of his behavior and wanted him home immediately or wanted a divorce. He gave her the divorce and married his girlfriend.

ROSIE AND ETHEL

R osie was angry but had spent so much time alone in the house, that not having Sam there wasn't as much of a life style change as she had expected. Besides, by then, Ethel was grown and lived nearby. She was there to help Rosie through the hard parts of the divorce. Rosie thought she'd sell the Long Island house but times were tough and there were no buyers.

Rosie often called Ethel with fear in her voice.

"I don't know what I'm going to do. I know we have bills due and I have no money to pay them. Any day now the bank will come, and I can just imagine them carrying me out on our couch and leaving me in the street. They did that in New York during the depression. Now your father has left me destitute. What will I do?"

"Has dad called you at all? Did you get any mail from the bank or from anyone asking for money?"

"No. But I have no idea why it hasn't happened, and I'm always pinching pennies on everything, worried that it's just a matter of time."

"We're here mom. We won't let anything happen to you. If you get any threats or a letter or anything like that, just call us. We're always here. You know that."

Soon, Ethel and her family moved into the Castle home to be with Rosie. Ethel didn't have to try very hard to get her husband to move in.

"It's a huge house right in the middle of Long Island. You'll love it," Ethel told her husband.

"I get it. I get it," he said. "But how will we ever afford to live on Long Island. Do you have any idea what the taxes are like out there? And what kind of a mortgage are we going to be saddled with if we make this move? I just don't know if we can swing this," he said.

"There won't be a mortgage. The house belongs to my family. We've never owed anything on it. Sam built it with money from his shirt store. We will only have to pay taxes. No mortgage, and mom has no debts to pay off. Dad took care of her well even after he left her," Ethel explained.

"I don't understand your family at all, Ethel. Where in the world did Sam get that kind of money? There's no way we could ever build a house like that out there. The property taxes are about all we could afford."

"And that's all we'll have to afford. What do you say? How about it? A house on Long Island. Wouldn't that be a treat in the summertime?" Ethel nudged.

"I guess I can't complain. No mortgage. A big house. Long Island. A prestigious address. Hum. Okay. It's a good place for Emma to grow up. She'll have plenty of sunshine and lots of room to play. I can invite my partners there to party. Okay. Okay. We'll do it."

And soon they moved in. Ethel's husband worked long hours in New York City and was only able to really enjoy the house on weekends. He didn't like working in the yard and let the lawn and gardens go to seed. He hired a lawn care company to mow around the front to make the place presentable when they did have company and rarely entertained out of doors. If Ethel or Emma wanted to barbecue, like the neighbors, they'd cook in the kitchen and eat on the small patio outside the kitchen door. Mostly, they just stayed inside. Occasionally, they went to the beach in Oyster Bay.

Before they moved in, they hadn't known that Sam sold some of the surrounding property to developers who planned to build colonials and ranches on small lots all around the clapboard house. Once they were settled in, houses were built right next door. The new neighbors were curious about the old place but mostly wondered when it would come down, so as not to detract from their skyrocketing property values. They put in modern asphalt driveways with Belgium block trim, mimosa trees, bright flower gardens and brick retaining walls, all creating rich and lavish curb appeal in the new suburbs. They knew this had been the Castle land purchased back at the turn of the Century. They figured the Castle family was very rich from selling off the land, but no one really got to know anyone in the Castle family very well.

Ethel and her husband began paying the bills. They had no idea what the neighbors were thinking since they were new to the neighborhood. They certainly didn't consider themselves rich. If anything, now that they were helping Rosie out, they were just scraping by.

One day, Ethel sat with Rosie over tea in the kitchen. Rosie pulled an embroidered handkerchief from her apron pocket and handed it to Ethel. Ethel could feel something heavy and rounded wrapped in the cloth. She opened it and waited for Rosie to explain.

"It's our ring," Rosie said. "Or at least I think it was ours. It has someone else's initials engraved inside. God only knows where your father got it or how many other women he gave it to before me. I like to think maybe 'P and S' were Percy and Sadie, but Sam never said. If so, I want you to have it. Take it. It's yours. It's my token of how much I care for you and dear Emma. It's my thank you to you for caring for me."

Ethel nodded and slipped the gold ring on her index finger. She got up, walked around to where her mother sat, wrapped her in her arms, and kissed her on her forehead.

"I love you, mom. Thanks."

Rosie died unexpectedly of heart failure three years after the divorce, and Ethel's family stayed on in the house.

ETHEL, SAM AND THE "TRUST FUND"

S am always loved his daughter dearly. He heard that Ethel was taking care of Rosie and that she was a resourceful and strong woman. Shortly after the divorce, about the time when Ethel's family had moved into the Long Island house, he wired Ethel. Sam asked her to visit him in Denver one last time, and bring her family along. Ethel had fond memories of her father and mostly overlooked his unusual ways. She wanted Emma to at least see him before he died of TB or old age or whatever it was that he was really suffering from—she loved him, but didn't always believe him. She and her family took a trip out west by train, essentially taking the same route that Percy and Sam had taken years ago on their respective first trips out west. When they got off the train, they rented a Buick and drove straight over to the Sanatorium where Uncle Percy had died and Sam was waiting.

Ethel planned to ask her father about the money and the bills so that she could help her mother relax and find happiness even if she was alone. She learned that Sam did in fact have tuberculosis. His TB was very contagious and it was too risky for everyone to go up to his room. She went alone into the hospital to see her father. Ethel had to put on a hospital gown, gloves and a mask, but they had a long visit. Their last.

"Looks like you are well protected," Sam noted. "Come here and sit next to me. It's okay. Just sit in the chair," he said and she pulled it over to be nearer to him.

"Ethel, thank you so much for coming. I've missed you terribly. I need to tell you, dearest, that I love you. I'm so sorry that I couldn't tell you how sick I was. I didn't want you to worry," he began.

"It's okay, pop. I understand," she said dutifully. "You're very thin. Are you eating anything?"

"Well, I have this pipeline to chicken soup," he smirked, pointing out the IV in his forearm. "You realize that it won't be long now, don't you?" He looked at her as if he might disappear any minute. He wanted to be sure she understood the seriousness of his intent as they talked.

Ethel clasped her hands in her lap and studied them as he spoke. "Are you in pain?" she finally managed.

"It's not too bad, really," he said. "Occasionally I can't stop coughing and my chest hurts then, but they give me pain killers and I sleep a lot. But I asked you to come for another reason. I have something important to tell you. To give you." He reached his hand out toward her but withdrew it. He wanted to hold her hand, but was afraid to touch her.

"What is it?" She said, wondering what he could possibly give her in his current state.

"First, he said, help me to the window. I want to see my grand-daughter."

Ethel called the nurse and together they lifted him out of bed and walked him to the window. He held onto the window frame as Ethel pushed the window open. They looked out and down to the street level which seemed far away from the 5th floor. Ethel and Sam smiled and waved to Emma and Ethel's husband.

"Okay. That's enough," Sam said. His hand shook as he held tight to the nurse, and nodded that he needed to go back to bed. "Thank you for bringing her so that I could see her," he told Ethel.

"She was anxious to see her grandfather but disappointed that she couldn't come in. Too young, they told us."

"That's good. Keep her out of here. You don't want her to get what I have, and she doesn't need to see all of these sick people." Sam settled back onto his pillow, coughing lightly. The nurse adjusted his IV and left.

Sam knew this would likely be the last time he saw his daughter and wanted to remember her mannerisms, the sound of her voice and the lines of her face. He was hypnotized by her blue eyes. In them, he saw something old and familiar: a spark of adventure, a black osprey skimming white caps in the bay. His eyes watered and his lips quivered as his bed rocked and white sails became white sheets gently covering him to keep him warm.

"What's wrong, dad? Why are you looking at me that way?" Ethel asked.

"Percy. Randall. Dad." Sam said almost inaudibly. "After all these years."

"Dad, you're frightening me. Should I get the nurse back here?" She asked as she finished tucking in his sheets and turned to get help.

Sam reached out and grabbed the sleeve of her plastic gown. She stopped.

"What?" she said.

"It's your eyes. They're 'Castle' eyes."

"Of course they are. I'm your daughter after all." She smiled and sat down again. He relaxed and seemed at ease. Returning her smile, he let go of the gown.

He weighed his contagion. "TB or gold fever? She's a Castle. Which one will claim her?"

"Providence will decide," he thought. "She has to know."

"So, what's this big important message you have for me?" Ethel prodded him.

Sam told Ethel the details about where the gold was and what she might do to keep it hidden. He referred to it as a "Trust Fund" and suggested she might use the same terminology so as to deflect any suspicions anyone might have.

"I don't know if having it makes us an accessory to the theft. No one can prove where it came from if they do find it, especially since it was stolen so long ago and both Percy and Rufus, are gone."

Sam went on.

"Because of the gold's origins, everyone who has known about it has kept it a secret, except to tell whoever would get it next. I want you to know that you have to be careful how you use it and where you keep it. I kept some of it hidden where Percy had stashed it. Some, I cashed out to keep us afloat back in the 1930s. And of course, some I used for the blue house on Long Island. But don't you go telling your mother that."

He tried to lift himself up on his elbow and started to cough.

"I won't say a word." Ethel was wide eyed and all ears. He was either crazy or her life was about to change in a big way.

Sam settled down and continued.

"Being careful like this might assure that no one family member will get overly greedy or suspicious of you. The gold will last a long time if you're careful how you use it. It is a terrific asset for the family, especially with education costs and taxes going up. Do you understand? Do you see that you'll need some ideas for how you might manage the gold in your own time?" Sam stopped and coughed a bit more.

"You okay?" Ethel patted him on the back.

"No. No. Don't touch me. Move away." He sputtered as he coughed some blood into a towel the nurse had left on his bed.

Ethel sat back a bit and watched. There wasn't much she could do.

Finally, his cough calmed a bit.

"Your mother doesn't know anything about this. I've paid her bills these past two years so she has nothing to complain about. But I want this to pass to you, not her, so that your family will benefit. Can you do that? Keep a secret from your mother? Can you?" He interrogated her.

"Yes, yes. Of course. If that's what you want," she said, only half believing all that he had told her.

"You'll be the new owner of the Castle Family Trust Fund, (ha, ha, ha) (cough, cough)," he squinted at her trying to see into her mind. "What do you say?"

Ethel studied her fingernails in her lap and a smirk slowly crept across her face. "Is there anything else I need to know?" she asked him.

"The gold, I mean the "Trust Fund", will have to pass to someone who you designate, and you'll need to choose wisely to be sure no one gets in trouble and only you and the designee know about it. Can you do that?"

"Well, yeh," she replied. "How was it passed on to you?"

"Percy told me before he died. Rufus, his son, told me where to find it. He couldn't wait to get rid of it. The poor guy was so nervous about knowing where it was that he could hardly wait for me to get my hands on it and move it somewhere he wouldn't know about. Percy ruined his son's life with that gold. He ruined his own life, as well….but that's another story. You're smart. You can take on this legacy and succeed. Just consider carefully who has it next, if it's still there to pass along."

Sam continued.

"There is government protected land in the hills where most tourists don't go, and it would be a pristine place to sit and meditate." He smiled and nodded, knowing that Ethel would like that. "It was wild, unclaimed property when Percy was there. It is ideal as a hiding place since, for the time being, it is forbidden to dig there."

Sam coughed uncontrollably and Ethel stopped their conversation and ran to get a nurse to help him.

PART 7

ETHEL AND PERCY'S GOLD

Ethel came outside shaken but with a bit of a new attitude that her husband and Emma were never able to put their finger on. Although she was sad about Sam's illness and impending death, she had a light air about her and smiled more easily, sometimes seemingly at nothing at all. It was like she and her father shared a sick joke that no one else could know.

Before going home from vacation, Ethel had a chat with her husband.

"You know how I always like to go and do something on my own when we're on vacation?"

"Yup. What this time?"

"I noticed the beautiful mountains outside of Denver. I want to take a hiking tour up there." She pointed out to the hills.

"You know Emma and I won't want to do that."

Ethel smiled. "Yes. I'm going alone, as usual. Do me one favor please."

"What's that?"

"Hire me a hiking guide so I don't get lost, and let me take the rental car for the day."

Her husband winked at Emma. "I guess tomorrow is our day honey."

Emma didn't have much time with her dad so this was fine with her, and the next day, Ethel got up early and left right after breakfast to meet the guide.

Ethel told the guide, "There's a place in the hills that my friend told me about. She said there's a great view and I should go and meditate there, and then take some pictures. Here's the map she drew for me. She said to go to this path. Do you know where this is?"

The guide knew exactly where it was and took her to the general area where Sam had told her to go. When they got to the beginning of the path, Ethel stopped and told the guide she'd rather wander about on her own for a while.

"It will be hard for me to have that special "spiritual" moment of meditation if you're standing there. Would you mind coming back in about an hour and a half to help me get back to the hotel? Here's an extra $20 for your trouble. Is that okay?"

The generous tip made him all too happy to go his own way, and soon she was following the landmarks Sam had given her to find the gold's hiding place. Camouflaged between the stones and the lichen, was a small thin piece of twine. Anyone else might have thought it was just a piece of string dropped by a bird on its way to its nest. By pushing aside some smaller stones, with shaky hands, Ethel was able to free the cotton bag from the wall of rocks. The bag was right where Sam had said it would be. Looking over her shoulder to be sure the guide hadn't followed her and that no one else was around, she had a sudden fearful pang of guilt and excitement. She was very alone in her mission, and imagined this must have been the feeling that her uncle Percy felt when he stole and hid the gold.

Ethel took three small pieces of gold. Each might be an ounce or more, and at the current exchange rate, that would pay off her credit card debt and the family's vacation. Taking just a few would make them easier to sell without bringing attention to herself. She tightly closed the bag and hid it in the same place, piling the stones back where they had been, and wedging the tiny twine between some rocks nearby. If someone else pulled on the twine, it would come loose, and the bag would be unnoticed. She just hoped no one did. Without the twine, Ethel wasn't sure she could find this place again, so she made sure the twine was wedged tightly. Sam had clearly found a good hiding place. Next, at a picturesque lookout, Ethel took some photos she could show her family later on. Finally, she sat down, strategizing instead of meditating, while waiting the 45 minutes for her guide to return.

"I'll sell the pieces an ounce at a time. If someone asks me, I'll say I got lucky on a tourist gold digging excursion. People might believe that for an ounce or less. Any more and they might start to wonder. I'll drive out of town to a gold exchange; the one Sam told me about."

When she got back to the rental car, she drove to the exchange right away so that she wouldn't be late and have to answer all sorts of questions her husband and Emma might ask. Instead, they oohed and ah-d at her pictures, believing that she had had a wonderful meditative experience.

Ethel realized that she'd have to come out to the Denver area many times to deal with the gold and couldn't possibly imagine what sorts of excuses she'd need to do that, or how many different places she'd have to go to, to cash it out. She was lost in thought on the way home, considering how to proceed. "Maybe I'll come out on my own, bring back a large amount and hide it somewhere closer to home. I could sell it in New York City. Sam made it work. I can do this."

There was still a significant amount of gold left. She'd have to think hard what to do.

Ethel talked with her husband on their way home.

"I really enjoyed my solo excursion into the hills around Denver. I think it would be really neat to take a vacation with my hiking friends sometime in the future."

"That sounds like fun, honey," he said, half listening, and patting her knee. He just wanted her to stop talking so he could take a nap. He was exhausted from all the driving they had done and the train ride was a relief.

The first trip back to Denver was sooner than Ethel had expected, as Sam died just 3 weeks later, and she wanted to go out for the funeral.

THE VALUE OF ETHEL'S GARDEN

S ubsequently, she enjoyed two fabricated vacations "with her friends" during the next two years. Each time Ethel got home from a hiking vacation, the family property on Long Island became a bit more valuable. When Ethel got home from the first one, she told her husband that it was always her dream to have a beautiful garden in the back yard.

"Seriously," he said. "You never mentioned gardening before."

"Yes I have. You just don't listen to me. I think it will be beautiful to have roses and penny plants and tulips all lined up out here," she said as she slowly extended her hand gracefully across the yard area where the flowers would be. "It would be a great help if you could create the beds for me. I'll plant the flowers."

"I want to help as well," Emma piped up. "I love flowers!"

"No. You can make your own garden when you grow up, dear. This is mommy's garden. You can watch in here from the window," Ethel replied, stunting Emma's enthusiasm because she couldn't risk Emma's finding out about the gold.

So Ethel's husband created three large beds in the yard. He hated yard work but hoped to keep her happy for a while with her new hobby. Emma watched from her perch on a kitchen chair pulled up to the back window. She noticed that Ethel dropped little packages in each hole before she put in the flowers.

"What's that you're putting in the holes, mom?" Emma called out the window.

"Shush, Emma. It's just a special fertilizer to help the flowers grow. I don't want all the neighbors to know about it. Then their flowers will look better than mine. So shah," she said as she held her forefinger up to her mouth, looking over at the Colemans' house to see if they were also watching.

Sure enough, the neighbor, Mrs. Coleman was hanging out of her window about to shake out a bathroom rug. "Hey there, Ethel. What's that you're doing now? You actually planting something in a garden? Well, will wonders never cease?" Mrs. Coleman shook the rug hard and pieces of lint and dust flew out over the fence right into Ethel's face and onto her new flowers.

"Now look what you did," Ethel whined.

"Oh. Oops." Mrs. Coleman chuckled as she closed her window. "Pop, she's planting a garden. Imagine the Queen of England on her knees planting flowers...."

Ethel pulled off her gardening gloves and hit them together to clean them. She stood up as the dirt flew. "Ugh," she grunted. "I must be getting old. My knees are stiff."

"That's just because you've never done this before." Emma was still watching from the kitchen window.

"Aw, just shut the window and draw up a bath for me. That nosy Mrs. Coleman is a real pain in the you-know-what," croaked Ethel, wobbling from side to side as she waddled back into the house with her knees straight.

"Are those annuals or perennials?" asked Emma, ignoring what she said about Mrs. Coleman.

"What-ennials?"

"Well, you know, in science class, we learned that annuals get planted again every year and perennials will come back next year."

"Now you tell me."

Ethel figured that she might have to dig up a few flowers to pay for Emma's first semester in college. Then she'd have to plant some more. "It's a bit of a bother," she thought, "but I'll keep an eye on the garden to be sure no one digs up any of those little packages. I want to *fertilize* Emma's education."

Ethel's husband was surprised when he finally noticed the backyard. "No one in this old Castle house ever planted anything but potatoes, tomatoes and stones. The backyard's been crabgrass and overgrown weeds for years. I'm proud of your new hobby, dear." He pecked her on the nose.

"Did you notice how mom put in small packages of fertilizer?" Emma said. "Those flowers will be beautiful. Mom really knows what she's doing. We'll have the best garden on the block."

Ethel spent hours in the garden even after it was all planted.

"Aren't you spending an awful lot of time out there?" Emma asked as she walked out the back door.

"Get back in the house," Ethel said. "Don't go near those flowers."

"Aren't you a bit preoccupied with this, mom?"

"No." Then, masking her concern, Ethel added, "I like watching them grow."

After forty years of messy vines, there was a veritable botanical garden. The neighbors knew this was hard work, and strange for a family that hardly ever went out of doors. It was an opportunity for their neighbor, Mrs. Coleman, to sustain her rumor-mill.

"She's burying dead animals, talismans and charms."

"Why else would she put them in little bags and bury them?"

"She probably buried her dad in the backyard. You know, he disappeared years ago."

Even after the gardening was done, Mrs. Coleman's rumors were only beginning, and stranger things started happening in the house.

HOME IMPROVEMENTS

One day, after returning from one of her hiking vacations, Ethel was careless in the kitchen.

Ethel knew Emma was upstairs studying, but she called out just the same as she went out the back door to water the flowers.

"Emma, watch the fish. It's frying on the stove."

But Emma didn't hear her and there was a frying pan fire. Emma got out safely. The fire left the kitchen wall and bathroom above it charred. Both were opened down to the studs and, subsequently, fixed over with a new stove top, new cabinetry and new bathroom wall board and tiling. Ethel picked out the new cabinetry and even helped put in the bathroom tiling herself-hot pink, her favorite color. She said she wanted a new hobby to add to her gardening.

"Mom, you really have to pay more attention to what you're doing."

"Sorry dear. You should have watched the dinner like I asked."

"You know I didn't hear you."

"Well, okay, okay. Don't tell your friends how we fixed up the kitchen and bathroom. Times are hard and people may get nasty when they see us spending money like that. Mrs. Coleman will start making up stories when she sees the workmen coming and going. It's none of her business."

"I understand. Okay, mom."

After that, for many years, the family led relatively secluded and frugal lives. Ethel's hiking trips stopped and the Castles didn't do any more renovating, other than basic painting and necessary electrical updates.

One day, when the electrician was working in the attic, he called down to Ethel to join him.

"Mrs. Castle, that old stairway to the Captain's walk is beginning to rot out. See those cracks and black lines there in the wood? It's not safe anymore. It's going to cost a bundle to get that back to its original condition. I could take care of it if you want me to do it."

Ethel went up the rotting stairs and looked at the space that was in the attic. That evening she spoke with her husband.

"He wants over a thousand dollars to fix the stairway up by the Captain's walk and he's not even a carpenter."

"Well, given that you don't use it to see when I'm on my way home, I think we can just forget about fixing it. I'm not paying that kind of money for something we never use. It's too hot up there to sit in the summer anyway."

Ethel agreed.

The next day, the electrician came to finish the work he had started.

"We decided not to fix that stairway, but we'd like you to take it down and leave the hole open. We'll use a ladder if we want to go up there. Before you remove the stairway, would you mind just putting this box up there for me?"

"Sure." The box was open at the top. He peeked inside and saw a pile of old toy money, and shook his head. "People keep the dumbest things."

"What did you say?" Ethel asked from below.

"Oh, nothing."

Ethel retired from her teaching job, but her husband still commuted to New York City and worked long hours even when he was home. Because of this, they never made friends with any of their neighbors.

"Are you lonely here all day?" her husband asked.

"Sometimes. But I don't want Mrs. Coleman and her friends coming in here and dropping crumbs or coffee in the kitchen, or wearing their scratchy high heels on the new bathroom floor. They just judge everything and talk behind my back. There's so much gossip about the garden. I really don't want them out there trampling on my beautiful flowers."

"Life is short. You are being awfully protective of your territory and not having much fun in the process. You're becoming a 'shut-in'. I thought you fixed up the house and garden so you could have friends over and enjoy it."

"You're one to talk. You never stop working."

"Taxes are getting higher. You want to live here? I have to work."

Ethel knew that the old blue clapboard house stood out in the neighborhood for its lack of curb appeal and old fashioned, New England style. The only landscaping it had was her gardening in the back. People joked that it was a haunted Nantucket house transplanted in the center of middle class suburbia. In their eyes, the family took on the same character as the house and no one cared much to get to know them. Ethel did feel lonely.

ETHEL'S SECRET; EMMA'S HEARTACHE

Perhaps because of the bullying, the secret she had to keep, or her creeping illness, there was a certain madness in Ethel's planting.

One day, when Emma came home from school, she heard her mother talking to herself in the yard.

Ethel was pacing back and forth and wringing her hands. "What will happen if someone finds the gold? They'll say I stole it. What if I go to jail? What'll happen to Em….."

Ethel froze. Emma was coming up the path. Squinting her eyes, she looked from side to side as if checking for intruders. Finally, she turned to greet her daughter. Surely the garden would be all right for ten minutes while Emma explained her homework for the evening.

"Hi mom. You look kinda stressed. What's up?" Emma said.

Ethel knew her daughter was right about her feelings. She knew there was a secret she was keeping from Emma, and tried to remember what it was. She felt confused. Usually her memory was sharp.

"Huh? You say something dear?"

"Mom? You okay? Why are you upset?"

"I don't know what you're talking about. You know I don't like you to be in the garden. Now let's go inside and see what sort of homework you've got this evening."

Emma felt her mother's uneasiness and didn't want to make a fuss.

"Okay. I don't really need your help today, but if that's what you want to do, let's go inside."

GETTING TO KNOW THE COLEMANS

Not being allowed to be in the backyard made Emma feel like a recluse. She also wanted to get to know the neighbors so, without telling her parents, she offered to babysit for the Colemans' kids. When the time came, she quickly told her mother where she was going and ran out of the front door. Ethel promptly forgot what Emma told her, but figured she'd be okay because she was a bright girl.

When Mr. and Mrs. Coleman left for the evening, Emma sat down to tell the kids a bedtime story about her vacation.

"Once upon a time there was a family—like mine—that went on a very long vacation trip," she began.

"That was you! You went on a trip! What kind of a trip was it?" Emma smiled and nodded as Susie scooted up next to her on the couch.

"It was a very special trip. We saw big parks with mountains and antelope and bears," Emma said.

"Bears? Weren't you scared?" asked Susie, wide-eyed.

"No. Not really. They stayed outside of our car. When they put their paws up on the car," Emma put her hands up to mimic the bear's paws, "we just made sure the windows were closed. But there was an even better part of our trip."

"What was that? Did you see cowboys?" asked Susie, wanting more details about the bears but knowing that Emma went to the "wild west."

"I saw my grandfather for the first time," said Emma.

"That's no big deal. I see my gampa all the time," said Susie. "He comes over for dinner every week." She waved Emma off, and began twisting her hair with her index finger, as she lost interest.

"Well. I've never met mine. But I was able to see him. He was high up in a hospital building, and he waved to me. He's the person who built our house, and owned all of this land before the other houses were built," explained Emma.

"That's not true. My mom said your grandfather is up in your attic and that we always owned this property," teased Ron, Susie's brother.

"Does she?" Emma coaxed them to say more.

"Yes. And he haunts the house and your mom killed him and puts pieces of him in the garden."

Emma didn't reply but her anger was burning.

"Okay, Ron. That's enough. Go to sleep now, and I don't want to hear anymore nonsense from you."

Susie and Ron laughed but they went to sleep right away.

Emma now understood why the neighbors never came over and why her parents didn't talk to them. They weren't nice people and made up stories about her family. When Mr. and Mrs. Coleman came home, they paid Emma and she said everything went okay. But she didn't offer to come back and babysit again.

When the kids woke up, Ron fed the rumor fire.

"Emma yelled at us."

"Is that true Susie?" Mrs. Coleman asked, putting toast on their plates.

Susie just shrugged. Mrs. Coleman was buttering the toast. Then, she spooned Sunday's scrambled eggs on their plates. Ron stuffed his mouth and continued talking with his mouth full. "Emma went on a big trip out west and saw mountains and parks."

"We want to go on a vacation too," said Susie, crunching on her breakfast.

Mrs. Coleman had heard enough. She figured that the Castles had some money stashed away from selling all the land that surrounded the house when it was built. That's how they paid for fancy vacations. She wished Emma had just been quiet and let the kids watch TV while she was out.

"Wow. Sounds impressive." She poured some orange juice into each child's cup. "Okay then. Let's just forget about Emma's vacation. If you really want to know about Emma, I'll tell you what's what."

Now Mrs. Coleman was leaning in close to the children's faces, hands flat on the kitchen table, and whispering. "There are ghosts from the wild--west who haunt Emma's house."

She looked from Susie to Ron as if she was telling a secret, her green eyes flashing as she brewed her story.

"They sleep in the backyard next door." Mrs. Coleman pointed out back. "You saw Mrs. Castle digging out there?"

The kids nodded, not missing a word. Susie's mouth was open and a piece of soggy egg was hanging from it.

"She was making them beds under the flowers. Emma doesn't have any friends but she knows all of those ghosts personally. Her parents went out west to get them and bring them home for her. So, of course, if you want to have ghosts living in our backyard...."

Mrs. Coleman was done and stood up, dusted the malice off of her hands, and crossed her arms over her chest. Susie was crying and Ron, his forehead creased, just shook his head no. Neither finished their breakfast, and that was that, until the next day in school.

The kids whispered to their friends, who in turn told their older sisters and brothers. Soon the bullying and teasing began. Emma's classmates said that she lived in a haunted house with a scary witch for a mother.

When Emma wrote a paper for the school newspaper about how much she respected and loved her grandfather, her peers taunted her that he must be fertilizing the gardens in her yard.

"Did you hear about the ghosts in that big old house?"

"I'm making friends with Emma so I can go over there to see the ghosts."

"Hey, ghost-girl, do the flowers dance in your backyard?"

"How come your mom doesn't let us in the yard?"

"Are there really ghosts back there?"

The stories were enhanced so much that they made it home to neighborhood parents. That summer, at a cocktail party down the block, people were laughing, and loud music was blaring.

"There must be a dead body," said Mrs. Coleman, a bit too loudly, above the music.

"(ha-ha) Yes, and buried treasure too! Why else would anyone in *that* family be digging up so much of the yard," added Cynthia.

"That land had nothing but potatoes and stones for forty years and all of a sudden the botanical gardens are growing there."

Mrs. Coleman pulled an olive out of her drink and yanked her spandex swim suit down over her ever-expanding derriere.

"And the only person who is doing the gardening is the mistress of the house. No one else is allowed to touch those flowers, according to what Emma told my daughter," said Cynthia, taking Karen's arm and pulling her along.

"She never says hello but always reminds me not to come in the yard. "Don't step over that line. She yells. She's just a paranoid witch!"

And at that Mrs. Coleman and Cynthia sipped their drinks and laughed their way over to the pool.

Some of the neighbors started spending more time in their gardens to compete with the Castles, but Ethel was on a mission and her garden always surpassed the others.

Between school and the neighbors, Emma was miserable.

In time, she graduated, went away to college, got married, had a son named Jason, and began her own life. She was relieved to finally be free, but sad to feel so distanced from her mother because of silly rumors about a garden. Even when she came home to visit, her mother was too preoccupied to spend time with her in any meaningful way.

ETHEL PROGRESSES

Instead, Ethel had spats with the neighbors about anything that touched their property....a new fence, new telephone wires, a cable post in their yard, a cat that dug in the flowers.

"Mrs. Coleman, stop looking out your window at me!" she hollered as she did her daily watering rounds in the garden.

One day, Ethel was in the garden and did not remember what the trowel in her hand was for. She picked some flowers for the house, leaving the trowel in the kitchen, as she put water in the vase. Later, Emma was visiting and found the trowel under the sink.

"Mom, why is this muddy thing in the kitchen?" Emma wrinkled her nose, holding up the trowel which still dripped with thick brown goop.

Ethel gasped. "They must have been in the house again. I can't believe it. Those neighbors of ours! Now they're sneaking in and moving my stuff around."

Emma gave her the trowel to put back outside. Ethel looked around the garden and remembered that she had to do something with the flowers, but couldn't think of what it was. She figured,

"Tomorrow, I'll remember," but deep down her confusion made her angry.

The next day, Ethel saw the holes in the ground that she dug the day before. She threw the trowel across the yard, stomped into the house, and sat at the table waiting for Emma to show up.

"Yesterday, the Colemans moved my stuff around. Now Emma must be in cahoots with them, digging up the flowers and bringing them next door for their dinner table vase." She brooded all afternoon.

All hell broke loose when Emma came home from shopping.

"What are you talking about, mom? I haven't spoken to that Coleman woman in years. Why are you yelling at me?" Emma went up to her childhood bedroom, frightened by her mom's senseless accusations. She called her husband, George, and told him that something was up with her mom, requiring her to stay over for another evening. He understood.

"Emma, dinner is ready," her mom called an hour later.

Emma sheepishly poked her head out of her door and slowly went down the stairs, expecting her mom to yell at her.

"Oh, hi Emma. I'm so glad you're here. Come sit by me and eat. Your father's late again tonight."

Emma could tell there was something very wrong about how her mother was behaving, but she had no idea what it could possibly be. Emma's father was oblivious because he wasn't home to see Ethel's late afternoon tantrums. When he came home, Ethel was already in bed, and Emma put out his cold dinner.

On another visit, a few weeks later, Emma said, "You know mom, I don't want to hurt your feelings but I don't really like being in this house. I probably won't keep up the family tradition of living here. I don't think George will want to move here either. Maybe you and dad should think about downsizing."

Ethel just shook her head at that and abruptly left the room. A while later, she came back.

"Emma, do you think some day you would like to move into the house? Dad and I could use your help."

Emma looked at her, dumbfounded, threw her hands up in the air, and took her turn at leaving the room.

Later that day when Emma and Ethel were in the kitchen, Ethel grabbed Emma's hand and swung her around. "Come on Mirabelle. Dance with me. The music's great."

Emma danced around with her. "Mom, you're crazy." They laughed.

When Ethel left the room, Emma thought to herself, "She really is crazy. What am I going to do about her? There wasn't any music and Mirabelle was grandma's friend."

THE LEGACY OF A TRUST FUND: ETHEL'S BOND WITH JASON

When Emma's son, Jason, turned 18 and was about to go off to college, Emma invited Ethel to dinner.

"Some of my friends were talking in school about who was coming to graduation. One of my friends has great grandparents who are still alive and may come. I was surprised at that because you've never mentioned your parents, grandma. Are they still alive somewhere? Maybe they would like to come to my graduation," Jason asked Ethel.

"No. No. I'm sorry to say, they both died years ago. Your great grandmother Rosie died right here in this house," Ethel looked around the dining room as if Rosie might appear right then and there. "And your great grandfather, Sam, died out in Denver," she replied. Emma and Jason looked at one another. They weren't in Ethel's house, where Rosie died.

"How come you never talk about them?"

"Well. You see…hum…well, how to tell you. I guess I'll just come out with it. Your great grandfather was a real lady's man, even in his old age. He was in his 70s, at least, when he met another woman and left your great grandmother." She dabbed her lips with her napkin and paused, thinking how to go on.

"In those days, it was a real disgrace to get divorced, so Rosie never told anyone what happened to Sam. He just never came home again as far as anyone knew. But I have the divorce papers upstairs in the attic, in a box. I'm sure you've heard your mother tell stories about the rumors that people spread about Rosie, and me. Those rumors were very hurtful and just kept being passed around in the neighborhood. People picked on us for all sorts of reasons-all nonsense." Ethel patted Jason's hand to reassure him that the rumors were not true.

"Yeh. Mom told me about some of the rumors. I don't know what to think. The house is kind of creepy sometimes. It's so old," Jason complained.

"Well, your grandfather and I have kept it in the best shape we can. Nowadays, people just move in and out of other peoples' homes. They don't care who lived there before. But you'll always know that this is your family's home," Ethel reassured him, still confused about where she was.

"Do you have pictures of my great grandfather Sam? I want to know more about him and great grandma Rosie."

"I can do better than that," Ethel exclaimed, thinking that here was an opportunity to get out to Denver without having to make up fake excuses. "Come with me to Denver. It can be your graduation present. We'll travel out west like your ancestors."

Ethel pretended to be riding a horse, pulling on the reigns with a smile on her face.

Then, she added, more seriously, "We can take the train. We can visit Sam's gravesite and see if the old family store is still standing near the railroad station. What do you say?"

"Wow! I like that idea. We can bond," Jason teased, poking her gently in the ribs.

She swatted him away laughing. "Is that my dad? Sam?" she thought, as if Jason was a stranger. She shook her head and then looked down at her hands in her lap. "No, no. I know him. It's, it's.....what's his name?" Her forehead creased, she looked over at Emma and, then back again at Jason, and said out loud, in an after-thought, nodding "It's ummm..."

"What Grandma?" asked Jason.

Ethel ignored his question. "Should I come to your gradua-tion?" she said.

Emma and Jason looked at each other. Jason took on a serious face.

"I'd like that, and then we'll go out to Denver. No offense, but you won't be around forever, and I want to learn as much as I can from you about our past ("while I still can," he thought). Is it okay, mom, if we go? We can wait until school ends and then take a summer trip before I have to go to orientation. Okay?" he asked Emma.

Emma was glad that her mom had gotten along so well with Jason all of these years. She was proud that her son was willing to go on a trip with his grandmother, knowing she could be difficult for an 18-year-old to care for. She was a bit concerned about what he'd do if she had one of her tantrums, started 'sun-downing' or forgot where she was. Emma would often say that her mother was "in and out these days."

"Yes. Of course you can go. Are you sure you want to travel with grandma? You'll have to take care of her a bit as you go. She can be forgetful, you know." She was trying to be tactful.

"Don't worry, mom. We'll take care of each other," Ethel grinned, nodding authoritatively at her dad, or was it her husband?

While in the hotel room in Denver, Ethel took Jason aside and told him about the "Trust Fund".

"Now understand young man that this is a very serious responsibility that you would be taking on. Your great uncle Percy stole that gold. If anyone were to ever find out where it came from, you might be in big trouble, and imagine what would happen to the family name. And you'd never finish college. Do you understand?" Ethel grilled Jason.

"Well, yeah. Of course. But what would happen if they do find out?" Jason was hesitant.

"I'm not sure," she shook her head, backing off a bit. "I guess it belonged to someone, maybe the government. I don't know if they want it back or even remember about it. I guess they could arrest us or ask us to give anything back that was bought with it. I don't know. It was so long ago...."

"Should I give it back?" Jason asked.

"I have no idea. That would be up to you. But I can tell you, it carries a heap of trouble whether you keep it, ditch it or return it." Ethel frowned and looked at him trying to size up what he would decide to do.

He sat silently in thought. "Was she fabricating all of this? Was this real?"

"There are a few other things I want you to do if you keep the gold," she said. "First, you must promise never to tell your mother about it, ever. She can't handle secrets. She cares too much about what people think and wants them to know everything. She'd blab the whole story to her best friends and it would show up on Facebook in no time. Then we'll all be wearing orange!"

"Don't worry about that," Jason smiled, proud of himself. "She doesn't know half of what goes on in my life. I'm good at secrets."

"Okay. That's good." She patted his knee, not considering all of the implications of what he had just said.

"Anything else?"

"To keep the family "Trust Fund", keep the family name," she said emphatically waving her forefinger in the air at him. "When I die, change your name to Castle, and I'll stipulate in my Will that you can have everything I own, except the house itself. That will go to your mom so she's not suspicious. She hates that house, but she has to develop a back bone. Cleaning out that place will make her deal with all sorts of things she can't stand. But the land will sell well, so she'll get her share of the wealth. Don't worry about her. So, what do you say, young man? Can you keep it out of your mom's hands? I have to trust you, to "Trust Fund" you," she laughed and then eyed him with serious scrutiny that took him aback.

"Grandma. If there's one thing I love, it's money! I don't have any problem with any of this. Where is the "Trust Fund" hidden?" he asked forming quotation marks with his fingers in the air, and eager to learn more.

"Ah. Now that's the question. I don't really remember where I put it all. I was hoping coming out here would remind me, but I'm drawing a blank. You know how the neighbors are always coming around and poking into everything. First my fence, then my flow-ers. They've probably been here too," she cowered looking around her. "But, I can tell you, if you look, you'll see that the house and its property are filled with treasure." She said this while rubbing her hands together like a miserly old woman.

Jason had a worried look on his face.

"What? What's wrong now? Why are you looking at me that way? Were you here with the neighbors before? You know some-thing you're not telling me. You know where it is?"

Was she just putting him on? Jason knew he could be greedy at times, and maybe she was just playing him. Was she slipping into her psychotic mode? Lately, he noticed that she would be fine one moment and in 'outer space' the next. Emma had warned him to watch her closely. She knew that her mother was forgetful and not at all aware anymore that her memory was slipping. Sometimes she got angry and blamed Emma or the neighbors for taking things or moving things she herself had hidden away but could no longer find. She could get very paranoid. Ethel's sudden angry moods were the most difficult for Jason to handle, and he hoped she would not start yelling at him now, in the hotel room.

"Um. No grandma. I love you. You can trust me. Let's just go to dinner now. I'm hungry. Are you hungry?" He gently led her by the elbow.

"Yes, I guess I am. We can lock up the door so no one will get in while we go eat. Do you have that key card?"

"Sure grandma. Let's get some dinner." Jason was relieved that he was able to redirect her, and they would actually get to eat dinner without stirring her up. He'd figure out what was true and what was just grandma's dreams later.

When they got home, Emma was amazed when Jason told her that she and her husband wouldn't have to pay for his college education. He said he would work and pay for it himself.

THE END OF A GENERATION

Emma never moved back into the house but she often came to visit and help her parents. A while after Jason left for college, Emma came to take Ethel shopping. While she was in the kitchen and Ethel was upstairs, getting ready to go out, Emma found a piece of paper with her phone number on it. She saw words scrawled and scribbled repeatedly in her mother's handwriting, "Call Emma, call J~~, call J, Emma. 555-349-~~~~." The paper was bunched up in her mother's kitchen silverware drawer, the one nearest the phone on the wall. She guessed her mother wanted to remind herself how to get in touch with her but couldn't remember the number, although she had called it hundreds of times over the past few years. Emma held it in her hands for a minute, her eyes tearing. It was harder and harder dealing with her mom who refused to get help in the house. Emma gently put the paper back in the drawer, tucking it away like so many other lost opportunities....she was lost in thought.

She remembered a few months back when her father became too ill for her mother to care for him. They moved him into a nursing facility that was close by Emma's house, and Ethel stayed behind in the family home. She refused to leave it except to briefly visit him, always wanting to return quickly. When Emma asked her why she wouldn't move closer to where her father was, or at least visit longer, she emphasized that this was her home and her neighbors would take it over if no one was there.

"Oh, mom. You are really becoming eccentric in your old age!" Ethel retorted in a tirade.

"What do you know? You're not here all the time! The Colemans threw rocks through our windows. They took our fence down and put up a different gate. Karen even dug up my yard—MY yard! I worked so hard at making it look presentable."

Ethel was suddenly very quiet. She was concerned about something else in the garden, but she couldn't remember what it was.

Later that week, Emma came over again and couldn't park on the driveway because Ethel's car was in the street blocking it. She walked in the house, throwing her coat and pocketbook on the chair next to the door.

"Mom," she called.

Ethel came down the stairs.

"What are you doing here?"

"I told you I was coming over. Why'd you block the driveway? I had to park in the street."

"That way, they won't know if I'm home or not, and they won't be able to come in here again and move my things around," Ethel said.

"Who's they?"

"You know exactly who I mean."

"But mom, maybe you just forgot what you did? We all forget sometimes."

"You mind your own business," Ethel stabbed at Emma with her index finger. "For all I know you are in cahoots with them!"

"With whom ma?" Emma sighed.

"Now I'll have to walk to the store and the bank because I can't move the car away."

"Maybe letting me help you out for a while wouldn't be a bad thing," said Emma, assuring her that she would be there first thing on the weekend to help her do her grocery shopping, get stamps and do anything else she wanted to do. Ethel would have none of it and walked everywhere when Emma wasn't around.

The following weekend, Emma was on her way to see her mother and there, walking on the sidewalk, was someone in an oversized coat, and baggy pants, bundled to the tip of her nose in a pilled scarf and hat, carrying a huge pocketbook and groceries in a white plastic bag. It was freezing outside. As she went past, she realized it was her mother. Emma slowed the car and stopped next to Ethel who swung her bag at the car, yelling, "Get away from me or I'll call the cops."

Emma couldn't convince her to get in, so she slowly followed her home. As she pulled up to the house, and her mother came up to the side of her car, Mrs. Coleman opened a window and shouted out, "Hey, bag lady. What'd you bring me today?" Emma could hear laughter as the window was slammed shut and the drapes were drawn.

Looking at her mother, Emma could understand why people might think she was wandering or homeless. "Why can't neighbors help out when they see this?" Emma thought to herself. But, Mrs. Coleman was elderly and spiteful, and had her own problems. Emma was worried that someone might harm her mother or that Ethel would forget how to get home. But, miraculously, Ethel always got home safely, and refused any help Emma offered, including the offer for her mother to move in with her.

Before she had come, Emma searched the web for information about Alzheimer's and dementia to learn a bit more about what her mother might be experiencing. She also spoke to a geriatric psychiatrist to get advice. But nothing prepared her for her own emotional turmoil as she watched Ethel morph and waste away.

As they came into the house, Ethel removed her coat and scarf and Emma was surprised by what she saw.

"Mom, why are you getting so thin? I brought you lots of food last week." She ran up to the kitchen to check the refrigerator.

"You're just trying to poison me."

"It's all still here in the fridge. Didn't you eat anything this week? Tell me. What did you eat?"

"I ate plenty. Take home your food. You eat it."

A week later, Ethel called Emma and sounded upset. She said there was an emergency.

"The neighbors broke in and started a fire in the house. The fire department was here."

"I'm coming right over—but it will take me time to get there. What happened?"

"I don't know. I think the microwave exploded. It's broken."

"Is the fire department still there?"

"No. They're gone."

"Why do you think the neighbors were there?"

"I saw them."

"When did this happen?"

"Just now. No. Wait. Maybe last night. No. Today. Well, I don't know. You're confusing me."

"Are you in the house? Is there smoke?"

"No. Why are you so upset?"

"I'm on my way over."

"You don't have to come over. I'm fine."

When Emma got there, the house smelled like burnt popcorn. The microwave looked fine. There was no sign of damage or a break-in. The plants were watered and the house was clean. Ethel had no idea why Emma was there and the accusations began again.

"They searched my house."

"Who?"

"You know who. That Mrs. Coleman." Pursing her lips, Ethel punched her kitchen table.

"My front door was open in the morning. They probably came in and set it. The kitchen was on fire."

Emma looked around the kitchen. There was no sign of a fire.

"But you said it was in the microwave. Mom, are you remembering the grease fire we had when I was a kid? Did you make popcorn in the microwave earlier and cook it too long? Did you smell it burning? That's what the kitchen smells like to me."

"No. I'm not an idiot. I know what happened. The fire department was here. I told you that. Why would they be here if I made popcorn? What do you think, I don't know what goes on in my own house?"

"Did you call the fire department?"

"Of course I called them. There was a fire!" Ethel was getting very upset.

"Oh. Okay, okay. How about I stay over to be sure everything's okay tonight?"

"Where else would you stay? Of course you'll be here tonight!"

Emma stayed over and hoped Ethel would be calm in the morning. She came down to breakfast and stood at the counter to make some coffee. Ethel was huddled in the corner of the kitchen at the table with some papers and the telephone. She was telling someone the most specific details of where she deposited her pension checks. Emma remembered what she had heard on the news about elderly people and phone scams.

"Mom, who are you talking to?" she whispered to Ethel.

"Go away, Emma. I'm on the phone."

"Who are you talking to?"

"Um. I don't know. It's important. Go away."

"Mom, hang up and talk to me. Tell me who you're talking to." Now Emma was concerned.

"It's a close friend. I don't know her name."

"Then how do you know it's a close friend?"

Emma convinced her mother to hang up. Later in the day, the conversation was forgotten. Emma also noticed that Ethel could no longer balance her check book, although she used to be a math whiz. Some bills were adding up and others had been paid twice over.

Emma came over later in the week and made dinner. While she was stirring the tomato sauce, Ethel came into the kitchen and took Emma aside. She had a pen and a piece of paper that she had torn from a shopping list. She whispered to Emma, "I think it's this."

Ethel bent over the table, looked around the room and wrote a shaky letter "A" on the paper. They were alone in the house, but she checked to see if anyone else was in the room or listening. Then she whispered, "It's the 'A' thing. It's horrible. He has it."

"Who has it? What mom? Do you think you have Alzheimer's?" Emma saw that her mom was paranoid.

"No. No, not me. Not me," she whispered. "It's him. Your father. He has it. It's that. I don't want to say it. Then it will be true."

Seeing that Ethel was becoming agitated, Emma put her arm around her mom's shoulder, both to comfort her and to get her attention. She asked again.

"Mom, are you saying that you might have it?"

"Oh. No. Not me. It's someone else." Ethel, insulted, pushed Emma away, crumbled the paper up and threw it across the kitchen. She stomped out of the room and never brought it up again.

Emma took vacation days from work to stay with Ethel, seeing that it was not safe for her mother to be alone. She realized that she needed help from additional family members. She remembered how Ethel and Jason had taken a graduation trip together. She called Jason.

"Jason, I need your help. Actually, grandma needs your help. Her house is close to school and your job. Would you mind staying over there with her a few days a week?"

"I don't mind doing that one or two days a week as long as I can get my work done."

"I really appreciate your help. I think it's important for her to stay in her own home for as long as possible since she gets disoriented so easily."

A few days later, Jason called Emma to give her a progress report.

"Hi mom. I'm over here at grandma's like you asked. If she comes in, I'll have to hang up quickly. I'll call you back if that happens. Grandma has these awful mood swings. She gets really confused and angry, and man, she's messed up! Yesterday at dinner, she kept calling me Sam. Today when I came home, she had taken all of my clothes out of the closet, put them in a plastic bag and was getting ready to give the bag to Goodwill. She didn't know whose clothing it was and didn't remember I was going to be here. I'm not sure she knows who I am. I don't know if I can realistically handle this. I love her and all, and I know you need my help, but aren't there people trained to do this sort of thing whom you can hire?"

Emma hired some companions for Ethel but they couldn't keep up with her progression either. Ethel didn't want strangers "nosing in her business."

One afternoon while her companion was cooking lunch, Ethel was confused.

"Who are you? Why are you in my kitchen? You can't eat my food!" she suddenly yelled. "Get out before I call the police!"

Susan, Ethel's latest companion, went to her bedroom and called Emma. "She's screaming at me and I'm afraid she might hurt me. She thinks I don't belong here and she said she'll call the police. You have to come. I'm leaving. Wait. Now she's banging on my door."

"Okay. Okay. Just stop and breathe," Emma replied. "She's just a small person. She can't hurt you. Don't yell back at her. Ask her if she'd like to have lunch with you. Tell her you're making her lunch and helping her. If that doesn't work, change the subject. Talk about something else she might be interested in like flowers or traveling. Try to redirect her."

"I did but she said she doesn't need my help and told me to get out. I can't do anything for her. She's outside my door yelling. I'm trapped."

"Okay. Sit tight. I'm coming," said Emma, who was 45 minutes away, trying to take a break while the companion was with her mom.

Emma drove over and helped the companion leave the house while Ethel continued to yell uncontrollably. Ethel accused Emma of helping the companion break into her house and steal her pots and pans and food. Emma took the companion to the train station. When she got back to the house, Ethel was cleaning up the kitchen. She had no idea why Emma was there or why she was so upset. Emma stayed overnight again and realized that recently, she also had trouble calming Ethel when she became upset. She needed more experienced helpers and had to come up with a plan but really didn't know where to turn. She tried a different home care service but it was a strain on Ethel to have strangers in the house.

By the time her husband passed away, Ethel moved into a nursing home. Out of her familiar surroundings, Ethel was enveloped by confusion and Alzheimer's consumed her quickly. When friends at work asked Emma how her mom was doing, she replied, "The adventurer who hiked in Denver on her own, taught first graders for years, and created a magnificent garden from a potato farm no longer knows who or where she is." The ones who had lost a parent said, "I understand." But Emma doubted that they did unless that parent also had dementia.

To decorate Ethel's room in the nursing home, Emma brought family pictures and labeled them to help her mother remember relatives' names. She went through the pictures with Ethel whenever she visited. Each time was like the first time. When Emma saw that Ethel didn't remember a name right after she told her, she took the labels off and let her mother decide who was in the picture, rather than having her ask over and over again, "Jason? Who is Jason?" Ethel's favorite question was, "So, what's new?" Emma might answer that question three or four times a visit, each time hoping a bit more of the information might be remembered. But then Ethel asked, "So, what's new?"

When performing groups played at the nursing home, Ethel remembered happy times as a teacher, and implored her nursing home friends to "be quiet in class and listen to the pretty music." She let one special nurse's aide water the plants Emma brought her. While she could still speak, she said, "Hello darling," to Emma, and smiled at Jason as he greeted her with a kiss. When she did this, Emma felt less guilty about having her in a nursing home and she thought her mother was happy to see her. But then her mother said, "Hello darling" and smiled at the nurse's aide when she came to get her for dinner, and Emma was devastated to realize that she greeted everyone the same way.

Ethel spent most of her time in a wheel chair and her face soon wore a glazed façade. Emma called it her "look of dis-connecting." Then, one day, Ethel forgot how to swallow her food….

Emma loved her mother. At her funeral, the family encircled Ethel's casket and told each other loving, and fun-filled memories.

"Grandma always said she had money in the sugar bowl, and that I could come to her if I ever needed anything," Emma said.

"Do you have a sugar bowl, mom?" Jason asked, putting his arm around his mother's shoulder.

Emma considered Jason's question. In her illness, Ethel never let Emma get close enough to the "sugar bowl" to see for herself if there was anything but saccharin to be found. Ethel would say, "Hello darling," or "Have you met my beautiful daughter?" and then keep her at arms' length, later, not fully remembering who she was, or why she wanted to hold her off. Emma felt the full weight of time-passed-by. She realized she would never enjoy a closeness to her mother that she always longed for.

"Yes, Jason. Dad and I are here if you ever need us," she replied, hugging him back.

For the time being, the family home was vacant. Because Ethel had no friends in the neighborhood, no one knew what became of the Castle family. Neighbors went so far as to step out into the street, off the sidewalk, when passing the house. It had an ominous appearance because it was so unkempt.

PART 8
(2008-2011)

EMMA AND THE HOUSE

Mrs. Coleman could hear the second hands on her kitchen clock as they counted all the time in the world. She slowly dipped her tea bag in and out of the flowered china cup. Her husband sniffled deeply, then cleared his throat as he turned the pages of the daily paper retrieved from their doorstep.

"Anything new today?" she said, peering across the top of the newspaper as it gently shook in his hands.

"Neh. Nothing ever new. War, guns, death, fashion. Nice picture of Hillary here." He held up the picture to show her.

"Eh. Who cares! We'll be dead by the time she's ever president."

Mr. Coleman pulled his reading glasses down a bit as he looked across at her.

"You bored?"

"What we need is some good gossip going on. I just can't stand the quiet over there." She slapped her hand on the table, rattling the cup on its saucer. "I don't get it. Where are they?" she said, turning and pushing her nose just past the edge of the kitchen curtain.

A car pulled up. Watching this new visitor arrive would give her something to do for now, and might be something she could gossip about later. She wondered if it was another Castle.

"Hey Pop, come look at this." Mrs. Coleman jostled the paper in her husband's hands.

"What's up mum?" He rose, stopped to put water in the cat's dish on the floor, then shuffled over to the window.

"I think it's that Castle girl, come back to check out the house," she said, waving him over to her, and pulling back a bit more of the curtain. "Just look at her. There's nothing special about her. Her car's just ordinary, maybe a Chevy or Buick and what an awful color beige it is."

"Looks to me like a Toyota Corolla, mum. Maybe two or three years old. Not a bad car. But you're right. Boring color." He pushed in next to her at the window as he chimed in, wanting to see more.

"I haven't really seen her up close in years. Move over. I want to see her face. Oh, goodness. Move over. Oh, now look what you've done. I think she's seen us."

She pushed her husband over to the side and whipped the curtains closed, turning her back to the window.

"Now she knows we're looking at her."

She tied her flowered robe tighter around her undefined waist more out of annoyance, than need.

"Come upstairs. Here. Let's try this window. I don't think she'll realize we moved over here," he said, pulling her with him.

Mrs. Coleman pulled up close to her husband, stepping on his socked feet as they started peering out the side window.

"Ah. Now I see her. She's so plain, like her mother. You'd think she'd dye that dark hair to brighten up her face a bit. Her hair is square and straight. There's no style at all. What a disappointment, what with all the rumors. You'd think she'd look like a movie star. And look what's she's wearing, ugh."

Mrs. Coleman scrunched up her face, shaking her head in disappointment.

"Beige car, beige coat, beige bag. Good God she's boring. What a sight. Oh look she's waving. She must know we're here. Look how's she's rotating her hand in the air. Ha! Like she's someone important," Pop commented.

"Oh brother. I guess we should let her go for a while," Mrs. Coleman feigned a smile, waving her hand once back. "She obviously knows we're watching and is just being up-itty with that Queen of England stuff. Anyway, I've gotta call Gladys and let her know the Castle 'ghost' family is back. She'll wanna tell her neighbor and her daughter, Cynthia, as well."

"Now don't go starting anything again, mum. You did enough harm with that girl's mother. You must have driven her crazy with your peeping out at her all the time in that garden."

"Okay. I guess you're right. Anyway, that Ethel is gone now. She never was a bright star at a party. Good riddance to her. Let her daughter pick up her pieces. Hopefully, she'll have some common sense and level that monstrosity of a house before the property value on ours goes down any more."

Mrs. Coleman swung the curtain closed and carefully stepped down the stairs, grabbing the railing with both hands.

"I second that. And anyway, just look at Emma. She's so 'beige'. She probably wants to disappear into the background. Doesn't want anyone to see her. She had so many troubles when she was growing up," he added. "Poor woman. Just think of what she'll have to contend with now, with that haunted house to take care of."

He followed Mrs. Coleman to the kitchen table and sat across from her again. They looked up at one another and burst out laughing.

No one in the neighborhood sent condolences when her mother died. It was like they were relieved to be rid of her….but there was also something about the house. Now, Emma looked back up at the Colemans' window and thought to herself, "This doesn't matter anymore. Now I have my own life in my own home, where I blend in. For as long as it takes me to clean out the house, I'll have to remember to ignore them, and keep my cool."

Emma inherited the house. She wanted to empty it, sell it and move on. Although she loved her parents, they had strange expectations when she was growing up, and happy memories of them were hard to conjure. Neighbors rarely waved, let alone said hello. Everyone peeked through their windows like Mrs. Coleman, but no one said anything.

As she closed the car door, Emma looked up at the family house and around at the neighborhood. Her house was older, larger and bulkier than the surrounding colonial and ranch styles. The outside of the house had a seafaring look about it with an enclosed Captain's walk in the shape of a parabola, at its top. Emma knew that some of her ancestors had come south from Nantucket, and a distant relative worked on a whaling boat. Maybe she would find clues in the house as to who he was and how she was related to him. On the outside, the Captain's walk was bordered by decorative tooth molding with miniature Corinthian columns on the corners, and wooden windows, framed with tiny squares of blue, red and green stained glass. She never really looked at it before, but now, she marveled at the artistry of it.

Under the Captain's walk, the house was a large two story rectangle with wooden shutters and window flower boxes displaying weedy dead branches. The clapboard house was a tired teal blue, presumably the same color it always was. The window glass, original in most places, gave off a rainbow of translucent shine in the right light and a foreboding ghostly hue at other times. Emma wondered if that's what made the neighbors spread rumors that the house was haunted.

The faded blue house wanted reawakening and caught your eye like a conspicuous wart on the neighborhood. Emma looked back up at the detailed architecture and recalled that it was the first house in the area. It towered over other houses with its turret of a widow's walk. They didn't make houses like this anymore.

Emma thought, "The neighbors seem in awe of it. Or maybe afraid of it." She glanced over at the Colemans' house, with its manicured stone walkway and new custom windowed front door. "Or maybe they think having it here will lower their property values."

Emma looked up at the Colemans' window again. "I hope they saw me waving. I guess I'll just have to be as confident as royalty and brush off their glances. I'll be coming and going for a while; Why not amuse myself?"

She held up her head and walked up the crumbling driveway.

The integrity of the house withstood the years. Rumors, spread mostly by Mrs. Coleman, fulfilled their function and, even when the house was empty for months at a time, no one ventured near it. No vagrants moved in. No one vandalized it, even though the Colemans themselves had been robbed. It would have been easy to break into. It stood at the corner on the edge of the neighborhood with little protecting it. Bushes grew wild by the front door. You could stand there for an hour and no one, except maybe Mrs. Coleman, would know you were there.

Emma opened the door and went in. Locking the door behind her and throwing her coat over a nearby chair, she checked out the front hallway. Things hadn't changed much. The air was dusty and stale. The heat had been left on and a plant drooped near the door. A fungal looking smelly goop grew around the bottom of the planter. As she walked through the family room, to the bathroom sink, she remembered drowning the plant on her last visit. Filling the watering can, she returned to the ailing plant and beseeched it, "Hale ghosts of the past! Come to life!" and dutifully doused the plant anew. She sneezed as dust flew up from the pot.

She felt the age of the house in her lungs as she inhaled, holding her hand to her throat. The wall in the front hallway was soft to the touch. Black mold grew in a corner of the game room walls where there was a console color television dating back to the mid-70s, and a cushy reclining chair. She imagined her father napping there wrapped in a plaid wool blanket as the voices of Metropolitan

Opera stars burst from oversized wooden speakers on either side of the room.

Her parents called this the family room, but mostly only mom and dad sat there. The pool table was long gone. A semi-detached stable was next to the family room. It doubled as a parking garage as the years turned. Mold also parked there. "Wow. That mold is really seeping in all over the place. That will have to be removed," she thought. "And the sooner the better." She didn't want to inhale it as she spent the time it would take to clear out the house.

Emma knew that the Castle Family Home was built in the early 1900s, and had nooks and crannies where nick- knacks, books, a shoe stretcher and a cane, a heavy vacuum cleaner and other questionable items were stashed or hidden away. An old typewriter with black, round, metal keys was in a bedroom, and a black, metal sewing machine was in the attic from Emma's grandfather's shirt store, along with boxes and boxes of papers. How would she ever go through it all?

She continued walking through the house taking it in, as if for the first time. Curtains were pulled closed and even when the lights were on, there was a gloominess about the place. Two major expressways framed the neighborhood just down the block, but inside, it was eerily quiet. Emma went upstairs. It was brighter there. She noticed that the blinds were broken and parts had fallen off, allowing in a sliver of sunlight. Dust floated in the air.

"Just like mom to close this place up like a fortress."

She wondered how long the blinds had been broken. She didn't remember them this way from her last visit. Now in the living room, she turned in circles, scrutinizing this portion of the house.

"Ugh. Cobwebs."

The floors were still polished and she knew her mother had scattered area rugs over them to protect the original planks from aging. Some were expensive hand-made rugs and some were of Woolworth vintage. She doubted Ethel knew the difference or cared.

Heavy plastic covered the couch and chairs from when they had cats as pets. The plastic had a greasy smell to it as if french-fries and fried chicken were cooked a hundred times in the nearby kitchen. The far wall showed spots of a mystery leak that no one had taken care of.

As she roamed around, Emma considered where to begin. Before she came, the plan was simple. She made a list:

1. *Look for anything of value. Take it home.*
2. *Hire a company to take out the furniture that has no resale value.*
3. *Hold a garage sale.*

But now, she wasn't sure how to attract anyone to come as far as the driveway for a sale. Shaking off her discomfort, and figuring she would deal with the sale later, she decided to start in her parents' bedroom. Her mother spent a lot of time alone there. Maybe there'd be interesting things to discover.

Emma felt like an intruder in her own house as she wandered up the stairs to the bedroom. Everything was the same since the last day her mother was here. Emma felt chilled. She hugged herself and looked around almost expecting someone else to join her. "Just the ghosts we left behind," she thought, and remembered her mother chasing her friends out of the house.

Her memory of that day was fresh in her mind. Her mother had forbidden Emma from having friends over to the house unless she was there. When friends did come over, she watched over them like a hawk, being sure they didn't touch anything or look in any closets. The attic was forbidden space, as were the living and dining rooms. The garden was off limits as well. And if they had to use the bathroom, they had to go home. That's what happened the last time Emma had friends over.

Emma remembered how she ran into the house with Billy and Cindy after school. The three threw their bags on the floor in the front hallway and crept up the stairway, keeping an eye out for Emma's mother. All of a sudden, there she was, right in front of them. Billy and Cindy shuddered.

"Where are you going? Did you wipe your feet off? Why are you coming upstairs?" Ethel asked sternly with her hands on her hips.

"Hi mom," Emma replied. "We're just going upstairs to my bedroom to play."

"Well, take off your shoes and don't stop in the living room. If you want to come out of the bedroom, call me first," Ethel said. As she stared at each child, they cringed and walked by.

"Why is she so stern and angry," whispered Billy to Emma. "We didn't do anything."

"Oh don't mind her," Emma replied. "She's shy of strangers and doesn't like us kids all over the house."

"My mother lets us go in the living room on the way upstairs. Why doesn't your mom? Oh, you know what? I need to use the bathroom. Where's the bathroom? I held it in all afternoon at school. I really have to go," asked Cindy.

"Well you can't go here," whispered Emma. "Mom doesn't let anyone use the bathroom."

"Did you say someone has to use the bathroom?" asked Ethel in a crescendo. They hadn't realized it but she was following them up the stairs to be sure they went into Emma's room. "You'll have to go home then. There's no bathroom here that you can use. Go ahead. Go along now. Go, go home." And Ethel pushed her way to the top of the stairs and shooed them down again.

"But mom. They just got here and we want to hang out for a while. Why can't she just use the bathroom? It works fine! The toilet flushes and we just got here," Emma retorted.

"Don't talk back to me. Your friends will have to go home now. They need to do their homework anyway and so do you. Good night Billy. Good night Cindy. Go on. Go on." And Ethel shooed them back out of the house the way they came in.

And that was that!

Pretty soon Emma's friends started turning down her invitations to play. They told secrets behind Emma's back about her mother's strange behaviors and how she was probably hiding secret treasures or a dead body or something awful that she feared they would find. They made fun of Emma in school and generally, made her life miserable. She was the kid who, they said, "lived in the old blue haunted house on the Indian burial mound."

Now, climbing those same stairs, Emma felt lonely and rejected as she recalled that time in her life. She turned and in her mind saw Billy and Cindy running out the door. Dark feelings bubbled up even after all of these years.

Emma opened the door to her parent's bedroom and sat on the edge of the bed. She slowly opened the dresser drawer, expecting her own childhood loneliness to slither out into her hands. She was astonished at what she found, and for a few minutes, lost her inhibitions about what she was doing. Whispering to herself, "I can't believe this," she pulled lacey lingerie from her mother's dresser. She always thought her mother was prim and private having dressed with the bedroom door closed tightly. Ethel hid herself even from her daughter until she was fully dressed. She never taught Emma anything about her body or even what sex was. Ever. When Emma got her first period, her mother followed an old superstition and slapped her face, brought her a sanitary napkin and helped her put it on. She gave her a pamphlet about how to keep herself clean and fresh. Then she left Emma to figure things out for herself.

Emma couldn't believe how old fashioned and naïve her mother was and thought that that was as far as things went. Until today. Who would have known that her mother wore black lace, and cream colored satin with pale blue lace trim? Emma had never seen such fine lingerie, and so delicately embroidered. As she aged, her mother had worn old slacks left behind in her father's closet. Like her mother, Rosie, Ethel was a good seamstress. She could make anything fit her trim waistline.

Emma closed her eyes and imagined her mother dressing in a long lacey slip and slinking across the room. She opened her eyes and put her hand over her mouth, gasping and laughing at once.

She thought about her mother's appearance over the years. She remembered her mother young, with blue nail polish—way ahead of its time. It matched her blue silk dyed shoes and magnificent sky blue dress of satin, lace and pearls. Her parents attended ritzy dinners with her father's clients. Her mother was strikingly beautiful at those times, in contrast to her frumpy middle age, when she wore tied shoes, wool skirts, and jeans, well before they were fashionable, as well as bulky scarves she had knit herself. Emma believed that once she hit 65, her mother never went clothes shopping again. She used her sewing machine and redid old clothing she found in the closets.

How could the same person have invested in so much sexy, delicate underwear? It must have cost her a fortune. Her mother was always frugal and modest, bringing change to the bank to exchange for dollar bills, buying the cheapest, roughest toilet paper on sale and then using just two squares at a time to save money... having powdered milk at breakfast and storing away half a slice of toast for lunch.

Emma continued looking. In the next drawer, she found gold earrings with pearls nestled next to plastic beaded necklaces in torn and worn boxes. Gold next to plastic pop-beads. It seemed that they held the same dearness and value to her mom. Emma was baffled. "What went on here?"

Emma folded the lingerie carefully and gingerly placed it back in the first drawer, thinking, "I'll never be that petite or that femininely exquisite. No point in keeping it or taking it home. Maybe someone else will want it. I'll give it to Goodwill or sell it at a garage sale. Ugh. How will I face that garage sale?" Emma sighed deeply, slumping on the bed and looking baffled at her mother's things.

She closed the dresser drawers and sat back, gazing around the room. She took in her thoughts, and feelings about the bedroom. Her parents lived here well over 50 years and their parents before them. The room wasn't very large but big enough for twin beds pushed together to form a king sized platform with book shelves lining the headboard and night tables under them on either side. The furniture was darkly stained pine, and a huge rectangular mirror sat on the dresser. There were mirrored trays with perfume atomizers and lipsticks and even an electric toothbrush, plugged in and waiting for the owner to return. But she never did.

Emma looked carefully around the room for anything she might want to take home that day. On the bureau, a dark brown shell hairbrush still held grey hairs in its bristles. Emma cleaned it off and wrapped the brush in soft towels to prevent it from cracking. She found a matching mirror. The mirror and brush dated from her grandmother's time. She held the mirror in her hands and stroked the shell finish with her fingers the way her grandmother used to brush and then braid her long dark hair. She wrapped it to take home.

Turning to go, Emma noticed the metallic round powder box on the shelf above her mother's night table. She could barely believe it was still there. Its finish was a worn combination of silver, purple and white hues, with a pastel water color picture of a man, woman and child painted on the top. Without opening it, she knew it held a soft cotton, pink powder puff that smelled of rose petal baby powder, and when you took off the lid, it played a soft tune from Swan Lake. Emma associated it fondly with her grandmother whose house this was when she was a little girl. Humming the tune in her head, she gently wound the music box and the familiar tune played. Emma smiled through the tear that slowly found its way down her cheek. Hugging the box, Emma closed her eyes, breathed deeply and remembered with affection, another time she spent with her grandmother. She must have been but 3 or 4 years old.

"Emma eat your breakfast," her mother scolded. She was always in a hurry.

Emma looked at the toast on her plate. It was dark and had something wet on it.

"Yuk," she replied. "I don't want it."

"Eat it now so we can get going. Come on or you won't go out to play."

Emma took a quick bite out of the soggy, burnt tasting bread.

"Good girl. Now let's go to grandma's," Ethel said, taking Emma's hand and pulling her along to the car. Ethel recently went back to school and her mother, Rosie, was babysitting while she was in class. Ethel and Emma drove at least a half hour to get to Long Island from Brooklyn every time Ethel had class. It wasn't until Emma was in first grade that she and her mother and father moved in with Rosie to the Long Island family home.

On one occasion, Emma woke up in the car as they arrived at the house.

"There she is. My princess. Come on in little Emma. Come with me," Rosie coo-ed to her.

Rubbing her eyes, Emma smiled and baby-kissed her grandmother. Still half asleep, she held her grandmother's hand all the way into the house as her mother drove away.

"I have something very special for you today," her grandmother said as she worked at preparing some new concoction at the kitchen counter. When it was done, she turned and with a big smile on her face, handed Emma a piece of white bread with something creamy on it.

"Now, close your eyes and take a BIG bite," said her grandmother.

Emma did. She could feel the white bread melt in her mouth with the creamy substance creating a blissful taste. She licked her lips and her eyes opened wide. "Yum. I want more. What is it?" she asked.

"Just eat it all up. I'll tell you what it is when you've finished," her grandmother replied. "Isn't it heavenly?"

It was.

Now as she held the music box in her hand, Emma had her eyes closed and could still taste the butter melting on her tongue. Her grandmother had that special touch. Rosie had died years ago but Emma could still feel the strong bond between them.

Carefully and tearfully, she lovingly packed up the powder box, and realized that the house held some good memories for her to rediscover.

Emma remembered how excited she was, sitting in her bedroom, as she packed a trunk to go far away to college, anxious to get out of this house. Once she had a family of her own, she complained about having too much to do with taking Jason to activities, going to work and cleaning the house. She never realized how busy she could be until her run-of-the-mill life was interrupted with visiting Long Island to take care of her parents who both succumbed to dementia.

When the Will was read, Emma learned that the family home was hers but a Trust Fund was passed to her son, Jason. Her mother knew how she detested the old house, and yet, now she was stuck with it. Her own life was flying by so quickly and she didn't want to waste time in this old clapboard shell. "How will I deal with this?" she thought.

Emma decided that accepting familial and historical responsibility for at least archiving her family's heritage would give her a positive goal to pursue as she emptied the old house, and maybe it would help her feel less overwhelmed. She remembered how her father also had second thoughts about living in the Long Island house. Out of nowhere, the memory of Mrs. Coleman calling her father Mr. Castle came to mind.

At least once a week, the young mother from Brooklyn remind-ed "Mr. Castle" to mow his lawn.

"Good morning Mr. Castle!" Karen Coleman called. "How are you this beautiful morning?"

"It's not 'Mr. Castle', thank you very much," Ethel's husband mumbled back. He was sick and tired of people assuming he was Sam and Rosie's son. But he didn't want to admit that the house belonged to his wife and that he couldn't afford 'a big place like that'.

"Just trying to be friendly," Mrs. Coleman replied, looking at him out of the corner of her eyes, wondering why he was always so grumpy. "Gonna get that grass cut soon, are ya? Eh? The crab grass is going to seed and will bleed over into our lawn. How about it Mr. Castle?" Mrs. Coleman said.

"Yes. Yes. I'll take care of it," Ethel's husband replied, thinking, 'since when is she my landlord, telling me what to do to take care of my own property?' He got in his car brusquely and drove away to catch the Long Island Railroad commuter train. He could care less about the lawn or about Mrs. Coleman's lawn. As far as he was concerned, that was her problem, not his.

And so it went over the years.

Roaming through the house, now hers, Emma thought back to when she and Jason had met with the lawyer after Ethel's funeral.

As they left the lawyer's office, Emma was curious, and turned to her son. "So what was that all about, meeting with the lawyer alone?"

"Aw mom. If he wanted you to know, he would have told you to stay in the room with us," said Jason.

"Well. So, I want to know. And anyway, it sounded like it was you, not him, who wanted me out. So tell me. I'm your mother. Just tell me what's going on." Emma turned and faced her son.

"I'm an adult now. I don't have to tell you everything. But, I don't see why you can't know part of it. I don't want you to feel left out or anything. It's a Trust Fund. Grandma left me a Trust Fund. I wanted to ask the lawyer about it. That's all. Okay?" Jason replied.

"A Trust Fund! What the….." Emma stopped herself. "What kind of Trust Fund? Grandma barely spent any money. They couldn't have had anything left when they died. They paid hundreds of thousands of dollars for that nursing home over five years and never went on Medicaid! What are you talking about? Are you playing games with me?" Emma stood with her hands folded across her chest, looking up at her son's face. She couldn't imagine what that Trust Fund might entail, but if it had anything to do with her mother's family, she had real concerns. Ethel wasn't "all there" in the end. What kind of story did she make up about a Trust Fund? Whatever it was, it couldn't be real.

Jason crinkled his forehead, took on a serious frown, considering what his mother might be thinking, and shrugged. "It's nothing. Just a joke from the old folks. You really don't need to worry about it."

"God. You've got such a sarcastic sense of humor. I don't know what I'm going to do with you," she said, but kept her eyes on him just a minute longer to see if he really had anything else to tell her. She smiled at him then, and giving him a kiss on his forehead, ruffled his hair.

Then she gave up.

Remembering that conversation and looking around again, Emma shook her head. "No. Just another story that mom made up from something she read or saw on TV. If there was any money, this house would have been kept up and reno'd over the years. It couldn't be anything valuable, or, knowing Jason, he would have had financial and legal proceedings in the making before he left the legal offices. Hum…."

She thought about Jason. He was a serious, caring and industrious individual, but he certainly loved money. In social situations, he could be painfully quiet. But when business was involved, he was charming and charismatic, and she knew he would get what he wanted in his career. She mostly was concerned that he take a break from gathering his assets to find true happiness in his lifetime.

"Nah," she said, shaking her head 'no' in response to her thoughts.

"If his grandparents left him a small nest egg, good for him," she thought. On her salary, she could never leave him anything of substance. They probably figured that was the case and wanted to help. She just wished they had sold the house before they had to move out. That money could have been used for the funerals. Now she was stuck with cleaning up their stuff, putting the house on the market, and paying off debts. Her resentful feelings were between her and her parents, not between her and her son.

"It's been over a month. I wonder if Jason did tell me the truth. Trust Fund! Phuh!" she puffed, looking around. "I guess I got the booby prize," she said out loud to herself, gathering up the few things she was taking home with her that day. Most was left right where it was for another visit.

MRS. COLEMAN'S PERSPECTIVE

O n her next trip to Long Island, Emma promised herself not to care about the neighbors. She wore a blue shirt-to match the house-and sneakers, so she'd be comfortable moving things around. "Who cares what they think," she said to herself. "It won't matter what I wear. I can't hide. They'll still be peeping out that window and wanting me and the house gone. My life has nothing to do with them. They should mind their own business."

Right on cue: "Hey Pop, she's back!" Mrs. Coleman called, picking her teeth with her forefinger. They had just finished their coffee and an English muffin with preserves that they shared.

It was a clear day and the window was open. Half the neighborhood probably heard Mrs. Coleman, "the Town Crier."

Mr. Coleman shuffled over to the window. He elbowed Mrs. Coleman out of the way and looked. "Uh huh, uh huh," he said. "Get away from the window mum. Now, move, just get away." He pushed her back pulling the curtains closed, while taking a peek himself.

"She doesn't look so beige today does she?" he muttered. "Watch out. She's liable to come over and ask you for some sugar or something." He was poking Mrs. Coleman out of the way in a jesting motion.

"She's not getting anything from me—you old lug. She'll have to fix up that garden again for me to pay attention to her. Maybe she's got herself a body in the trunk of that car and she can go dig up that garden and plant some nice rose bushes…" She was about to chuckle. "—oh wait. It's not beige either," Mrs. Coleman said, pushing open the curtains again and looking out at Emma's car. "What's she up to?"

Meanwhile, Emma gave them her Queen of England wave, swirling her hand in the air, just short of favoring a certain finger in their direction. She was feeling a bit more confident today.

"There she goes again, Pop. She's waving at us with her hand all in a circle."

"Get away, get away," he said. "Just close up that curtain. Maybe she'll empty that house and be done with it if we leave her alone."

"We'll be dead by then," Mrs. Coleman mused, looking at him hard in the face.

"I'll kill you now if you don't get away from that window!" And he shoved her away and pushed both the window and the curtains shut.

Out in the street, Emma could hear them bickering, and looked up at their window half worried and half smiling. "What a bunch of losers," she thought. "How ironic would it be if they die before I empty the house and sell it!" Then she flicked them off her shoulders like imaginary dandruff. "Can't be derailed. Gotta get this done." And with that, she went into the house.

Halfway through the day, she began to realize that it would take much longer than she had thought to clear all of the things out of the house especially since both her parents and grandparents had lived there. What would she keep? The plastic toy fish from young bathtub days, the newspaper headlines from President Kennedy's inauguration and assassination, the boxes and boxes of papers in the attic? More boxes of who-knows-what were carefully stored on shelving in the basement. All of the closets were full of clothing and boxes of hats and albums and toys. There was a deer skin jacket eaten by moths with brown stains on it in a garment bag. Some items were antiques and some were just junk. Often enough Emma couldn't tell the difference. Dollar bills were hidden in pants pockets. Jewelry was falling out of suit pockets. Picture albums lay in ruins on closet floors, the pictures frail and cracked.

Emma took a break. She made a cup of instant coffee in the kitchen and dwelled on the situation. Part of cleaning out the house, would be removing her personal cobwebs about how things had gone. She didn't remember the house looking like this in her childhood. Ethel sure made a mess of the place as her paranoia grew in her old age. Emma felt bad. Maybe she should have spent more time with her mother toward the end. But then she remembered what it was like when she did try to help. Her mother got angry and pushed her right out the door, out of control and screaming at her. Ten minutes later, her mother invited her in, happy to see her, as if no altercation occurred. No. She did her best. Putting her coffee down, Emma walked from the kitchen into the dining area which opened into the living room.

Nothing was on the walls anymore. Framed pictures, her mother's favorites, were piled high on the living and dining area floors. Her mother took them down when the house was painted more than two years ago, but never put them back up. Some pictures told the stories of great grandparents or other relatives, long gone. There was a picture of a confederate soldier that Emma just couldn't figure out. She knew her grandmother was an immigrant and her grandfather came from Nantucket. How did a confederate soldier get into the family? There were all sorts of rumors about the family, and the pictures reminded Emma of holographic specters. She lined some of the pictures up on the dining room table so that she could see them all in a row. Each had a story to tell. Emma speculated that maybe some of the rumors were true. The house had a life of its own and it was never friendly to Emma, but at least now, she had the freedom to explore it. She reminded herself that before she sold the house, she would do her best to learn about her family's history, and not precipitously throw out the pictures.

Weeks went by as Emma returned several times to explore, and though there were no problems in the past, Emma didn't like coming into the empty house alone. It was creepy, and she began to understand why Mrs. Coleman spied on it through her windows and never came over to see it for herself. It would be better if someone watched over the house to keep it secured as she came and went. After all, she never really moved in and felt she never would.

One day when Emma pulled up to the house, Mrs. Coleman shuffled across the lawn, startling her. Emma did her best to be cordial. She was curious about what made this awful woman leave her window perch to actually make contact with her.

"Good morning, Emma. You are Emma, aren't you?" Mrs. Coleman cross examined her.

Emma did her best to smile and acknowledge Mrs. Coleman. "Yes. I'm Emma. How are you Mrs. Coleman?"

"Oh. I'm fine dear. Just fine. But I hear your father has gone into a nursing home. How is he doing?" she seemed genuinely concerned.

"Oh. Well. Dad passed away a few years ago. And now my mother..." Emma started out.

"Well, I don't really care much about your mother," Mrs. Coleman cut her off. "She wasn't a very nice person. So I don't really care much about her. But your dad was a nice man, a very nice man. I'm so sorry to hear he passed away. That's just awful." Mrs. Coleman shook her head in mild concern. "So you moving in or selling it or what?" Mrs. Coleman said.

Emma was so taken aback by Mrs. Coleman's rudeness concerning her mother that she took a minute to think; "Why should

I give her any information or satisfaction. She never came over when it mattered. She only cares about herself. She doesn't deserve my consideration."

"Why, Mrs. Coleman, what would you like me to do with the house? Because I'm all ears," Emma challenged.

"Well, sell it, of course. To a developer so we can all get our property values back. No one would ever want to buy the place. I mean really," Mrs. Coleman muttered dismissively as she returned to her own house. She really didn't care what Emma might say next.

When Mrs. Coleman got back inside, Emma heard her call, "Pop, she's back." And then Mrs. Coleman brusquely shut her door.

Emma just stood in shock on the front lawn. Karen Coleman was even more hurtful than she had imagined. How dare she say to her, their daughter, that one parent was worth her concern while the other was not? Who did she think she was to judge people like that, and have so little sensitivity?

After this conversation with Mrs. Coleman, Emma felt a bit paranoid herself. She glanced around at the other neighboring houses and wondered how many other people thought the way Mrs. Coleman did. If that was the case, they might try to damage the house or burn it down, just to clear the Castle name off its property and theirs. She had to admit the house was an eye sore, but that wasn't their business. She had her hands full just doing what had to be done.

Emma decided to change her attitude totally. She would not be cowed by Mrs. Coleman or anyone. This was her house and her grandfather had owned all of this land at one time. On the next visit, she wore a red shirt and jeans with her sneakers. Why try to look sophisticated or try to blend in? She would be herself. She would be comfortable. As far as she was concerned, from now until the house was sold, she would think of her neighbors as squatters on her land. During the next hurricane, she hoped the rotted fence would fall in the direction of her neighbor's yard. And, if it did, she would let Mrs. Coleman shuffle out and pick it up so her lawn wouldn't yellow! Emma transferred her resentment from her parents to the neighbors.

JASON AND THE HOUSE

Emma decided to ask her son, Jason, to move in so that he could be close to his job and house sit, preventing vagrants and others from exploring the contents of the old homestead, and returning life to the cold structure. Jason gladly jumped at the opportunity, although Emma wasn't quite sure why a young man would want to live in such a dilapidated old place that had poor lighting, marginal heating, and about which the neighbors incessantly gossiped. He hired someone to get rid of the mold, and soon the workmen were patching up the front hallway wall. While they were there, Jason called Emma on his cellphone.

"Hey mom. How's it going? I've got Rick and Joey over here fixing up the wall in the hallway. As you suspected, it was pretty bad," he said.

"What's the damage? What did they have to do? Was there water in the wall?" Emma asked.

"They had to clean out some mold and put in a new two-by-four. They're putting in new sheetrock now. I think you'll like it when it's done."

"Are they going to paint it?" Emma asked.

"No. The wall board is such a close match to the white walls that it's better to just leave it spackled until you're ready to paint the whole room. Otherwise, it'll be splotchy when you do go to paint. It's looking really good. I think you'll be pleased," Jason continued.

"How much will I owe them? Should I send you a check for the whole amount? Will they do the garage area as well?" Emma asked.

Jason hesitated. "No. Nothing. It's fine. I've got it covered. They work with me all the time. Yes. They've already done the garage," Jason replied.

"But it has to cost something. It's a big job! Who bought the materials? Really. You shouldn't have to pay for repairs. What can I do to help?" Emma couldn't imagine they'd do the job for nothing.

"Uh. Well. Um. You don't really have to pay anything. Uh. Okay. Let's see. How about you tip the people doing the work? I think they'd like that. Can you do that?" Jason was searching for some way to bring closure to her questions. He wanted to quell her curiosity about the money.

"Sure. How much of a tip is reasonable for a job that's this big? About $50? They were there for two days. That's a lot of time. Is that enough?" Emma asked.

"Yeh. Sure. That's plenty. More than enough. Just either stop by to see the job when they're done tomorrow, or leave me some money the next time you're out here, and I'll make sure they get it, and know it's from you. Okay?" said Jason.

"Yes. If you're sure. That's fine with me. Jason, are you sure you aren't spending too much of your time and your own money on this? Please let me know if it's an issue with you. You're doing a lot to fix up the old place."

"Everything's fine, mom. Really, fine. Let me go now. I've gotta get back to work." And they hung up.

Jason was relieved that Emma wasn't going to press him further about the money.

After that, Jason never asked his mother for money to pay for the repairs and she assumed that since he was an architect, he knew people in construction who were helping him get the work done. It made it easier for him not to have to explain where the money came from. There were so many places around the house where little "surprises" were hidden, and he was getting to know them a little at a time. He hadn't found large amounts of money or other saleable things tucked away, but just enough to do the work he needed to get done. Ethel had told him the house had "assets" hidden in it, but she never told him how much or where. It was a veritable treasure hunt for him. He figured she was "half crazy" in her forgetfulness, and had hidden things all over the place and had forgotten where she put them. He found whatever he could.

In Emma's eyes, Jason was a young Gen X man in search of family ties and history. After all, he inherited the Trust Fund, whatever that was! She took into consideration that his grandparents clearly wanted him to carry on the family line, so why not let him explore and enjoy the house as well, if it could be enjoyed. Also, Jason knew about houses and he loved this one. He was slowly moving in for just two weeks now, and had already fixed the front hall wall, the broken toilet, the motor on the furnace and the leak in the washing machine, which definitely predated his arrival on this earth. Emma wouldn't have to worry about the house if he was there. It would be in better condition when it went on the market than it was now. She could clean out its contents slowly or not at all, if she decided to wait….as long as he stayed on. She could help her son save some money on rent and he could help her feel comfortable as she did what had to be done. Moreover, the house would remain secured from Mrs. Coleman's prying eyes and remain in the family for a few more months.

Emma put in a cable line so that she and Jason could do online research about the family, especially if they found anything interesting in the house. Jason was particularly good at using ancestry.

com, Wikipedia.org, Craig's list and eBay. He could work from home so he appreciated having high-speed Internet.

Jason was dependable, a trait he shared with Emma. He was like his great grandfather, Sam, in that he was slight of frame, somewhat self-consciously vain, and good with numbers and money. His hair was a light brown, even reddish in the summertime. His eyes were deep, deep blue. His smile was broad and white and he could hide all of his emotions behind it. He loved animals and was gentle and caring toward little children, but could be compulsive and even irrational when irritated. He had a strong will, but his loyalty was stronger, and his friendships were deep and meaningful. He was also streetwise and could take care of himself, having answers for everything and never living vicariously. He was a Castle through and through. He belonged in this house. He belonged to the house and its family and felt a deep emotional connection to his ancestry.

When he moved in, he chided Emma about her fears and taunted her into calling him Jason Castle, after the family name. Emma played along and addressed him as "Mr. Castle" for as long as he lived there, not realizing that he had actually already changed his name legally, as he had secretly promised his grandmother, Ethel, he would do. He was indeed a "living specter" who roamed the house when Emma was away.

One day, Jason decided to have a look in the attic. The drop down stairs were old and rickety, so he used a ladder instead of the built in stairs to get up into the attic. It was cold and damp. A large tinfoil baking pan, the kind you cook a turkey in, was suspended from the ceiling by a wire hanger. He pulled the ladder up into the attic, and used it to climb up and pull down the pan. A few old bills floated down from the pan as he threw it carelessly away across the room. Two bills landed by his feet as he stepped down. They looked a bit larger than normal dollar bills-probably play money from an old game. He picked them up and noticed a picture of someone that looked like his grade school textbook picture of Andrew Jackson on one bill. The other bill had a picture of workmen with a hoe and a shovel. He stuffed them in his pocket and figured he'd have a look at them later since they did look a bit old.

There was a hole in the roof above where the pan had been. He figured that an attic fan or other appliance had been removed from the space recently. He craned his neck to see what was above the hole and suddenly realized that it was another room. It must be the Captain's walk, visible from outside of the house. But the stairway up to it was gone. He'd go to Home Depot later on and get supplies to put in a hanging staircase or patch up the hole, as well as fix the attic stairway. Jason sneezed from the dusty odors and wiped his face with his sleeve. A spider ran across his hand and he jumped momentarily back from it.

"Ugh! This place is disgusting!" Jason couldn't help but exclaim out loud to himself as he gently brushed it away.

Although it upset him, he remembered that his grandmother always told him that spiders were good luck and that you shouldn't kill them. He left it alone and wandered away through the boxes and trash in the space, all the while shaking off the crawly feeling of the spider. He knew his mother wouldn't want to have to deal with the dust and bugs, so he kept track of what he saw so he could tell her the next time she came.

Jason poked through the boxes. One box had photos piled up to its top. He pulled over another box and sat on it while shuffling through the pictures, using his flashlight and a bare light bulb that hung from the ceiling to make out the figures in black and white. One picture in particular caught his eye. He imagined that this picture might be a hundred years old or more, and was fascinated. Pictures were rare and expensive to shoot back then. He wondered who might have taken it.

A man and a woman were in the picture. They were probably husband and wife. In front of them were two boys, most likely brothers, one much older than the other. The younger one looked a lot like himself, with slicked back hair, and a huge mischievous smile. In a moment of playfulness, Jason caught a glimpse of himself in an antique mirror that leaned against the attic wall. He smiled at himself and ran his hand through his own hair, comparing himself to the boy in the picture. Then he looked back at the picture.

The older boy was not smiling and had his hand on the younger boy, perhaps holding him still. In back of them were trunks and a carriage with a horse. His eyes traveled up to the top of the picture and then, he saw it. Behind the family loomed a large house, much like the house he was in. Maybe it was even the same house. Jason knew that his great grandfather, Sam, had built the house he was in now. Jason had seen pictures of Sam, and the man in the picture was not him.

Jason dropped the ladder down again, looking around warily for spider webs, and took the picture out of the attic. He held it up to the light and examined it closely. The man was dressed like Rhett Butler in Gone with the Wind, a movie Emma made him watch when he was younger and acting in plays. He held a wide brimmed hat and had an ornamental walking stick or maybe it was a sword in a leather case-it was hard to tell. His coat was long and ended mid-thigh, like an old-fashioned riding jacket. He displayed a wide bushy mustache that he might have shaped with candle wax. His boots were knee high and must have been leather. The woman in the picture was dressed in a different style. Her dress was a light color, maybe a pastel. It covered her up to her chin and down to her toes and was plain, except for the sleeves. Her arms were covered and the sleeves puffed at the shoulders and tapered at the elbows. They went over the backs of her hands with lace around the edges. It almost looked like she had added embellished sleeves to an everyday dress. She was small and delicate. Her hat was flat and it seemed as if the picture was faded where her face had been. He couldn't tell if she was pretty or plain, smiling or severe. Because of how the picture had worn, it looked as if the man had a three dimensional character and the woman was flat like her hat.

Jason looked more closely at the house and then took it out of doors to make comparisons. He shaded his eyes against the sun, looking up at the top of this house. Then he looked down at the picture. The Captain's walk had a spire at the top, something his family house was missing. The shutters on the old house were a bit larger than the Long Island house, and had hooks on them holding them open, as if they might shut if left on their own or be clasped shut in case of a storm. The window area was square and did not fan out at the bottom. Jason estimated that the current house could probably seat four in the Captain's walk. The old house was just wide enough for someone to stand in. No, this was a different but similar house.

He went back inside and started to search online. Both the house in the picture and the house he was in had a New England style to them. The Captain's walk would place the old house near the water. Because of the things that his mother had said, Jason thought the picture might be Sam and Percy's boyhood home on Nantucket. However, Google Earth was not successful in finding the exact house. It was probably gone by now.

Jason's eyes shifted back to the boys in the picture. The younger one had a wide winning smile like his own. He wondered if this was his great grandfather Sam. He had heard that Sam had a brother Percy but no one in his family really talked much about Percy. He was deep in thought as confederate bills floated down into the attic from the box in the widow's walk above his head.

Jason spent over a year living in the Castle family home while Emma fussed with what to keep and what to toss. Together they found family albums that showed people and events that Emma remembered from her childhood. Other pictures, taken in the 1800s, were few and far between and very dear. Only the one Jason had found in the attic showed Emma's great grandparents. There were a few other old pictures with Sam and Rosie at a beach that might have been near Oyster Bay or Setauket Harbor. Emma wasn't sure. There were rocks in the sand like the north shore of Long Island and it would have made sense that aging Sam and middle-aged Rosie would have vacationed near the house Sam built. In these pictures, you could tell that Sam was content as well as much older than Rosie, and Rosie was always smiling and happy to be with him. In several pictures, Rosie was alone. Ethel must have taken those.

Emma recalled that her grandmother, Rosie, had mixed feelings about Sam.

At times she would tell Emma, "He was a two-timing, no good liar, and I should have left him sooner."

At other times, she'd say he had the interests of the family at heart and was a "very dear man. He really meant a lot to me."

Although Emma had seen him once, she never actually met him, so she couldn't judge for herself.

One weekend, when she and Jason were going through the closets, they found the deerskin jacket that Emma had seen the first day she was there. It was wide and long, and had fringes on the bottom. Jason pulled it on in sport. It had a tear in the back with large oddly shaped brown spots around it. Emma gasped and insisted he take it off immediately.

"Those are blood stains. Take it off! Take it off!"

Jason shook, his whole body feeling really creepy about it, and dropped it to the floor off his back.

"Where do you think it came from? Whose was it?" he asked, holding it up with distaste, in just his thumb and forefinger, a distance from his face.

He examined the spots and agreed that it looked like dried blood, although he wasn't at all sure how he knew that. After scrutinizing it for a minute or two, he brushed it off with his hands and with a sly grin, said, "So, Goodwill?"

Emma pushed him away in jest and, pointing to the pile they had started, told him to lay it across the bed. She avoided touching it. They'd think about it.

"It must be very old and have some history to it," Emma said. "Grandma would have kept the jacket only if it had some special meaning. We can't just throw it away. It's so odd. It's got to be significant," Emma considered.

"I guess we'll just keep everything and pass it along so the next bunch of Castles can figure it out," Jason teased her. "You're keeping everything. Are you superstitious or something? Why do we have to keep this?" He was losing his patience with her indecision.

Jason looked at Emma who was lost in thought. Maybe she inherited her mother's madness. He shook his head and thought, "better move on."

Jason and Emma took a break and sat in the kitchen drinking coffee. Jason left for a minute and returned with the picture he had found in the attic. Holding it up, he showed it to Emma.

"That must be your great grandfather, Sam," she said.

"He's the one who built this house?" Jason confirmed.

"Yes," she replied.

"Do you see how the house in the picture looks like this one? It's not this one though," Jason pointed out. "See how the widow's walk is a different shape and the shutters are older?"

"Oh my goodness! I never would have noticed that. It really looks like a house on Martha's Vineyard or Nantucket. I remember hearing stories about a house in Nantucket and one of my great, great grandfathers, or someone like that, being a whaling mate or Captain. I don't really know for sure."

Emma took the picture from Jason and looked it over more carefully. She put it on the table and pointed to the man in the picture, pushing it over, as she did, so as not to drip any coffee on it.

"But that must be the house that Sam and Percy grew up in on Nantucket. Who's that other guy in the picture? He sure looks out of place. Hum, he looks familiar. I think I've seen a picture of him somewhere in the house. I'll have to see if I can find it again."

Emma looked from side to side as if the picture would be right there in the kitchen. She sighed, exasperated, got up and went into the dining room. She had gone through so many things and left several pictures strewn across the dining room table in the next room. She probably wouldn't find the other picture of this man in this mess. Putting the family story together seemed impossible while pulling the house apart. She went back in the kitchen.

Emma looked back at the picture of the house, and remarked to Jason, "You look a lot like your great grandfather." Now, she was holding the picture with both hands, and staring into it trying to regain some of its history. "I'll bet Sam would have loved to meet you, had he lived to be a hundred and fifty or whatever his age would have been by now!" Emma smiled and gave the picture back to Jason. "I'll frame it for you so that it will last longer."

Jason took the picture, smiled and nodded, still looking at Sam in the picture. It was hard to imagine this little boy as an old man. Jason wanted to know more about the other boy in the picture. Emma told him that the other boy was likely Percy, Sam's brother. Emma told Jason that Percy was probably the most enigmatic character in the Castle family.

"Maybe that deerskin jacket –the gross one—had something to do with Percy?" Jason questioned.

"We'll never know," Emma replied.

"How come you know so much about Sam and nothing about Percy?" asked Jason.

Emma explained further. "Grandma told me that Percy once came to visit for just one day. Imagine that. He came all the way from Colorado for one day. Rosie and Sam were still living on Stone Avenue. He heard that his brother Sam had a daughter and wanted to meet Ethel, your grandmother. He made the long trip east from Denver to see her and, unfortunately, he showed up on a day when Sam wasn't around."

Jason and Emma sat back down to finish their coffee as Emma continued the story.

"For some reason, Percy couldn't stay longer. So, Sam and Percy didn't get to see each other that day. I wonder why he couldn't stay. It just doesn't make sense. It's like he was in a rush so no one would know where he was."

Emma got up to see if there was milk in the fridge. When she didn't find any, Jason found some powdered milk in one of the cabinets and they laughed, remembering how Ethel insisted that powdered milk saved them money. Emma sprinkled some into her coffee, and sipped it, grimacing at the taste.

"In any case, my mother, your grandmother, was too young to remember having seen Percy but Rosie—my grandmother-- described him as being chipper for his age. She told me his eyes –blue like yours--melted with nostalgia when he met her and Ethel, probably thinking of Sam. He was a scruffy looking fellow. Grandma said she almost didn't let him in the house, he was so disheveled. But, he must have had a heart, because she said he was devastated that Sam wasn't there. He said he had something very important to show his brother, but that he couldn't stick around and wait. My grandmother told me that she thought this was very odd but he left anyway. According to Rosie, there was something not quite right about him."

Emma sipped her coffee and then continued, "In any case, when Sam came home, my grandmother told him about Percy's mysterious visit, and that Percy said he had something to show him."

"Is he really your brother?" Rosie asked Sam. She had noticed that Percy was so much older than Sam.

"Of course he's my brother," Sam acknowledged. "Our mother tried to have other children after Percy was born and lost three children before I was born and survived. Because of that, Percy was several years my senior. He was like a father to me when we were growing up," Sam remembered warmly. Nodding his head, his eyes became moist, looking at nothing in particular and seeing into the past. "I can't believe you let him go. I just can't believe Percy was here and you let him go." Sam was upset.

"Well, you should have seen him, Sam. I didn't want to let him into the apartment at first. He looked like something the cat dragged in. You could tell he tried to fix himself up-he slicked his hair back-but he was a mess. His boots were worn and his clothes were old fashioned, and he smelled. I can't imagine how he lives way out there in the middle of nowhere. What's he do out there anyway?" Rosie said.

"I hear he runs a general store," said Sam. "I just don't understand why he ran away. I really wanted to see him."

Rosie saw that there was a strong bond between the brothers, although they were so very different from one another.

"Well, if you ever have a chance, I suppose you could visit him. But don't expect me to go dragging along out there to the end of the earth," Rosie said.

"And, later when Sam did want to go, she let him go on his visits to Denver whenever he chose to." Emma continued telling the story of Percy's visit.

"When my great uncle Percy came, I guess, that's what you'd call him," she said, "my great uncle….he brought your grandmother (Ethel) a gift of a small doll in a grey velvet dress. Percy told Rosie that Sam would recognize it. My mother told me that Sam did remember it. Sam told her that it was special and from his mother, Mamie, hoping she would keep it. So, if that's the case, the doll went way back to your grandmother's grandmother…" Emma stopped and thought. "So that's your great, great grandmother, Ethel's grandmother, who was Mamie," she said. Emma continued, "Grandma said it was worn even when she got it, but she cherished it as her only token from her uncle Percy and her grandmother, whom she never met. Ethel told me that Rosie explained that Percy had been a frontiersman who helped slaves escape in the Civil War. Apparently, my grandmother also told my mother that Mamie, or Mamie's slave probably made the doll. So, the doll is really old and probably has some historic value. It would be fascinating if we found it."

Jason agreed.

Emma went on.

"Maybe we know less about Percy because he was a bit different from the other Castles. He wasn't bound by formalities or by what people thought he should do. He was a free spirit. My mother told me that Sam believed that Percy thought deeply about most of his actions. However, because he wanted to really feel "alive," playing pranks, being in danger and taking risks were what he ended up being known for in the family. Everyone who spoke of him loved him, especially Sam. He did what everyone wanted to do but was afraid to do."

Jason looked again at the picture he had found in the attic. Sam was the one who was smiling. Percy must have been the older boy. He looked intense.

"We found that old picture of your great grandfather. Maybe we'll find a picture or something else, somewhere that will explain whose deerskin jacket that was and what happened to the person wearing it," Emma concluded, talking about the jacket they left in the pile on the bed.

"I don't think there's much question about the answer to that," mumbled Jason, thinking about the brown stains near the hole in the back of the jacket. To his mother he said, "I guess we might figure out where it came from, but there's just so much stuff in this house, I'm sure there are some family stories we'll never know."

Thinking about his mother's story of Percy, Jason knew he had inherited the same sense of adventure, and not unlike his great,

great uncle Percy, he wasn't above a good prank. When Emma went home that day, he slipped the deerskin jacket out of the pile they had made. He thought he might wrap it up in a big box with pretty wrapping paper and a bow, and leave it on the Colemans' doorstep as a Christmas present, with a note saying that it was a gift from the ghost in the Castle attic. He chuckled at his sadistic idea and then went back to exploring the house. All the while, he wondered if Mrs. Coleman would survive the shock.

Emma explained to Jason how she wanted to learn about their family history. They pulled out old albums and looked online for the names they found in the family bible. Nothing surfaced about the train theft and its suspected connection to Percy and Rufus Castle, so Emma stayed in the dark regarding the gold. Emma knew that Sam already had had a shirt tailoring store in Manhattan when he built the house on Long Island. She and her husband could barely afford to keep one house afloat with a mortgage and New York State and Federal taxes to pay. How on earth did her grandfather afford his store, an apartment and a new huge house on Long Island? She knew she must be missing something. Jason knew what it was, but he had made a promise not to tell, so he suggested that Sam might have been frugal like his grandma. Emma was satisfied because her mother was very, very frugal.

One day, picking through papers in the attic, Jason found a diary that Sam kept. But it seemed like it was cut short. The diary described Percy's death, but nothing more. Jason passed it along to Emma to keep in her family archives. Emma's curiosity was captured by the diary and she ventured into the spider-ridden attic to look around.

She found some immigration papers for Rosie and a moving van receipt for a pick- up in Mobile, Alabama as well as a drop off in Brooklyn on Stone Avenue. Jason checked the directory at Ellis Island for additional information. Emma remembered her earlier memory of Rosie getting her to eat butter, and about the music boxes that Rosie kept throughout the house. Just about any container you picked up could be wound and played. It was a game for Emma to go through the house and find the magical boxes. She alerted Jason to be careful in the event that he found some packed away in the attic.

THE *TRUST* FUND

Once Ethel moved out, Jason lived in the house for well over a year. In his free time, he dug around the front garden, giving the house curb appeal in preparation for putting it on the market. He fixed the attic ladder so that it was safer to go up and down, replaced the toilet in the upstairs bathroom and called roto-rooter when the sewers backed up into the basement slop sink. He told Emma that the old oven needed replacing, but she just told him to fix it. A suggestion for a new stove was also over-ruled. Whenever Emma spoke to him on the phone, Jason always had something new to report about the house.

"You know, I really think we should just keep the house. I can renovate it and make it more modern. We'd get a better price."

"I'd get a better price," Emma reminded him.

"Aw. Come on mom. I really want to keep the house. I want to fix it up and just live here. It'll be a beautiful house when I'm done with it."

"Oh, honestly. Why would you spend so much of your time and money on it? I just want to get rid of it."

"It'll be worth so much more money if I fix it up. Come on. Please? Don't you trust my judgment?"

"Jason, the house is mine. The Trust Fund is yours. We're selling the house."

He conceded.

One day, when Emma was at the house, and Jason was there, at his computer, she asked him to come into the kitchen to sit with her for a while.

"Have some tea."

She put out his favorite cup and one for herself, and poured some hot water in each.

"I've done all I can do." She sat across from him. "I guess I'll leave the rest to the movers."

"Oh." Jason was disappointed. "It's been tough for you, mom, hasn't it?"

"It was so hard for me to distance myself from grandma's aggressive and accusatory behaviors. I wish I had known how to handle it better." She pushed her hair behind her ear and leaned forward to sip the hot tea.

"Don't be so hard on yourself. I don't know that anyone really handles Alzheimer's well. You did all you could." Jason knew that most of Ethel's early paranoia was probably due to hiding the gold. He was already feeling the stress of it. But the last seven or eight years of her life were most likely due to her illness.

"I had no idea that she was paranoid because she couldn't remember where she put things or even what things were at times. She just kept blaming me or the neighbors, and I couldn't figure out why. Fear and distrust drove her behaviors, and she couldn't express what she was feeling. The one thing that really bothers me is why I was the object of grandma's anger and frustration. I really wanted to help her but she wouldn't let me do anything."

Jason sat quietly listening to his mother tell her own story. He remembered back to the first day he explored the house and found the ancient picture of the Castle family. He imagined a picture of his mom and himself in front of this house with a moving van beside them. He wondered if the new picture would last a hundred years. He sipped his tea and refocused on his mother.

"I always wanted to have a close relationship with grandma," Emma said.

Jason thought, "Is she trying to convince me or herself of that?"

"It seemed that in every step of my life something came up to prevent that from happening. I went away to school. I got married hundreds of miles away, and only visited for short periods of time. And there was always something distant and formal about the way grandma treated me even when we were together. I can't put my finger on it."

Emma sat for a moment thinking it through and looking around the kitchen at the flowered wallpaper Ethel had put up herself after the fire. Jason caught her eye.

"Grandma really loved flowers, didn't she?" Jason said.

Now eyeing Ethel's vintage mix-master, Emma said, "Gee. I wish we had had a chance to make sugar cookies one more time together. I can still taste the raw dough. She made the best cut out cookies, your grandma."

Emma bit her lip. She didn't want to cry in front of Jason, but the house triggered an aching emptiness.

Jason reached his hand across the table. "I'm sorry it turned out this way for you."

He felt bad for his mother and wished he could explain the secret that Ethel had to keep. But he gave his word not to say anything to Emma and was superstitious about breaking his promise to his deceased grandmother. He was glad his relationship to his own mother was close, and hoped he never had to go through what she had experienced.

"I've been watching you as you've been coming and going, cleaning out the place. You seem to be in awe of the house. Are you afraid of it or of something in it?" Jason knew he was prying, but he was curious about her feelings for the house.

Emma acknowledged her discomfort, nodding her head in agreement.

"I lived in this house for years when I was growing up, but I always felt like a guest."

"You know, I just have to say this. I hope it doesn't upset you. You've been here dozens of times and the house still looks like no one has been here since grandma left. Even after going through drawers, closets and boxes, you put everything back where it was. I know you took some things, but the outward appearance of the rooms hasn't changed. Did you know you were doing that? It's like you don't want grandma and grandpa to know you're here touching their things… and they're gone. Here. Look. I found this. I'm surprised you didn't notice it on my hand."

Jason slipped the gold ring from his finger and placed it on the table in front of his mother.

"I love you, mom. You should keep it. It's yours."

Emma was speechless as she checked the inscription on the ring.

"Another mystery," she finally said. "Thank you," and she slipped it onto her index finger. She was both numb and filled with wonder. She had told Jason he could keep anything he found that he wanted. Here was something of value and he gave it to her. She never would have known had he kept it for himself. "I love you too, very much," she said.

Jason wrapped his hands around the tea mug that was cooling off. He looked down at the cup, scooped it up and walked over to the microwave as they continued their debriefing of the house clean up. It felt good having his mom say that, but he also felt embarrassed. He should have given her the ring sooner.

"You told me not to go into some of the rooms. How come?" He added more water, put the mug into the microwave and pressed the one-minute button. He reached out his hand to take his mother's mug so that he could make another cup for her as well.

"I guess when I was here, your grandmother told me not to go into those rooms. I still feel uncomfortable about going in now. I didn't want both of us doing something that would make grandma unhappy."

"But she's dead." He hesitated. "I'm sorry. I didn't mean to be insensitive. But really, mom. Get over it. The house is yours. You can go into any room as much as you like and so can I. Grandma won't know."

"Yes. I'm aware." Emma smiled, looking down. "I also know you've been everywhere snooping around."

Jason sat down and squirmed in his seat, handing her a fresh tea bag.

"It's okay. It's just hard for me."

"Now, when the moving company comes, some strangers are going to come and clear out those rooms. Is that how you want it to be?" Jason looked at his mom to see how she was handling all of this.

"Yes. I guess that's how it will be," she said, sitting back in her chair and staring at the gold ring on her finger. "It's funny. Sometimes when I was here, I could see that you weren't really working on the computer. You were watching me pick through things. Other times, you followed me around like a puppy. Thanks for giving me some good advice and for helping to keep the house together all this time. I really do appreciate it. Actually, though, it was a little creepy having you looking over my shoulder at every step. You reminded me of your grandmother when my friends came over. I half expected you to tell me not to use the bathroom!"

Emma grabbed a tissue and blew her nose. "By the way, what ever happened to that gross buckskin jacket we found? You know, the one with the bloody hole in the back?"

Jason got up quickly, calling back over his shoulder, "Speaking of the bathroom. I've gotta go…" and he ran out of the room.

"Just as well," Jason chuckled to himself. "I guess she didn't notice the vacant house next door. That jacket and the Colemans are a conversation for another time."

On the last evening they were in the house together, Jason opened a bottle of Sambuca that he found in the living room hutch. Laughing at how old it must be, he and Emma added it to their coffee and toasted to the Castle family tree. The furniture would be picked up and moved out the next day, and the same company agreed to run a garage sale at a remote sight. Emma decided that the money made from the sale would go to the local school district for elementary arts programs.

Emma couldn't bear to watch the family's possessions being carted away. She left and went home in tears. Maybe she should keep the house for Jason or just for vacation times. But she had so many mixed emotions.

When the house was empty, Jason went in for a final good bye. He remembered everything his grandmother said about the secret legacy that he now carried. Although he had found some old confederate dollar bills in the attic, and gold coins in the front hallway wall, he never found the treasured "Trust Fund" that his grandmother eluded to. Maybe she was fabricating it, like so many other stories she made up to cover her memory loss.

Jason double checked all of the places that Ethel had worried about. Earlier, he even went back to the attic to check out the oversized dollar bills that had been hidden in the tin baking pan. He priced the old bills and they were worth just under a thousand dollars. He found more in a box in the Captain's walk. He used the money for repairs on the house to keep his mother's suspicions at bay. Nothing he uncovered was even remotely meaningful with respect to being a "Trust Fund." He began to agree with his mother. The trust fund was just another fabrication of grandma's that made her daughter feel estranged. He was a bit disappointed because now there were huge college tuition bills to pay off on his own since he had lied to his parents about how they were already paid with his summer jobs, which really barely paid for gas. In spite of everything, he was glad he had been close to his grandmother and was able to help his mom.

With all of the stress of moving out, and listening to his mom's angst, Jason's stomach was gurgling, and he had to use the bathroom. It was a good thing that there was a new toilet and the water was still on. The moving company even left a roll of toilet paper. He relaxed himself onto the seat and looked around at the bright pink tiling. He remembered what his mother said about the old kitchen fire that prompted the Castles to retile the damaged wall in the bathroom when they redid the burned out kitchen. He couldn't imagine why anyone would use such a bright pink tile in a bathroom. In his line of work, they used marble and concrete for countertops and floors. He thought, "Pink ceramic tiling is incredibly vintage. Why in the world didn't they ever change it out? 50 years is a really long time to be looking at hot pink every time you have to go!"

Just as his thoughts were sweeping him away, Jason noticed a fat brown spider dropping down from the ceiling. If it kept going at the current rate, it would land right in his lap. He cringed, thinking, "Ironic that there's a spider here since grandma always said they're good luck and the house is all but tinder and empty space now." He remembered that a spider landed on his hand as he removed the tin baking dish from its place in the attic. So instead of hurting the spider, Jason pulled himself up by putting his left hand on the sink next to him and the other on the toilet paper holder which was lodged into the tile in the wall. He thought he could slide out from under the spider and then gently move it somewhere else so he could sit down again.

As he moved aside, in an uncomfortable moment, Jason lost his balance and the tile broke away from the wall under his weight. He wasn't hurt and the spider got away. Jason was relieved to see it scurry out of the room. Then he groaned realizing that he'd have to fix the hole in the wall where the paper holder had been. Looking over at the hole to see what that would entail, he was shocked. A soiled white cotton bag was bulging out from behind the sheetrock where the paper holder had been attached.

A week later, Emma answered the phone in the early evening. She thought the voice sounded somewhat familiar but muffled. It was a call for George, so she put him on the phone.

"Hi dad. It's Jason. Why don't you move into the other room while we talk? Oh, and don't tell mom I'm on the phone."

"What's up Jason?" his dad whispered obediently.

"I want to start a property investment venture in the Hamptons. I've just signed a binder on a piece of property worth 3 million dollars, and I just need a bit of a small loan to start building. Will you go in on it with me? I'll pay you back very soon. I just have to take another quick flight out to Denver. I can be back and have the money for you in just four or five days," Jason said.

"What? Denver? The Hamptons? Where did you get that kind of money, and how in the world are you going to afford this? I'm not made of money you know," his dad looked questioningly into the phone as if he could see Jason's reaction on the receiver. "The kid's nuts," he muttered to himself.

"Quiet! Quiet! Don't let mom hear you. Don't worry about it dad, really. It's a long story, and I can't tell you all of it. Let's just talk. Meet me in Sag Harbor tomorrow for lunch. Oh, and remember, don't tell mom."

PERCY'S GOLD OR THE
TRUST FUND?

J ason talked his mother into keeping the house for another
month. Although, at the time, she didn't know what he found
in the bathroom, Jason knew he wouldn't be able to hide the fact
that the bathroom wall needed to be fixed. While he focused on
the repairs (and his investment venture), Emma went over to the
house for one last nostalgic look.

She went into the backyard and walked through the garden
that Ethel had worked on so diligently. The flowers were mostly
brown and dried from lack of water and feeding, but a lone daisy
was lying on its side, a splash of yellow in the mulchy, muddy bed.
She bent over and picked up the flower hoping to save it from
a soggy ending, plucking it, roots and all, from among its dead
neighbors. Hanging from the roots was a piece of white cotton. On
second glance, she saw the cotton had come loose from a small bag,
still in the hole where Ethel had left it. Emma picked up the bag,
remembering how Ethel had dropped "magic fertilizing" packages

264

in with the flower seedlings. Although the bag was small, its contents were hard and heavier in her hand than she had expected.

She opened the bag and reached her hand inside to feel the cold, hard nugget....

DISCUSSION QUESTIONS

1. What role does guilt play in the story?
2. What role does ethics play in the story?
3. Why did Mamie marry Stewart? What did she hope to gain by marrying Stewart? What did she trade for her marriage?
4. Mamie marries a bigot and later on, marries a carpet bagger. Yet, she has at least two redeeming characteristics. What are they?
5. Why do you think Mamie kisses the boys on their foreheads and not on their cheeks or lips or anywhere else?
6. Why does the house on Long Island look like the house on Nantucket?
7. What was Sam doing when he was by the river near the plantation?
8. Describe Stewart's relationship to Percy. At first, Percy does what Stewart tells him to do. Why?
9. Why does Jason search the house and why does he want to renovate it and keep it?
10. What is the symbolism behind the color of the clothing that Emma wears as she cleans out the house?
11. Why does Ethel skip Emma and pass the legacy to Jason?

12. What's the significance of the fire in the kitchen and the renovations that Ethel makes in the house?
13. What's important to Percy? What's important to Sadie? What are their guiding values and how do they differ? Do they always differ?
14. What's the significance of the buckskin jacket that Emma finds?
15. Jason's been working closely with Emma on clearing out the house. Why does he call his father and not Emma at the end of the story, and why does he ask his father not to tell Emma?
16. What is the biggest priority in life for each of these characters? Which ones are "Castles"? Which ones have something in common? Who do you feel has the most integrity?
    a. Percy
    b. Mamie
    c. Sam
    d. Rosie
    e. Ethel
    f. Emma
    g. Jason
    h. Stewart
    i. Sadie
    j. Rufus
17. Does Randall's gold ring ("Percy's gold") bring happiness? What is passed on with the ring? Does the "Trust Fund" (Percy's stolen gold) bring happiness? (to Percy, Sam, Ethel, Jason, Sadie, Rufus). What is passed on with the Trust Fund?
18. What would you do if you had a neighbor like Mrs. Coleman? Why do you think the Colemans moved out?
19. Ethel has Alzheimer's. What has she remembered? What has she forgotten? At the end of the story, what does Emma

remember? What has she forgotten—or perhaps has never known? What does she discover about Ethel?

20. Ethel and Emma are likeable people. Name something you like about Ethel. Name something you like about Emma. From the story, we can tell they love one another but they have trouble connecting. Why?

21. What would you do if you inherited stolen gold?

22. What does trust have to do with the stolen gold? (Ethel says to Jason, "I have to trust you to 'trust fund' you." When Ethel becomes ill she loses much of her ability to trust.) What does trust have to do with what parents pass on to their children?

SOURCES OF INFORMATION AS WELL AS POINTS OF INTEREST

1. Jack is a character not unlike the real John Jacobs, a famous scout who worked with John Bozeman to open the Bozeman trail for wagon trains. More information can be found at:

   http://www.wyohistory.org/encyclopedia/brief-history-bozeman-trail (Web site was begun in 2011 and copyright is by The Wyoming State Historical Society); or a popular site at http://en.wikipedia.org/wiki/Bozeman_Trail (last updated 9/4/15 and retrieved 10/7/15); Also at Bob Drury and Tom Clavin, "The Heart of Everything That Is: The Untold Story of Red Cloud, An American Legend," (New York: Simon & Schuster, 2013), Reprint edition (September 2, 2014).

2. Historic Background: Because it was essential to have access to the land for the railroads, the U.S. Government established agreements with some tribes, the Sioux among them. But the government broke and ignored treaty after treaty, leaving the Natives no gains for their sacrifices. As the Civil War wound down, war-time generals and soldiers

returned to the western forts to protect the railroad progress, as well as the emigrants and settlers. Violence became
commonplace. Learn more about this at: Bob Drury and
Tom Clavin, "The Heart of Everything That Is: The Untold
Story of Red Cloud, An American Legend," (New York:
Simon & Schuster, 2013), Reprint edition, (September 2,
2014); and

and https://www.youtube.com/watch?v=-kq1r27S5DU The
Transcontinental Railroad (American History Documentary)
May 24, 2014 pbs.org online.

3. The Native tribes recognized that settlers were not only
passing through their sacred lands. Men brought their wives
and families. They were coming to stay. All of these people
competed for buffalo meat. The Native Indians used all of
the parts of the buffalo to survive. The animals provided
meat, hides for housing, blankets, and clothing, among other things, that the Natives depended on for their economy
and life style. Settlers took the meat and left the rest of the
animal to rot, wasting valuable resources.

Natives saw that their lands were stolen, and their resources were wasted and depleted. They were pushed off of
their sacred territories, where they had lived for hundreds of
years, and were running out of space to settle and to hunt.
In addition, cavalry troops raided peaceful tribal camps and
burnt them, killing innocent women and children, while
the men were hunting or otherwise occupied. The Sand
Creek massacre of a peaceful Cheyenne village was an example of the ruthless disregard for Native Americans held
by the cavalry militia. The slaughter of their families, the
steady depletion of land and resources especially angered
the younger warriors who saw a dead end in the future of
their people. The Natives held the land as a sacred natural
resource with which people should interact and sustain. The

wasteful, disrespectful and ravaging behaviors of settlers, who believed you could own the land, were more than they could bear. Find more about this at: Bob Drury and Tom Clavin, "The Heart of Everything That Is: The Untold Story of Red Cloud, An American Legend," (New York: Simon & Schuster, 2013), Reprint edition, (September 2, 2014).

4. Margot Mifflin, "The Blue Tattoo: The Life of Olive Oatman" (from the Women of the West Series), (Lincoln: University of Nebraska Press, c2009), Reprint edition: Bison Books (eBook), (April 1, 2011).

5. Duncan Emrich Library of Congress, ed., "Mormon Handcart Song: Songs of the Mormons and Songs of the West from the Archive of Folk Song: The Handcart Song," (Washington, 1952), 4.

6. Learn about tattoo's and sailors:

   *Maori, along with other Polynesian peoples-http:// earthsign.com/docktattoo/tattoo-designs/maori-pacific-islands/, retrieved September 2015

   *http://earthsign.com/docktattoo/tattoo-designs/new-england-sailors/, retrieved September 2015

   *Not unlike Martin Hildebrandt who opened a tattoo store in NYC around that time period. http://www.needle-sandsins.com/2015/01/martin-hildebrandt.html, posted by Marisa Kakoulas, January 16, 2015; written by Michelle Myles, Daredevil Tattoo. Retrieved 9/29/16; or Popular source: Wikipedia: Tattoo: History in United States https:// en.wikipedia.org/Tattoo#United_States

7. Edward Feld, ed., "Mahzor Lev Shalem, Rosh Hashanah and Yom Kippur: Rosh Hashanah Musaf Service," (New York: The Rabbinical Assembly Inc. 2010) 144.

8. As Red Cloud realized that the cavalry was building more and more forts to help settlers move across the buffalo plains and the sacred areas of the Black Hills, he was able

to unite young warriors, and their attacks grew in ferocity. Red Cloud understood the value of strategizing and under his leadership, the tribes were successful in slaughtering hundreds of cavalry men during Fetterman's massacre and later, at the Battle of Little Big Horn. You can find more information about this at: Bob Drury and Tom Clavin, "The Heart of Everything That Is: The Untold Story of Red Cloud, An American Legend," (New York: Simon & Schuster, 2013), Reprint edition (eBook),(September 2, 2014).

9. Compiled by William Francis Allen, Charles Pickard Ware, Lucy McKim Garrison, "Slave Songs of the United States: We Will March Through the Valley," (Bedford, Massachusetts: Applewood Books, 1867), #95, 73.

10. Quaker prayer by William Penn 1693: http://www.mylastsong.com/advice/169/113/107/funerals/christian-funerals/quaker-funerals Retrieved 6-9-2015

SUMMARY

Percy's Gold or The Trust Fund is a multi-generational saga of familial love, infidelity and loyalty. Aided by his brother Sam and the underground-railroad, Percy runs from the encroaching Civil War and joins a wagon train headed west. He steals gold from the railroad as it makes its way through the Black Hills. Upon Percy's death, the stolen gold is passed to Sam and his descendants as a familial trust fund. To inherit stolen gold, each must be trusted to keep the family secret. Sam's daughter, who has Alzheimer's, Wills the gold to her grandson, Jason, but misplaces it before he can inherit it. How will modern-day descendants, Emma and Jason, come to terms with what they learn as their quests for parental love and material inheritance test their trust of one another?

"An amazing display of imagination that was impressive and held my attention." Richard Bronson, M.D.

"A poignant and personal story of a family legacy-told through a rollicking tale of youthful adventure and an intimate exploration of mature discovery." Michael Mitnick

Made in the USA
Middletown, DE
09 February 2017